"I've been lo...
Beverly said breathlessly

"I've got to have you to myself for a few minutes. Is there a way we can be alone?"

My God, Sonny thought. *Doesn't she know what it does to me when she talks like that?*

He acted bored. Unconcerned. "I was going to knock off for lunch after I made my rounds."

"We could have lunch together," she said, looking up at him, all blue eyes and happiness.

She's fractured all my hormones, he thought. *I'm dying.*

"I'll go to the supermarket deli. I'll buy sandwiches. Meet you at the park? In the gazebo?"

Beverly was so euphoric that she stood on tiptoe and tried to kiss him on the jaw. He dodged her, his heart hammering.

"Fine," he said curtly, but the smile in his eyes tempered his brusqueness. "Go buy me a sandwich. Turkey and Swiss cheese. Hold the mayo."

My God, he thought. *She tried to kiss me.*

If her lips had touched his face, even fleetingly, it would have been over. He would have pulled her into his arms and kissed her the way he hungered to. Then she would know how much he wanted her, and then he would lose her.

Bethany Campbell is acknowledged as the author of this work.

Special thanks and acknowledgment to Sutton Press Inc. for its contribution to the concept for the Crystal Creek series.

ISBN 0-373-82536-6

LONE STAR STATE OF MIND

Bethany Campbell

LONE STAR
STATE OF MIND

Harlequin Books

TORONTO • NEW YORK • LONDON
AMSTERDAM • PARIS • SYDNEY • HAMBURG
STOCKHOLM • ATHENS • TOKYO • MILAN
MADRID • WARSAW • BUDAPEST • AUCKLAND

Dear Reader,

For two years, hundreds and thousands of readers from San Francisco to Sydney to Milan have been taking a break each month to hang their imaginary hats in Crystal Creek, Texas. They've pulled up a chair in the homey kitchen of the Double C ranch, and rejoiced in the birth of Jennifer Travis McKinney and in the rehabilitation of Bubba Gibson. They've grieved at the deaths of Dottie Jones, of Jeff Harris and of our beloved Hank Travis. And they've celebrated lots of weddings! From the Texas rancher and Bostonian banker, the rodeo man and the boot designer, the jockey and the dentist, to the May-December union of Mayor Martin Avery and his Billie Jo, Crystal Creek has demonstrated with grace, surprise and excitement that love is forever and always the universal that inspires and delights readers around the world.

Congratulations and deepest thanks to Margot Dalton, Bethany Campbell, Barbara Kaye, Sandy Steen, Penny Richards, Kathy Clark, Sharon Brondos and Cara West—the authors who have produced this outstanding and ground-breaking series of stories. In stepping beyond the bounds of single series romance novels, they have created interlinked works of breadth and vision, each unique and yet, the whole series even more delightful than the sum of its parts!

As for *Lone Star State of Mind*—Bethany Campbell has created an absolute blockbuster finale to this fine series. Take a deep breath and plunge right in to this final installment of living and loving in Crystal Creek. And be prepared to be swept away!

Sincerely,

Marsha Zinberg,
Senior Editor and Editorial Coordinator,
Crystal Creek

A Note from the Author

For some of us, Crystal Creek has been an ongoing part of our lives for over three years. And challenging years they've been!

The longer we writers and editors lived with the characters, the more real and compelling they became to us, the more the town became an actual place. Although it may not appear on maps, it appears on the geography of our hearts and souls.

Some of us working on the series have a hunch there are still more Crystal Creek stories to be told. And maybe someday, somebody will tell them.

But for now, we've reached the end of this particular trail. With affection I will remember traveling down it, and I feel privileged to have been along for the trip.

So, as the sun settles slowly in the west for this series, I want to say some thank-yous. First, a tornado figures in this book. I want to thank my mother and my son for riding out the fearsome experience of a *real* tornado with me—that day, nature taught me what fear was, and they taught me what courage was.

Many, many thanks to Karin Stoecker and Marsha Zinberg for starting this immense and ambitious project and for guiding us along the way. Their vision was bold, their daring was inspiring and their support was unfailing. The Dynamic Duo—what writers could ask for a better, smarter or more gutsy pair at the helm?

Thanks to Zilla Soriano and Marsha for their editorial insight and guidance, and to our overworked copy editor, Darlene Money. Zilla, Marsha, Darlene, it couldn't have been done without you. Or you, either, Brenda Chin, editorial assistant on this project.

Thanks to the other writers on the series for their generosity and camaraderie: Barbara, Sharon, Cara, Kathy, Penny, Sandy—and most especially Margot Dalton, not only a good writer, but a good friend.

A special thank-you to Imat Amidjaja, wherever you may be. Someday I hope to find you again, laugh with you again and tell you how much you meant to us. If God gives gifts, Imat, one of the greatest he gave me was you.

Bethany Campbell

Who's Who in Crystal Creek

Have you missed the story of one of your favorite Crystal Creek characters? Here's a quick guide to help you easily locate the titles and story lines:

To my own Texas hero,
the man from El Campo

CHAPTER ONE

IN HIS VEINS ran the blood of princes, peasants, warriors, masters, slaves, mystics and pirates. He was tall, dark, handsome, and the most exotic person ever to set foot in Crystal Creek.

Born on the island of Java, he was half Chinese, one quarter Indonesian, and one quarter Dutch mixed with Australian. So mixed was his heritage that he had largely ignored it, choosing instead to invent himself according to his own lights. He liked America because it was as energetic, irreverent and independent as he was.

He spoke English fluently, with only the faintest trace of a foreign accent. Thirty-one years old, he conveyed a skeptical, mocking and slightly dangerous air. What was most dangerous about him was his mind, which was keen as a scalpel.

He stood six feet even, all lean muscle. His shoulders were wide, and he always wore jeans that hugged his hips. His belt had a silver buckle he'd bought in Bangkok, and his black cowboy boots showed scuffs from real use.

He'd done his undergrad studies at the University of Hawaii. Summers, for the hell of it, he'd worked as a hand on one of the Big Island's cattle ranches, and he'd turned out to be a natural. He could ride a horse, throw a rope, herd and cut cattle as if he'd been born to it.

He still rode when he could, but he was not a cowboy by any means. He was Crystal Creek's newest doctor, and he was not happy about doing grunt work in such a hick town.

Dr. S.J. Dekker was fresh from his residency in Austin and hungry for mental challenge. He was not meant for the slow life and dreary practice of a backwater clinic. He was a neurosurgeon, for God's sake. Crystal Creek needed a specialist like a horse needed ballet shoes. But here he was, stuck in a town full of tonsil cases and gas pains. He could tolerate the situation only because it was temporary—six months.

Dekker had been supposed to go to Denver at Hopkins-Sloane, one of the premier neurosurgical clinics in the country. But his appointment had gotten tangled up in a foul and infuriating knot.

The Denver position was one of the most desirable that a young neurosurgeon could snag. And it had been Dekker's, all but the contract, until the venerable Dr. Amos Hopkins had decided at the last minute he would *not* retire on the fifteenth of August as he'd announced. Rather Hopkins had decided to wait until his sixty-second birthday, which was an interminable six months away. Until then, Dekker would have to wait in limbo.

Dr. Amos Hopkins was a genius, of course, and one of the founders of Hopkins-Sloane, so he could do anything he damn well pleased, no matter how eccentric or inconvenient.

So for six months, Dekker would kill time in Crystal Creek. It had been the only place he could find desperate enough to hire a doctor who refused a contract and would only stay half a year.

The town had every reason to be desperate. Given its size, it should have had five doctors. Until he'd arrived, it'd had only two, the bright but aging Dr. Nate Purdy and the younger Dr. Greg Sinclair, who, on his best days, was close to competent.

Like a prisoner, Dekker marked the days off the calendar that hung on the wall of his cheerless apartment. Sometimes he made mental lists of everything he liked and disliked about Crystal Creek. The length of the lists differed dramatically.

He liked Dr. Nate and Rose Purdy and the pie at the Longhorn Coffee Shop.

He disliked the hospital, which was small, poorly constructed and in sad disrepair. It needed more room, more beds, more equipment, more everything. He disliked the clinic, which was always swamped with patients, disorganized and running late.

He disliked the clinic's malingering office manager, Peggy Sue Grimes. She hid her laziness behind a facade of sweetness and pathos that made him queasy.

He disliked Peggy's husband, Roger Grimes, the assistant football coach at the high school. Grimes was a muscle-bound hulk who thought he was God's gift to sports. Football was not a game to Grimes, but the one true religion.

Most of the town was caught up in the mania, because the Crystal Creek Cougars were on their way to their third statewide championship, and everyone was conscious of this glorious prospect.

The radio station had distributed printed football schedules, and they glared from every business's front window, ornamented the walls of every bar and restaurant. They bore a photo of Grimes posed with his team, approximately four tons of aggressive adolescents in shoulder pads and custom jerseys.

The radio station had also passed out blue and gold booster buttons that said, Go Cougars! Not to wear one was considered heretical. Dekker did not wear one.

He was depressed every time he drove past the town limits, because one could not avoid the signs reading: Crystal Creek, Home of State Champion Cougars! GO, COUGARS!

Sometimes he mourned this football madness over a beer with another newcomer to town, the high school band director, Tap Hollister. Hollister could be as derisive as Dekker.

The first time they met, Hollister had grumbled, "Those football gorillas have their own weight room. About a million bucks' worth of equipment. I think they have their uniforms hand-sewn in Paris. They got designer helmets, hundred-and-fifty-dollar cleats. Can I get squeeze a dime from the school for new band uniforms? No. I've got a tuba player who's split his pants three times. He mooned an entire stadium last weekend. And a full moon it was.

"What buttons we've got left are tarnished," Hollister muttered. "The sashes are rags. The hats are beat-up. Will the school board give us one red cent? No. We gotta have a chili cook-off to raise funds."

"Have fun," Dekker said.

"You'll have fun with us," Hollister warned. "The hospital's going to enter a team. They'll want you. To show your civic spirit."

"I have no civic spirit," Dekker said. "I don't want any."

"You'll be there," Hollister said. "Beverly'll make you."

Beverly, Dekker thought contemptuously. *Beverly Townsend. The beauty queen herself.* Why, of all the irritating things in Crystal Creek, did Beverly Townsend irritate him most?

"When hell freezes over," he said.

BEVERLY TOWNSEND and Dekker had gotten off to a bad start. A former Miss Texas and first runner-up for the Miss America title, she did volunteer work at the hospital when she wasn't off somewhere pursuing her career as a model.

A model, Dekker always thought in disgust. Modeling was high on his list of useless occupations, right up there with poodle groomers and mimes.

Dr. Nate Purdy raved about her. But Dekker couldn't see her charm. He considered her a beautiful, empty-headed twit. She had a phony, if brilliant, smile and an all-too-genuine streak of prejudice.

When she met him for the first time, her blue eyes had widened in surprise, and he knew why. She hadn't been expecting an Asian, and it showed. It showed big-time.

To his knowledge, he was the only Oriental in Crystal Creek. He understood the look on Beverly's face. It said, *You're different. You're alien. You're not one of us.*

She had recovered quickly and flashed him her megawatt beauty-queen smile. She shook his hand with too much enthusiasm, began to talk too effusively.

She pretended his first name, Sunarjo, was too difficult for her to pronounce and declared she would always call him Sonny Joe.

After that, whenever she saw him, in a voice of purest syrup she would say, "Oh, hi there, Sonny Joe!"

Sonny Joe, for God's sake. What next? A Confederate belt buckle, a shotgun, a hound dog covered with ticks? Perhaps he should lose a few teeth, learn to pluck the banjo and spit tobacco juice.

But the name caught on, which blackened his already dark mood about being in Crystal Creek. He became known, Lord help him, as Dr. Sonny Dekker. Bleakly he thanked the fates that she hadn't decided to call him Skippy or Bubba or something even worse. Bitterly, he resigned himself to being Sonny for the next six months.

Oh, there was no question Beverly was lovely. She had big azure-blue eyes, an almost too perfect little nose, a dewy pink mouth right out of a lipstick ad.

Her fabulous blond hair cascaded to her waist, and a tiny little waist it was. Her breasts were too good to be true, and he would bet she'd had a boob job. Well, if so, it was a damn fine boob job.

But she was so overgroomed and overwhelmingly glamorous that he couldn't take her seriously. She had perfected and polished herself into a glossy sex object. *Object* was exactly what she'd seemed to him, not really human and not really sexy. She was too flawless, too designed.

There was a rumor that she had been thinking of going to medical school. He could not, no matter how hard he tried, picture her as a doctor. She had no more depth than a teaspoon.

He found it improbable that Miss Beauty Queen was engaged to an oil field wildcatter who had little money and was often gone. But when he saw the fiancé, all was explained. The guy was handsome as hell. He and Beverly were two gorgeous creatures in a gorgeous, mindless, sensual romp. Ken and Barbie with glands.

Their romance was not smooth, and it kept hospital gossip lively. They would marry soon. No, they wouldn't. Yes, they would. Every time they weren't getting along, Beverly went into world-class denial and acted so cheery and friendly that it set Dekker's teeth on edge.

But then, the unthinkable happened. Something went violently wrong with the golden girl's life. Her fiancé, Jeff Harris, was killed in an oil field accident. The town was shocked.

Dekker didn't see Beverly for a long time after the accident. He heard she was devastated, stricken almost speechless, not even able to cry. He was surprised at how hard she was said to be taking it.

He also heard that within a month after Jeff's death, she'd had another severe blow. Old Hank Travis died in his sleep. Dekker had never met him, but everyone seemed unable to believe the old man was gone. He had been one hundred years old.

"Grandpa Hank" had not been Beverly's real grandfather, but he was the closest thing she had. Like Jeff Harris, he had been an oilman, and Beverly had grown close to him. She took his loss as hard as anyone in his immediate family.

Nate Purdy was concerned. "She's a sensitive woman. It took her a long time to get over her father's death. This is going to throw her badly. I know that girl. Too much dying. She's not equipped to deal with it. Poor kid."

Dekker wasn't inclined to be sympathetic. "If she can't deal with dying, why does she hang around a hospital?"

Nate gave him a sharp look. "Because she tries to fight her own weakness. And up till now, she's done a damn good job. You know your trouble?"

Dekker was taken aback by the older man's tone. "I don't have any trouble."

"Yes, you do," Nate snapped. "You and Beverly both have the same trouble. You're too much alike, dammit."

"Me?" he said, appalled. "Like her? God forbid."

"*That's* what I mean," Nate said, stabbing a finger at Dekker's chest. "Have you ever once looked at her? As a person? No. All you see is a beauty queen, a Southern belle, an airhead. She's not an airhead."

"You could have fooled me."

"See?" Nate demanded. "See? I know how she gets to you. It's your goddamn pride. And you've got a lot of it—wonder boy."

"Wonder boy? I never said I was a wonder boy."

"You don't have to say it. Your résumé does. And I know how you feel about being in this town. Like you're a Thoroughbred racehorse hitched to a plow."

That, of course, was exactly how Dekker felt, but he wouldn't give Nate the satisfaction of admitting it. "What's this got to do with Beverly Townsend?"

"You don't like Beverly because the first time she met you, she saw you as a stereotype."

"Right," Dekker said with a sardonic nod. "She gave me a look that said, 'Why aren't you in the kitchen making chow mein? Why aren't you in the laundry, ironee shirtee?' "

"Give her a break," Nate said, clearly at the end of his patience. "Her father was a good ol' boy, but he had a prejudice, a bad one, and he passed it on to her. She's trying to overcome it, dammit, but you don't give her a chance. You act like an iceberg around her."

"Look. I'm a person, not some blonde's Remedial Oriental 101. I don't want to be her token good deed."

"Crap," Nate said bluntly. "She's tried with you. You didn't know her father. He was a POW, Vietnam. You never saw his scars. I'm surprised the man didn't die."

"I'm not Vietnamese," Dekker shot back. "I didn't know him. Why should I pay for what somebody else did?"

Nate sighed and put his hand on Dekker's shoulder. "Look, son. I'm sorry. We're lucky to have you here. Damned lucky. But I want you to understand about Beverly."

"Why?"

"Because my wife and I love her."

"Why?"

"Because she's lovable. Give her a chance."

"She looks at me like I escaped from a Charlie Chan movie."

"She's doing the best she can, blast it. Her father wouldn't watch television if there was an Oriental on the screen. He wouldn't eat if there was rice in the *room*. I saw him walk out of church suppers, dragging Beverly with him, because somebody brought rice."

"He sounds like a swell guy. I wish we could have met, bonded."

"I am trying," Nate said with great deliberation, "to tell you what she's up against. Give her credit, will you? Her father was traumatized, he traumatized her. She was trying hard to get past it. Do you have to be such a cold fish to her?"

"I don't like her. Isn't this a free country? Can't I not like somebody?"

"You're a worse bigot than she is," Nate said.

"Me?"

"Yes. All you see is a stereotype yourself. Blond. Miss Beauty Pageant. She tried to look past the surface, at least. You don't even try. Hell."

"Me? Think in stereotypes?"

"When it comes to her, you do. And what's funny is the two of you really *are* alike. You've both got charm. And you can both turn it off and on like a faucet."

"I don't have charm, dammit. I've got a bedside manner. It's different."

"Ha," said Nate Purdy. "I have spoken." He walked off.

Dekker looked after him, frowning in consternation. He wasn't happy in Crystal Creek, but he'd come to like and respect Nate. The man labored like a workhorse; he had dedication; he was honest and said what he thought.

Could Purdy possibly be right? Had Dekker never really looked at Beverly as a human being? Had he judged her harshly? Even stupidly?

He couldn't abide stupidity in anyone, least of all himself. The next time he saw Nate, he apologized. "Okay," he said with a resigned sigh, "make me like this blonde."

"Ah," said Nate. "Let me tell you about her work with some of the kids...."

IT WAS TWO MONTHS after the accident, late October, when Beverly returned to the hospital. The only difference Dekker saw in her was that she had cut her beautiful golden hair. Now it only reached her shoulders.

But she was bright-eyed and smiling. Nothing at all seemed to have affected her. Nate was dubious. "Beverly, are you sure you're ready for this?"

"I'm perfectly fine," she said airily. "And I've been useless lately. I've got to do *something,* don't I?"

Nate agreed to let her stay, but later he took Dekker aside. "Watch out for her," he said gruffly. "I've got to go back to the clinic. Keep your eye on her."

Dekker nodded. Beverly went to the children's small solarium to help the kids cut out and color paper leaves. With her audience of children, she smiled a lot and seemed to be her old fiddle-de-dee, Scarlett O'Hara self.

He'd come into the solarium at the end of his rounds, under the pretense of checking on a boy with a neck injury. Beverly gave him a sunny smile and kept cutting paper and coloring and chattering with the children.

Unexpectedly a little boy with a leg cast said, "Your boyfriend went to heaven, didn't he?"

"Yes," Beverly said without hesitation. "He's with the angels now. He's in a wonderful place, and nothing can ever hurt him again. Oh! Look at that pretty leaf that Jenny made."

After a moment, she said a sudden and cheerful goodbye—too sudden, too cheerful, Dekker thought.

"I think I'll run on home," she said. "Y'all be good. That means you, too, Sonny. See you!" She flashed them all a smile, blew the children a kiss and left.

He strolled to the solarium entrance, leaned against the doorframe and watched her as she walked down the corridor. Her head was high, her back straight. With one hand she absently touched her trimmed hair.

She walked with perfect grace, as if she were on the runway in a beauty contest, parading before the judges' eyes. But when she reached the end of the hall, she turned neither right nor left. Instead, she went to the janitor's supply closet, opened the door and stepped inside, shutting it behind her.

He blinked in surprise. *Miss Texas just shut herself in the supply closet.* Alarm swept him. Nate was right. She was under too much strain. He had visions of her drinking cleaning fluid, trying to end it all.

He sprinted after her, flung the closet door open. She cowered in a corner, her hands to her eyes, crying in silent sobs that racked her body.

"Shut the door," she ordered almost pettishly. Gone was all pretense of cheer or charm. "I don't want anybody to see me. Leave me alone."

She shot him a resentful glance, yet her expression seemed full of need. He stared at her in concern. Her eyes were red, mascara ran down her cheeks, and she looked like utter hell. The closet was a large one and had a light switch. He turned on the light and pulled the door shut.

"I think you should go home," he said as gently as he could. "Do you want me to take you? Or would you rather somebody else did?" He offered her his handkerchief.

She didn't take it and didn't answer, only kept on crying soundlessly, her hands pressed to her face. Her chest heaved, and her fingers dripped with tears.

He didn't think twice. The most natural thing seemed to be to put his arms around her and draw her close.

She resisted for a moment, then sank against his shoulder, sobbing. Her tears were hot, soaking through the fabric of his jacket and shirt.

"He's dead—and I was mean to him," she choked. "I didn't know he was going to die—and I was mean to him. Now he's gone."

Her words went through him like an arrow. Twenty years ago he'd said almost the same thing when he'd learned his younger brother was dead. It was the last time in his life he had cried. "Hanafi's dead—and I was mean to him," he'd said in anguish. It had been in another language, another country, and, it now seemed in another lifetime, but he understood her emotion, all too well.

She sobbed so hard that her body quaked, so he held her tighter. She no longer seemed silly or less than human to him.

Later, he drove her home to the ranch, where she lived with her mother and stepfather. He walked her to the door. She seemed humiliated by her outburst. Yet it was also as if a wall between them had fallen down.

"I'd ask you in," she said, her voice still shaky. "But I'm not very good company today."

"Are you going to be all right?" he asked. "Is your mother home? Will there be somebody with you?"

She nodded and tried to give him a smile. It failed. She'd repaired her makeup so that her face looked nearly normal, but he still couldn't get used to her shortened hair, which was tumbled now. He resisted the urge to touch it, to try to smooth its gold back into some sort of order.

She took his hand to shake it goodbye. He felt a galvanic jolt go through him at the unexpected touch. Her skin looked almost ivory next to the bronze of his.

"I owe you an apology," she said, looking at their joined hands. "I acted stupid when I met you. And I've probably seemed silly and phony, trying to make up for it. But when I needed a friend, you were there. Thanks, Sonny. I hope we'll stay friends."

His heart took a long, awkward stumble in his chest. The nickname she'd given him no longer seemed hateful. He dropped her hand, but her touch still burned and tingled through him.

"Friends? Sure," he said gruffly.

"Good," she said and nodded.

Be careful, he told himself. *Friendship is all she could ever feel for you. Be careful.*

But it was too late. He, of all people, was already half in love with her. He, who had trained his mind to be as cutting as a diamond and his heart to be diamond-hard. He sensed his honorable ancestors turning over in their graves.

BEVERLY DIDN'T GO back to the hospital for a week. She'd stayed home, crying over Jeff, crying over their last argument, crying over everything. Now that her tears had finally come, it seemed they couldn't stop.

His death was senseless and unthinkable. That she had quarreled with him during his last hours was unbearable. She wept until she was sick. Then she remembered that Grandpa Hank, too, was gone, and wept even more.

Her grief was real and deep, and it was compounded by guilt. Jeff Harris had been an unlikely lover for her, but she'd adored him with all her being.

When they met, he'd had a bad-boy past, few prospects for a future, and everyone was surprised when Beverly, rich and privileged, took up with him. Nobody had been more surprised than Beverly herself.

Their romance had been tumultuous, their engagement even more so. The day before his death, she had given the ring back to him—for the third time.

By that night, she'd started to regret it. By the next morning she was ready to apologize. But then, unbelievably, he was dead. Dead. Him, so young and beautiful and full of life and quick desire. It had not seemed possible. It still did not.

At last, her tears were spent. She felt empty and numb. The pain was deadened, but so were all other emotions.

Only then did she return to the hospital. She walked in the front door, and there stood Dr. Sonny Dekker. She looked at him, and her cheeks blazed with shame. She'd been held in this man's arms. She had literally cried on his shoulder.

But he didn't act embarrassed. Instead, he seemed almost bored. "Hi. How ya doing?" he asked in his slightly husky voice. He stood with his thumbs hooked on either side of his belt buckle, his hip cocked.

He wore what she thought of as his hospital uniform, the black cowboy boots, faded jeans, white shirt, black tie, tan blazer. The outfit never varied, and she thought that perhaps he did not own many clothes.

She realized that she, in contrast, was overdressed. Nate teased her without mercy when her clothes were too fancy for the hospital, but sometimes she did not so much wear her clothes as hide behind them. Today she wore a little sky-blue dress that cost a fortune and was so sassy it seemed to say that she didn't have a care in the world.

Her earrings were diamond studs; she had on her gold necklaces and bracelets and Rolex watch, her sapphire ring. She had dressed like a million dollars because she felt like ten cents.

"How am I? Fine," she said a little too brightly.

When his keen black eyes settled on her mascaraed blue ones, he gave her a one-sided smile. It was wry, and it shook her unaccountably. He knew she was faking. She could feel it in the pit of her stomach.

Still, though his smile mocked her, she sensed kindness in it. "I'm taking a break," he said casually. "Can I buy you a cup of coffee?"

She didn't feel like it and started to refuse, but realized she might seem unfriendly. "Sure," she said and gave her hair a perky little toss.

They strolled toward the staff coffee room. He looked her up and down. "You're awfully dressed up," he said. "You look okay. Even kind of—attractive. Yeah. Maybe so. You almost look kind of attractive."

Beverly's eyes widened in surprise. She looked *kind* of attractive? Didn't this man realize she'd been a beauty queen, almost Miss America? Or by his country's standards, was she not good-looking at all?

She started to say, "Why, thank you" and give him a forced smile, but then she saw the devilish glint in his eyes. He was teasing her—quite expertly. His mouth curved into a fraction of a smile.

She narrowed her eyes. "You look quite sharp yourself," she said. "I admire your outfit. Very innovative."

"Touché," he said. "Actually, I have no taste in clothes. So I always wear the same thing. That way I can't screw up too much."

Beverly gave him a curious glance. The cowboy boots should have seemed incongruous, but they didn't. Some men were built to wear jeans and cowboy boots, and he was one of them. "Don't you get tired of it?" she asked. "Always wearing the same thing?"

"Nope," he said. "It simplifies life. I get up in the morning—no sartorial decisions. Absolute efficiency."

They'd reached the staff coffee room. No one else was there. He starting putting coins in the machine. "You take it black? Or how?"

"Black, please."

She sat at the little Formica-covered table. He brought two cups of coffee and sat across from her.

"So," he said, "let me impress you with my social skills. I can be very original in conversation. How's this? What's a nice girl like you doing in a place like this?" He made a gesture that indicated the hospital as a whole.

"I just do volunteer work. You know that," she said, suddenly feeling shy. Until the closet incident, he'd treated her aloofly, coldly, in fact. She hadn't suspected he had this sardonic, playful side.

"What's this about you going to medical school?" he asked. "Is it true?"

She shrugged. "It was only a wild idea. I couldn't really do it."

"Why not?"

Because, she thought darkly, *I don't deal with death and dying well. I thought I was over all that, but I'm not.*

"Oh, I'm just a flibberti-gibbet," she said. "I haven't got the brains for it. Let's not talk about me. Let's talk about you. Why, I don't even know where Indonesia is, for goodness' sake."

"Yes, you do," he said. There was irony in his voice, and his statement startled her. She met his eyes again. His gaze was so steady, so full of vitality and intelligence that again she felt oddly shaken.

"What?" she said, caught off guard again.

"You're smarter than you pretend," he said. "Nate told me you were a straight A student all through school—college, too. He likes to sing your praises. I know you got the geography medal three years in a row in junior high. I'll bet you know exactly where Indonesia is."

Caught, she blushed.

"Don't you?" he challenged, his gaze holding hers.

She gave him a slightly shamed smile. "Indonesia lies north of Australia, south of Vietnam. It's part of the Malay Archipelago."

He laughed. He had a nice laugh, a low, deep chuckle. She couldn't help smiling back.

"You fooled me at first," he said. "I thought you were the archetypal dumb blonde. Why the act?"

She toyed with her coffee cup, embarrassed that he'd seen through her. "My daddy used to say I'd scare all the boys off if I acted too smart. He said a real lady didn't parade her brains."

His dark hair had fallen across his brow. He pushed it back, an impatient gesture. "Your daddy may have had a point. Beautiful women can be intimidating. Smart, beautiful women?—doubly so. Is it hard, looking the way you do? I think it would be."

She stared at him with fresh surprise. No man had ever asked her such a question. It *was*, in fact, hard being beautiful, sometimes quite hard. Women often acted jealous or unfriendly. Men often *did* seem intimidated. Or overeager, wanting her only for her face and body, not herself. Jeff had been different.

"It has its drawbacks," she said, looking away. "But I really don't want to talk about me. What about you? Your English is fantastic. You must have studied like mad."

He took a sip of coffee, shook his head. "No. It came easy for me. Besides, I've been in the States thirteen years."

"That long? Really?"

"Yep. I started college in Indonesia, got a scholarship to finish my undergraduate work in Hawaii. Did med school and interned in California. Came to Austin to do my residency. I wanted to work with Swanson—he's one of the best. I'm supposed to be in a neurology clinic in Denver. But there was a screwup. So, I ended up here. Temporarily, thank God."

He said "here" with such obvious contempt that Beverly blinked. "You don't like Crystal Creek?"

"No," he said emphatically. "Bright lights, big city, that's my style. It's hard to get into a conversation around here that doesn't center on football. Every person on the staff wears a booster button. Even Nate."

"Oh," Beverly said. "Well that's partly because of Peggy Sue Grimes."

"The office manager who never manages the office?"

She smiled an acknowledgment. "Since her husband's the assistant coach, everyone figures her feelings will be hurt if we don't all wear our booster buttons." Almost guiltily she raised her lapel to show him hers. She tried to keep it hidden unless Peggy was around.

"I won't wear one. Know what?"

Beverly smiled again. "We're having a conversation about football. So let's change it. Tell me about Hawaii. I've always wanted to see it."

"You've never been to the Big Island?" he asked. "Or Kauai? God, they're beautiful."

"No," she said, putting her elbows on the table and resting her chin in her hands. "Tell me."

So he did. He told her of green mountains and sapphire-blue waves and forests of giant ferns. He beguiled her with descriptions of volcanoes and tall, lovely waterfalls. He described orchids growing wild and whales that sported in the harbor.

Beverly listened, enchanted. He'd seen dozens of places she'd only dreamed of, and he described them vividly and with humor.

He was telling her a wildly funny story about Thailand when his name came over the intercom. "Dr. Dekker to the emergency room. Dr. Dekker to the emergency room."

He sprang to his feet, looking at his watch. "Damn! I lost track of time. See you."

He was gone, the spell was broken, and Beverly found herself alone, marooned again in the small-town realities of Crystal Creek. She realized that for the first time in weeks she had escaped from thoughts of herself and Jeff.

What an interesting person, she'd thought about Sunarjo Dekker. *I'd like to talk more to him.*

And she did. Soon they were always together during coffee breaks. She saved up jokes, stories and observations to share with him. They became friends, but friends only.

After all, so close to Jeff's death, she was incapable of thinking of falling in love again. Sonny Dekker as a friend was a godsend. But as a lover? The thought did not even cross her mind.

CHAPTER TWO

IT WAS a rainy Saturday afternoon, and Belinda Dugan sat, solitary, in the Longhorn Coffee Shop. She had the place almost to herself.

Belinda, twenty-two, was the new speech and history teacher at the high school. She sat in a booth nursing her coffee and reading a depressing book about the Battle of Gallipoli.

She had come to the Longhorn before the rain started, simply to escape her lonely apartment. Her real home was in Waco, and she usually went back on weekends, but this week her parents were in Oregon, visiting their brand-new grandchild, their first.

Belinda tried to avoid spending weekends in Crystal Creek because it was too painful. She was in the humiliating position of adoring a man who barely noticed she existed. All the clichés fit: she had fallen in love at first sight, had tumbled head over heels, and bells had rung.

Today, she'd hardly noticed when the rain started, but now a clap of thunder boomed so loudly that she jumped.

"Wow!" gasped Kasey, the waitress. She'd been sitting at the counter, doing a crossword puzzle. "That scared me!" Belinda didn't have a chance to reply because another crack of thunder split the air.

Then the door burst open, and in came the man who was the object of Belinda's hopeless devotion. Even soaking wet, he looked so wonderful that it shook her to the heart.

Tap Hollister was the director of the high school's marching band. Tall and lean and wide-shouldered, he had chiseled features and the most beautiful eyes she'd ever seen, a startling and vibrant blue.

He wore his blond hair longish, and the rain made it curl around his ears. Water glistened on his biceps, had pasted his T-shirt to his chest and made his tight jeans cling more tightly. Raindrops made starlike points of the lashes of his remarkable eyes.

A lightning flash blazed, and simultaneously another thunderclap roared, making the walls quiver and the window glass rattle.

Tap leaned back against the door, his arms spread as if guarding it. "Thor is angry," he said ominously. "Quick—we need to sacrifice a virgin. Do either of you qualify?"

Kasey snorted. "Count me out."

"Then it has to be you, Dugan," he said to Belinda. "Can I buy you a last cup of coffee? It's the least I can do."

Belinda blushed. As always, Tap's presence made her tongue-tied and awkward. He was so different from her. Words came easily to him; he took the world with a sardonically merry attitude, and he never seemed hindered by inhibitions. He exuded life and a kind of high-hearted rebellion.

He sat down in the booth beside her, so close she could feel the heat of his body. He smelled like rain. When she looked into his eyes, they were so blue they made her dizzy.

"What's your book?" he asked.

Belinda's heart banged wildly in her chest. "I—I need to know more about Australian history. It's—it's about the Battle of Gallipoli."

"Heavy stuff," he said, nodding. "Did you ever hear that song about it? 'The Band Played Waltzing Matilda.' Tommy Makem sings it."

"No," she managed to say. She felt so breathless it made her panicky.

"Killer song," he said with feeling. "Come into my office sometime. I'll play it for you. But bring about eight hankies. Four for you, four for me."

She smiled, but felt her lip twitch nervously.

"Yo, Kasey," he said. "Coffee for me and a refill for my pal Dugan, here. Okay?"

My pal Dugan, Belinda thought bleakly. Was that how he would always see her? She supposed so.

She was in love with Tap, but Tap was in love with someone else, and he didn't try to hide it. That made him all the more enigmatic to her, because although he acted carefree, she knew his heart was broken.

Tap had been smitten by Liz Babcock, the former choral music teacher. Liz was tall, confident and beautiful. She was like a younger, more casual and Americanized version of Sophia Loren.

Belinda, on the other hand, was short, shy and unremarkable. She resembled no movie star at all, and the only person she looked like was her mother. She was so petite she felt minuscule. Her long hair was ordinary brown and straight as string. She had large, dark eyes that people sometimes told her were pretty, but when she looked in a mirror, she was reminded not of a gazelle, but of a faithful cocker spaniel.

She was, in short, not the sort of woman to make a man forget someone like the stunning Liz.

It didn't matter to Tap that Liz was eighteen years older than he was, or that she had eloped with another man. Belinda had heard that Tap had told Rex Carradine, the math teacher, that he would never love another woman.

He certainly didn't *look* at other women, Belinda thought gloomily, least of all herself. Almost every girl in the high school had a violent crush on him, but he didn't seem to notice. The unmarried women of Crystal Creek practically fell over one another trying to flirt with him. He wasn't interested; his mind was on Liz alone.

"So," he said, turning to Belinda. "How come you're here? I thought you went home every weekend. Where is it? San Antonio?"

"Waco," she said in a near-whisper. She stared at the tabletop so she wouldn't get lost in his eyes. *Oh, God,* she thought, *This is terrible. Why does he affect me like this?*

She was saved when two men walked into the Longhorn. She knew one of them only by sight. He was short, stout, gray-haired, and his name was Horace Westerhaus. He owned the local radio station and the controlling interest of the town's weekly paper.

The other man was Roger Grimes, the assistant football coach at the high school. He was arrogant and abrasive, and Belinda thought he set a terrible example for his players.

The two men stood in the doorway, dripping rain. Both wore their football booster buttons. Horace Westerhaus took off his billed cap, shook the water from it, then noticed Tap.

"Hollister," Horace said in a raspy voice, "you're that band feller, right?"

"Right," Tap said. Then out of the side of his mouth, he whispered to Belinda, "Is there no end to my fame?"

"I wanna talk to you," Horace said. "I got a grandson that wants an electric guitar. What should I buy him?"

"Depends," Tap said. "On his age, on what you want to spend, on a lot of things."

Horace didn't wait to be invited. He sat down and joined them. Roger Grimes sat, too.

Brusquely Horace introduced himself to Belinda, but he didn't bother to ask her name. Both men gave her a cursory glance, then seemed to forget about her, as men often tended to do. She was almost grateful. She could sit by Tap and say nothing at all.

Horace grilled Tap about guitars. He was a self-important man, humorless and full of opinions. Roger Grimes sat next to him, smirking at nothing in particular.

Horace changed the subject to Crystal Creek's football team, which seemed guaranteed to win its third consecutive state championship. Horace and Roger went on about place kickers and punts and quarterback options.

Tap tried to bring Belinda into the conversation. "We're ignoring the lovely lady. How are things in your corner of the world, Dugan? What's the debate topic this year?"

She gave a shaky smile and loathed her own nervousness. Taking a deep breath, she said, "It's on foreign aid to disaster areas. We've got three propositions to work on—"

"Now that's something I don't hold with," Horace asserted. "Giving aid to foreigners. If you want my opinion—"

"Hello, everybody!" caroled a jolly voice. "My goodness, it's raining cats and dogs out there."

Shirley Jean Ditmars stood just inside the doorway, water pouring off her clear plastic raincoat. She was a round, bright-eyed woman who worked at the telephone company.

"Kasey, bring me a cup of coffee, will you, hon?" Shirley said. She walked to their booth, pulled up a chair and sat down at the end of the table. Then she shucked off her raincoat and hung it on the back of her chair. Shirley wore two booster buttons, one for each of the nephews she had on the team.

"Have you ever seen such rain?" she asked, giggling. "Maybe we should build an ark."

Everyone smiled dutifully, but Belinda's heart sank. She didn't know Shirley Jean Ditmars in person, only by reputation. It was said that if the Olympics had a competition for gossip, Shirley Jean would be sure to bring home the gold.

Shirley's dark eyes glittered with curiosity as she examined Belinda. "You're the new speech teacher, right? And history, too? Belinda Ann Dugan? From Waco? Your daddy's the principal of a high school there? He retires next year? You graduated from U.T. in Austin?"

Belinda nodded numbly. The woman was uncanny and more than a little frightening.

"I'm Shirley Jean Ditmars," Shirley announced with pride. Her gaze darted from Belinda to Tap and back again, and her smile grew knowing.

"You two," she said, wagging her finger at them. "Are you seeing each other? Sitting so cozy like that?"

Belinda almost choked. Tap shook his head. "No, ma'am. I came in to hide from the rain, and Dugan was here. She was kind enough to share her booth."

Shirley studied him. "Hmm," she said.

Belinda cleared her throat uncomfortably. She was about to say, *In fact, I think I should be running along now.* But the rain was still pouring, and she hesitated.

Shirley tried to fluff her wet bangs. "I declare," she said. "I must look like a wet poodle dog. You know who I saw sharing an umbrella? Just as big as you please?"

"Elvis and Eva Peron?" Tap asked innocently.

Shirley made a shooing gesture. "Go on, you. Of course not. It was Beverly Townsend and that Chinese doctor."

"I wouldn't go to any Chinese doctor," said Roger Grimes with a snigger. "He'd stick those acupuncture needles in you. And put you on a chop suey diet."

Horace and Shirley laughed. Tap and Belinda did not.

Encouraged, Roger went on. "But that Beverly, she's something else. Woo!" His hands described the shape of an hourglass. "She's a looker, all right."

"She may be a looker," Shirley said, sniffing, "but she doesn't care how things *look.* It's one thing for her to carry on at the hospital with that man. But going out in public? My goodness, poor Jeff Harris is barely cold in his grave. Well, the beauty queens always do go after the doctors. But a Chinese one? My word."

Tap's voice was dangerously quiet. "They're friends. Dekker and the woman. Just friends."

Shirley lifted an eyebrow critically. "You know him?"

"Yeah," Tap said in the same tone. "I've played pool with him a couple of times. We have a beer once in a while. They're friends. That's all."

"I should hope so," Shirley said. "Anything else would be—unacceptable. Completely."

Kasey brought Shirley's coffee. "Sorry it took so long," she said. "I was making a fresh pot."

"Kasey, what do you think?" said Shirley. "Are Beverly and that Chinese man just friends? Or is something going on?"

Kasey put her hand on her hip and stared down coolly at Shirley. "First, he isn't Chinese. He's part Indonesian and part Dutch, and I think some Australian."

"Huh," Roger Grimes said, "a real mongrel."

"Well, whatever. He's foreign," Shirley said. "Are they having a fling?"

Kasey's face grew sterner. "It's my distinct impression that he's helping her get through a tough time. That's all. But if he wants more than friendship, I can name a dozen women who'd volunteer. I think he's a hunk."

"A hunk?" Shirley said, clearly horrified. "But, Kasey, how can a Chinese person be a hunk?"

Kasey tossed her head. "What about John Lone? Or Jason Scott Lee? Or Bruce Lee? Sonny Dekker looks a lot like Bruce Lee."

"Who's Bruce Lee?" Shirley asked, her hand pressed to her breast in shock.

"A movie star," Kasey said. "Stop at the video store on your way home. Give yourself a thrill. A big one."

"I'm sure I wouldn't be thrilled a bit," vowed Shirley.

"I don't believe in mixin' the races," Horace Westerhaus said firmly. "It's not natural. Do you see bluebirds mate with robins? See sparrows mate with jaybirds? No sir."

"Amen," said Roger Grimes with a sagacious nod.

"I'm getting out of this conversation," Kasey said grimly. "Before I get in deep trouble."

The thunder rolled. She walked away and sat at the farthest end of the counter, pointedly keeping apart.

"Well," Shirley whispered. "She didn't have to get huffy. Who did she say? Bruce Lee? Who *is* he?"

"A hunk," Belinda surprised herself by saying. "And she's right—Dr. Dekker's quite attractive."

The glance Horace gave her was hostile, but she didn't care. She hated this conversation.

"He's also damn bright," Tap said. "This town's lucky to have him."

"I wouldn't let him touch me," Horace said with conviction. "What's the matter with American doctors? Let him go back where he come from."

"That's a terrible thing to say!" Belinda instinctively reprimanded him, and then was shocked that the words had slipped from her mouth.

Horace narrowed his eyes at her. He studied her for a long and chilling minute, as if seeing her for the first time. "Dugan? That's your name? I know who you are. You're the one giving Joe Bob and Kayo such a hard time, aren't you?"

Belinda's cheeks burned. Joe Bob and Kayo Westerhaus were two of Horace's grandsons. Both were on the football team, and both had such mediocre grades that they were in danger of being benched. They were doing particularly badly in her history class and were unruly to boot.

"You've been givin' those boys bad grades," he said in an accusing voice. "And not just them. You keep it up, and you'll mess up their football."

Belinda's face burned more hotly. Horace was on the school board. Was he threatening her? Would he have her fired if she flunked Joe Bob and Kayo?

"They should study harder," she said defensively. "On their last world history test—"

"World history," Horace said in disgust. "What do they need to know about world history? Greeks and Romans running around dressed in bedsheets. Phew!"

"I got six players in your class," Roger Grimes said. There was warning in his voice, but his smirk was still in place, as if Belinda's discomfort amused him. "You should take it easier on them, you know? They work hard on that football field. Mighty hard."

"Excuse me," Belinda said, her heart pounding. "But why should I have a double standard? Why should players be treated differently from anyone else?"

"Because," Horace said contemptuously, "football teaches them about life. The give and take and the rough and tumble. It's got meaning. It's not memorizing a bunch of dumb dates."

Shirley Ditmars said, "I swear I don't remember one thing from history. Except Henry the Eighth had six wives. Or was it Henry the Sixth had eight wives? No, history never put any groceries on my table."

"I'd hate to see our team hurt by some brand-new teacher, still wet behind the ears," Horace said. He eyed Belinda malevolently. "I believe there'd be complaints."

Tap swore and smacked his hand on the table so hard Shirley jumped. "I've heard enough of this crap," he said, his eyes flashing. "Stop trying to intimidate her."

Horace glared at him in surprise. "I'm intimidating nobody," he retorted. "I'm stating facts. Who pulled your chain?"

"You did," Tap practically snarled. "Don't you the hell tell her how to teach. Leave her alone, dammit."

Horace glowered at him in disbelief. "Did you just cuss me, boy? Did I hear you right? Did you toss curse words at me?"

"I didn't toss them," Tap said rebelliously. "I hurled the mothers like rocks. Back off from her, Westerhaus. You, too, Grimes."

Shirley's mouth dropped open in shock. Roger Grimes's face took on a look of deep offense. Horace Westerhaus scowled. "You got a lot to learn, boy," he said scornfully.

"No. You do," Tap said, standing. He threw two dollars on the table. He glanced at Belinda. "I said I'd buy your coffee, Dugan. This should cover it. Come on. Let's find some fresh air."

"Absolutely," Belinda said, snatching up her book. Horace, Roger and Shirley glared at her.

Tap stalked to the door, Belinda at his side. Neither looked back at the others at the booth.

"Well!" Belinda heard Shirley Ditmars say. "Isn't he huffy? That sort of language, and they let him teach our children? Well!"

"Pinko," muttered Horace Westerhaus. "Long-haired leftist hippie freak. Probably smokes dope."

Tap barged out the door, Belinda right behind him. He strode to the sidewalk, and the rain immediately drenched him. It ran off his hair in small rivers, streaming over the intriguing planes of his face. He swore again, then put his hands on his hips and laughed.

Belinda stared up at him, blinking the rain from her eyes.

Tap laughed again. "My car's in the shop," he said. "I can't even offer you a ride. What a lousy sense of exits I've got."

Belinda pushed back a wet strand of hair. "I can't offer you a ride, either."

He laughed again and looked up at the gray clouds. "I think we just made enemies, Dugan."

"Who cares?" she said defiantly. "They were awful." *And you were wonderful,* she thought. *Just wonderful.* "Thank you," she managed to say.

He shrugged, as if it were nothing. He turned to her again. "We could get fired, you know. Horace Westerhaus is on the school board. We could be done, doomed, past, finished."

"Who cares?" she repeated, feeling reckless.

"Attagirl," he said and slapped her back encouragingly. "At least we'll have our honor. We may starve, but we'll have our honor."

She nodded. Her hair, she realized, was soaked, and she probably looked like a small, drowned rat. Her spirits suddenly sagged and grew as damp as her clothes.

"You shouldn't have gotten involved," she said. "I'm sorry. Really. You shouldn't have."

He wiped the rain from his mouth with the back of his hand and said, "Forget it."

She would never forget it, and he was so handsome she could think of nothing to say.

"Where do you live?" he asked.

"The Enderby apartments," she said, ducking her head. Her heart was beating far too wildly, and she was afraid to look at him any longer.

"I live at Minnie Wollenhaupt's," he said, trying to toss his hair out of his eyes. "We're only about two blocks apart. I'll walk you. Okay?"

"Sure." She nodded, still not looking at him. She clutched her book tightly to her chest, trying to protect it.

They began to walk. The rain still fell in a flood, and the sidewalk was deserted. They went half a block in silence.

Then Tap smiled his careless smile. "Know what this reminds me of?"

"No," she said, giving him a sidelong look.

"The movie *Singin' in the Rain*. You know, where the water's pouring, and Gene Kelly goes stomping through puddles and swinging around lampposts, singing his head off."

She smiled. The movie was one of her favorites.

"You know it?" he asked.

"Oh, yes. I love it."

He seized her hand. "Then let's go for it. Come on."

Belinda felt an almost unbearable thrill when he touched her. Drenched but dazzled, she gazed at him.

Tap headed for the street, where a swift stream ran in the gutter. He plunged into the water and began to walk, splashing as much as possible. He sang with gusto about singing and dancing in the rain.

Belinda, delighted, joined him. Together they stamped through puddles, swung about lampposts, did an improvised soft-shoe down the sidewalk.

Still hand in hand, they stood beneath a store awning so that the runoff could spill over them, soaking them even more thoroughly. It was mad, spontaneous and silly. But Belinda was too bewitched to care. When they came to a corner, he took her in his arms and led her in a polka step through a puddle that extended from curb to curb.

"One-two-three, one-two-three," he said, laughing down at her as they sloshed through water past their ankles.

Belinda could only smile back, too euphoric to speak. She thought if she lived to be a hundred, she might never have another moment as marvelous as this—dancing crazily in the rain, held in Tap Hollister's strong, warm arms.

BEVERLY HAD BEEN drifting through downtown Crystal Creek with no particular purpose when she'd bumped into Sonny. Somehow, it seemed natural for them to walk together.

When the rain didn't let up, they took refuge in the white gazebo in the park. Beverly sat on the ornate wrought-iron bench and hung her dripping umbrella on its arm.

Sonny remained standing, one hip cocked, watching the lightning play on the horizon. He wore faded jeans, a white T-shirt and a red windbreaker. He'd joked that he was in James Dean mode.

The blowing rain had dampened his dark hair, and it fell over his brow, as usual. A tall, Eurasian version of James Dean wasn't half-bad, Beverly thought; it was quite a nice variation. All the nurses said he was handsome, and she supposed he was.

At the hospital, he and she entertained each other with an exchange that had become second nature to them. She told him about Crystal Creek. She wove its stories into a continuing melodrama, and she used all her ingenuity to make it amusing.

"Scheherazade," he'd tease her. "You almost sucker me into liking it here."

In turn, he told her of the great world outside her little hometown. This rainy afternoon, he'd been describing Java, which sounded full of marvels. He'd talked of the seas, the countless volcanoes, the jungles, ruined temples, leopards, orangutans and even pythons.

"Pythons?" she asked in awe. "Do they eat *people?*"

"Well," he said with a shrug, "there was the unfortunate case of the jeweler from Burma. But we don't talk about it. Bad for tourism."

"A python ate a jeweler?" she said, taken aback.

Sonny shrugged again. "Maybe he needed more carats in his diet."

"You're completely awful," she said, laughing. But he swore the tale was true and went on to spin her another, even more fantastic, about tree-climbing fish.

"Now it's your turn," he said. "You tell me a story."

The rain beat down on the roof of the gazebo.

"I can't think of any," she said. "I think I've told them all. Unless you want to hear about Mary and Bubba Gibsons' ostrich farm again."

"Why didn't you want to go into the Longhorn and warm up, have some coffee?"

"Oh, I saw that awful Horace Westerhaus go in with Roger Grimes," she grumbled. Usually she hid any negative opinions about people, but with Sonny she could be honest.

"Who's Horace Westerhaus, and why's he awful?"

"He considers himself the media mogul of Crystal Creek. He's the one putting out all those football booster buttons. You know, the kind you won't wear."

"Another fan of the glorious fighting Cougars?"

"He played when he was in school. Back in the neo-lithic age. Both his sons played. Now he's got four grandsons on the team. I get sick of it—this fixation on football."

"My," he teased, "you're downright heretical to-day. Any more blasphemy?"

She sighed. "When I was younger, I never thought about it," she said. "It seemed as natural as the air I breathed or the water I drank."

Sonny cocked a pessimistic eyebrow. "This town's no different than most. It wants something to be proud of."

"I know," she said. "But most of the little boys were brought up to think the peak of success was making the football team. And little girls dreamed of being home-coming queen. Some people acted as if that was *it*, the pinnacle of accomplishment."

His eyebrow crooked more cynically. "You were homecoming queen, of course?"

"Of course." She shrugged, surprised at her own sarcasm. "But here I am, all these years later, still in Crystal Creek. And I've never had a steady job. Is there life after prom night?"

"Thus passes the glory of the earth. And you didn't want to join Roger Grimes, either? We could check out the latest episode of the poor, pitiful Peggy Sue saga."

"Poor, pitiful Peggy Sue?" Beverly echoed. "Now *you're* the heretic."

"You're not pulling any punches today," he com-mented. "Why should I? I don't like her."

Beverly looked at him in surprise. "You don't? Most people love her to pieces."

Peggy Sue was young and small and sweet-faced; her manners were so exquisite that she seemed every inch a lady, and she showed the greatest solicitude for each patient that came into the clinic.

Almost everyone admired her exceptional graciousness, as well as her equally exceptional courage. When she was eighteen, a car crash had killed all of her family except herself. She had suffered a back injury that still kept her in constant pain. She tried to smile through it, and refused to take painkillers.

"Peggy's life is a soap opera," Sonny said, his mouth taking on a scornful twist. "And I wish she'd take something for her damned back. Nate always sends her home early or tells her to take half a day off. Then she's running off to her specialists in Austin. She gets full-time wages for part-time hours."

"She's never going to take painkillers," Beverly said, crossing her arms in resignation. "She's trying to get pregnant. She says she'd rather be in pain then take a chance on hurting the baby."

"The baby," Sonny said, staring off into the rain again. "More soap opera. For somebody who never asks for sympathy, she manages to get a hell of a lot. Last month two of the patients brought *her* flowers."

Beverly nodded. Peggy wanted a child so badly because she had no living blood relatives. She mentioned this often and with great wistfulness. The whole town seemed caught up in her drama, and people frequently said they were praying for her.

"I shouldn't say this," Beverly murmured, "but old Mrs. Munson practically gave the Grimeses that acreage they live on. Because she was so taken by Peggy. I heard her son in Toledo was upset. He thought they took advantage of her."

"Yeah. I've got this older woman, a stroke patient. She doesn't have much money. But she had a nice ring.

Peggy gushed over it so much the woman gave it to her. A lot of older people seem to give her stuff.''

"I've never said this to anybody on the staff," she admitted. "When Grandpa Hank was in the hospital after his truck accident, about a year and a half ago, *she* came flitting around. But he didn't like her. He called her that 'nicey-nice she-buzzard.'"

"The more I hear about Hank, the more I think we would have gotten along. Sounds like a man after my own heart."

Beverly smiled. Sonny was often irreverent, and Hank would have appreciated that. "He said something odd once. He had second sight, you know. He said, 'That woman's undoing will come by wind and water.'"

"What did he mean?"

"I have no idea," she said.

Sonny shook his head. "Another thing I don't like is the way those football kids are always coming in to talk to her. Nate's not paying her to play den mother."

"Well, she *is* their den mother. Haven't you heard her say, 'I think of them as the children I can't seem to have'?"

"Yeah," Sonny said. "And her chin always quivers when she says it. And her voice breaks. I thank God I have a heart of stone. And a stomach of iron."

Beverly gave a guilty laugh. "Oh, lawsy, Sonny, the town'd string us up if they heard us. *Nobody* ever says anything bad about Peggy. Roger may be overbearing, but Peggy's sacred."

"I calls 'em as I sees 'em," he said.

"That's what I like about you. And you let me say anything I want. Sometimes I feel that for years and years I've been such a priss that I'll go straight to hell if I say anything mean, even if it's true."

He turned to her, gave her a slow smile. "I'm corrupting you."

"Maybe. But it's nice to be honest."

His smile grew sardonic. "I used to think you were like her. Peggy, I mean. Too nicey-nice. It's good to find I'm wrong. I kind of enjoy you when you're sharp-tongued."

Odd emotions tingled in her midsection. She toyed nervously with her necklaces and discovered they were tangled. "Oh, drat," she said in frustration.

He looked at her in concern. She liked it when he did that. He pretended to be cold and skeptical, but he wasn't. Of all the doctors at the hospital, he had the best way with patients, and he charmed the children completely.

"What's wrong?" he asked.

"My locket," she said. "It's twisted up with my pearl. I hate when that happens."

She frequently wore two necklaces, and the pearl was one of her favorites. But if she was restless, she would play with her jewelry, and the pearl's chain was prone to catch.

"Let me get it," he said. "You're making it worse."

He crossed the gazebo, sat down beside her and started untangling the chains. He had beautiful hands, strong and skilled, perfect for a doctor.

"Why do you wear this locket so often?" he asked. "It's not much. Not your usual style."

"Oh," she said, tensing slightly at his sure touch. "Jeff gave it to me. It was a valentine present."

"Maybe," he said gruffly, "you shouldn't wear it for a while. If it brings sad memories."

She shrugged.

"Hold still," he said, his fingers accidentally brushing her throat.

"It has good memories, too," she said, trying to stay motionless. "I've got Jeff's picture in it."

"Ah," he said with a sigh that stirred her hair slightly. "Jeff."

Beverly swallowed. "I know a lot of what I feel is guilt. Because I broke up with him just before he died."

"You couldn't know," Sonny told her. "Wow, Blondie. You really are all tangled up."

The outward symbol of the inward me, she thought unhappily.

"We'll get you untangled," Sonny said. She didn't know if he was talking about her gold chains or her emotions.

"It's going to haunt me forever," she said unhappily. "What if I hadn't broken up with him? Maybe the accident wouldn't have happened. Maybe he was distracted or thinking how mean I was—"

"Shh," he said. "Don't talk like that. It wasn't your fault. That piece of equipment went out of control—he wasn't operating it, he didn't make it happen. You know that. We've been over that."

She knew Sonny was right. She'd brooded over the details a hundred times. It had been a freak accident, and it was nobody's fault.

"This is stupid," Beverly said, tossing her head in frustration. "Why do I make you listen again?"

"Because you've got to get it out of your system. Hold still, will you?"

She swallowed again but held still. She could feel the warmth of his hands near her throat, smell his scent, which was sandalwood. "Um," she said. "You smell good."

"I know, I know—it drives you mad with desire, et cetera. My God, how did you do this? You've invented golden Velcro."

"Maybe you're right," she said, holding her head higher. "Maybe I shouldn't wear it. At least for a while."

"No. You shouldn't. Ah, there you go. Free at last. Only the skilled hands of a surgeon could have done it."

"Thanks," she said and managed to smile. For a moment his fine-featured face was close, his dark eyes intent on hers. It gave her an unexpected dizzying feeling. She looked away.

Slowly he drew back. "So what about the future?" he asked, his voice coolly challenging. "Old Hank with second sight—did he ever tell you what lay in store for you?"

She stared at her hand. Jeff's brother had insisted on returning the engagement ring to her, and she always wore it. She felt naked and disloyal without it. She might take off the locket, but not the ring.

"Hank took Jeff's death awfully hard," Beverly said. "They were partners, you know."

"I know."

"Hank was failing badly when it happened. I wonder, really, if that wasn't the final blow. That the great oil adventure was over."

"I asked about you," Sonny said.

"The last time I saw Hank, I was holding his hand. And I had a little shudder. Down here, when that happens, people say, 'A possum must have run over my grave.'"

"And?" he prompted. She could feel him watching her.

"So I said that. About the possum. And Hank said, "No, girl. That's Jeff, kissin' your ear.' His ghost is holdin' you tight. He don't want to let go.'"

As she said it, she shuddered again, exactly as she had that night. It really was as if Jeff were kissing her ear, telling her not to forget, not to stop loving him.

"Ah, Beverly," Sonny said in his husky voice. "We were born in the wrong countries, you and I."

She looked at him, surprised by the edge in his tone. "Why do you say that?"

"Because it's written that Indonesia's haunted, full of ghosts. If you live there, you have to believe in them. But I never believed. Until I met you."

Again she didn't want to meet his eyes. She turned her gaze to the rain-flattened grass.

Sonny was right. A ghost lived with her. Jeff wouldn't let her go. Nor could she let go of him. Not now. Maybe not ever.

CHAPTER THREE

IT WAS A WARM, cloudy Sunday afternoon in early winter, and Beverly and Sonny were on horseback. She'd teased him that she intended to see if he really could ride. He could, and she was impressed.

She reined in her Palomino, Dandi, atop a small rise and surveyed the hilly country. She'd always loved this land and found comfort in its sometimes stark beauty.

Sonny was beside her on Outlaw, a big, black horse that belonged to her stepfather, Vern. It was a handsome horse, part Arabian, with a fine head and a flowing mane and tail. It was high-stepping and mettlesome.

She stole a glance at Sonny as he stared out over the rolling acres. He was hatless, and his dark hair stirred in the breeze. He wore his usual weekend uniform, jeans, white T-shirt, the red windbreaker.

"You sit a horse well," she said. "Like it's in your blood."

He gave her a sardonic look. "I think that driving a water buffalo through a rice field is what's in my blood. My God, what was it like to grow up with all this space?"

She shrugged and urged Dandi to a walk. Sonny kept pace. "I don't know. It seemed natural. I thought everybody lived like me. What was it like growing up in Jakarta?"

"Crowded," he said. "It seemed natural. I thought everybody lived like *me*."

She gave him a musing smile. "When I got older, I dreamed of going to someplace fabulous. An island with palm trees and volcanoes. Like where you were."

He let his gaze rest on the horizon. "It might disappoint you. I dreamed of coming here. To the States."

"Has it disappointed you?"

"I don't let myself be disappointed."

He was always strangely closedmouthed about his past and had told her little. Today she decided to try to learn more. He, after all, knew everything about her.

"Do you mean it about staying in this country?" she asked. "Giving up your native land and everything?"

He nodded. "I'll apply for citizenship when I get to Denver. Either that, or start looking for Miss Green Card."

He turned to her with a wicked half smile. "Want the job? I'd be an interesting husband. I *am* a doctor. I know many stimulating things about the body."

"You *thing*," Beverly said. "I'm serious. You won't miss Indonesia? It's home, after all."

His smile went away. "No. Not anymore. I don't have anybody left there. I don't need a home."

She nodded, but felt a surge of sympathy. She knew both of his parents had died when he was young and that he'd lost a brother, as well. But he never spoke of the details.

"Sonny, what happened to your father and mother and brother? Why do you just have your uncle's family?"

"Ah, Blondie," he said, not looking at her. "We grew up very differently, you and I."

"I know that," she persisted. "But tell me. Or don't you want to talk about it? Does it bother you?"

"Nothing bothers me," he answered. "I don't let it."

She shook her head, not understanding how he could feel that way. She pulled down the brim of her white Stetson. Like Sonny, she wore jeans, T-shirt and windbreaker, only blue, not red. "What about your father and mother?" she asked. "Will you tell me what happened?"

He kept looking straight ahead. "It's hard to explain. Did you ever see the movie *The Year of Living Dangerously?*"

"Yes," Beverly said. "Mel Gibson played a reporter in Indonesia. But I don't remember it that well. I just remember being terribly jealous of Sigourney Weaver."

He arched his brow sardonically. "Do you remember what the title means?"

"No."

"President Sukarno was in power. He was more like a god than a president. Nationalism was intense. He named each year for a challenge that the country faced."

She nodded, watching him.

"The Year of Living Dangerously was just that," he said. "Sukarno was spitting in everybody's eye. He withdrew from the United Nations. There was an attack on Malaysia, skirmishes in Burma. Emotion ran high. He kicked all the British and American journalists out of the country."

"Why?" Beverly asked innocently. "What had we done?"

"You were *Nekolim,* the 'neocolonial imperialists.' He'd defy you at any cost. At that time, as someone said, 'All white faces are bad.'"

Beverly straightened, slightly stung. It seldom occurred to her that other races might look down on hers.

"Don't be hurt," he said cynically. "That included my father, of course. He was half Dutch. With some Australian thrown in. But he was also half Chinese, and that made him a two-time loser."

"But why?" Beverly asked. "What had the Chinese done?"

He spoke coolly, as if none of this affected him. "It's complex. It's political and racial and economic and cultural."

"Oh," she said, stung again. "You mean it's too complicated for me to understand."

He gave her a sharp look. "No. That's not what I mean. I grew up in it, and *I* didn't understand it. I wasn't really white or Chinese or Indonesian. I didn't fit anywhere. I didn't want to fit. Except in the medical community. That's my country. That's my family."

Beverly glanced away, feeling vaguely guilty. She had never been the target of prejudice, and all her life she'd fit in, perhaps too well for her own good. "You don't want to belong anywhere? Ever?"

He gazed up at the sky. "I belong to medicine," he said. "Not to any person or place. Just science."

"It sounds so cold," she objected.

"It's pure. Race doesn't matter. Or nationality. Or politics. Only the search for truth counts. That's all."

She took a deep breath. "You still haven't told me what happened to your parents."

"They were killed. They were shot."

Beverly recoiled in disbelief. "You mean murdered?"

He shrugged. "There was a coup. Then a bloodbath. Maybe half a million people were killed, many

Chinese. My parents among them. They were both part Chinese. I was very young. I can't remember it.''

He said this so calmly that it stunned her. ''But why were they killed?''

''Like I said—race, politics. My brother and I'd been sent to my Javanese grandmother. It saved us.''

''Sonny—I'm so sorry.''

His face was dispassionate. ''Don't be sorry. My grandmother took good care of us. She was a house-keeper for an Australian diplomat. He let her take us in. Later, he married an American woman. She'd been a teacher, but the government wouldn't let her teach. She had no children, so she worked on my brother and me.''

Beverly looked at him with incomprehension. Her childhood had been so calm, so protected, so privileged, that his seemed incredible to her.

''She taught you English?'' she asked. ''The American woman?''

''She taught us a lot. She used to call us her 'little scholars.' ''

He spoke of it so nonchalantly that Beverly was puzzled. ''Were you fond of her?''

''Sure. Although later people claimed she gave me big ideas and made me *kasar*—rude. Too frank. Asking too many questions. Laughing at tradition.''

''And,'' Beverly prompted.

He suddenly flashed his one-sided grin. ''They were right. I question everything. I say what I think. To hell with tradition.''

''What happened to her, to the American woman? And your brother? And your grandmother?''

''I'm sick of talking about myself. You talk. What's the story behind that carousel down on the square?''

''I want to know about *you*,'' she said.

His smile died. He looked out at the hilly horizon again. "My brother died. He was hit by a car. Traffic's terrible in Jakarta. People drive like maniacs. Accidents happen."

He hesitated, looking moody. "We'd had a fight that afternoon. A quarrel. I'd made him cry. Three hours later he was dead."

"My, God," she said, stopping her horse. "That's why you understand. About Jeff, I mean."

"I suppose," he said without emotion.

"Did you blame yourself? For the accident?"

"Yeah," he said, turning his gaze to the cloudy sky. "Sometimes. I got over it. You will, too."

She doubted that she would, but didn't want to think about that. And he still hadn't told her everything.

"What about the American woman?" she asked.

He kept his eyes on the clouds. "After Hanafi died, she sort of poured all her efforts into me. She helped me get the scholarship to Hawaii. And then she died. She wasn't really very old. But she died. Meningitis."

"And then?"

"Two years ago, my grandmother died. That's the last time I went back, when she was dying. I'm not close to my uncle's family. He thinks I'm too westernized."

"You've got nobody to love," she said softly.

"I don't want anybody to love," he said.

"But someday, you'll find somebody who—"

"No. I don't want to. If I ever marry, it won't be for love. It'll be for convenience. I decided long ago."

"But—"

"I told you. Medicine is what I love. Science is my country. Science is my religion. I'm meant to be a research doctor, not a people-person doctor like Nate. That's how I am, that's what I'm like."

"You're *good* with people."

"I'm better with ideas. And they're not as messy as people. No. I don't like caring about people too much. It's not my style."

THAT NIGHT IN BED, she thought a long time about what he had said. She believed him. He was a man in perfect control of his emotions. He would never yearn painfully after any woman.

Like her, he was beyond the touch of love. It was comforting that he was that way. It made him safe. Nothing could complicate their relationship, and that was good. That was how she wanted it.

She slept and dreamed, as almost always, of Jeff.

A WEEK AND A HALF later, Beverly came dashing down the hall of the hospital, smiling brilliantly. As soon as Sonny saw her, his heart did something painful and acrobatic. He struggled to keep his expression under control.

She ran to him, seizing him by the arm. Her touch jarred through him like electricity.

"I've been looking all over for you," she said breathlessly. "I've got to have you to myself a few minutes. Is there a way we can be alone?"

My God, he thought, *doesn't she know what it does to me when she talks like that?*

She looked beautiful, of course. She wore the simplest of clothing—jeans, a pink sweater, a blue windbreaker—but on her they looked anything but simple.

Her breasts thrust out enticingly underneath the windbreaker; her hips and long legs filled out her jeans as perfectly as champagne fills a tall, finely curved glass.

But what most intrigued him was her smile. She looked radiant, happier than he'd ever seen her.

He acted bored, unconcerned. "I was going to knock off for lunch after I made my rounds."

"We could have lunch together," she said, looking up at him, all blue eyes and happiness.

She's fractured all my hormones, he thought. *I'm dying.*

"Whatever," he said. "Let go. I've got to inspect the former site of an appendix."

She squeezed his arm. "I'll go to the supermarket deli. I'll buy sandwiches. Meet you at the park? In the gazebo?"

"In half an hour," he said, not looking at her. "And it's got to be short. We're having a blue light special on head colds at the clinic."

"It's a deal," she said, smiling. She hugged his arm. *Be still, my sperm,* he thought darkly.

Beverly was so euphoric that she stood on tiptoe and tried to kiss him on the jaw. He dodged her, his heart hammering.

"Don't," he ordered and pulled away from her.

"I'm sorry," she said, obviously chagrined. She put her hands in the pockets of her blue jacket. "I didn't mean to offend you."

"Fine," he said curtly, but the smile in his eyes tempered his brusqueness. "Go buy me a sandwich. Turkey and swiss cheese. Hold the mayo."

"Aye, aye," she said. She gave him a mock salute and turned away, half running, half skipping down the hall.

His heart followed her, half running, half skipping, half dying. He did not allow himself so much as a blink to show what he felt.

My God, he thought. *She tried to kiss me.*

If her lips had touched his face, even fleetingly, it would have been all over. He would have pulled her into his arms and kissed her the way he hungered to. Then she would know how much he wanted her, and then he would lose her.

SONNY WAS ALWAYS so calm and cool, Beverly thought in frustration.

He wouldn't be nearly as excited as she was. Still, there was no one else she wanted to turn to, except him. She had a new idea, and it excited her until she bubbled with it.

They sat in the gazebo. The day was bright, the sky blue, and the park ducks haunted the gazebo's edge, hoping for bread crusts.

"Here's your sandwich," Beverly said, thrusting it at him. "There's your coffee, and there are potato chips. I'm taking charge of my life. I'm embarking on a career."

He raised an eyebrow skeptically. "This sounds like a major conversion. Are you becoming a nun?"

"No," she said, wrinkling her nose at him. "But I'm sick of modeling. It's never been a steady job, anyway."

"Didn't I tell you to hold the mayo?"

He was being perverse for the pure pleasure of it, she could tell. She ignored him. "I'm too short for a model anyway. And I'm not thin enough. I'm too round where I should be flat."

He threw a potato chip to a duck. "You're of a roundish persuasion here and there."

"I fooled myself into thinking I could be a doctor."

He sipped his coffee, unperturbed. "You'd give more men heart attacks than you'd save. It's your roundishness."

"Thank you, I suppose. But I really was deceiving myself. I couldn't pith a frog, I don't think."

He looked her up and down. "No. You couldn't. Or dissect a cat. Let alone a cadaver. You're a marshmallow-heart."

"Listen. I was lying in bed last night, and I couldn't sleep."

He gave her a mocking look. "For wanting me? I'm flattered. You should have called. You might have got lucky."

"You *thing*," she said and swatted his arm. "I'm serious. I'm not cut out to be a doctor, but I've got a degree in business, which I've never used."

"And?" he asked.

She took a deep breath. "And the idea hit me. I've got a business degree. I like the hospital. A hospital is a business. I should go back to college and take courses in hospital administration. What do you think?"

His smile had been teasing. Now it died. His dark gaze settled on her face. He was silent for the space of three heartbeats. She waited in suspense, wishing she could read his expression.

Then he said, "I think *yes*. You've got the brains. Good administrators are hard to find. Go for it."

She was almost wriggling with excitement. "Do you really think it's a good idea? You think I can do it?"

"It's so brilliant I'm surprised I didn't think of it. I don't think you can—I know you can. I mean it, Blondie."

"I feel like I've sprouted wings," she said, rising and throwing out her arms. "Jeff kept telling me I could be a doctor, but deep in my heart I was afraid. But this—this feels right. It's like after all these years of drifting through a fog, the fog lifts, and there's a path. Does that make sense?"

He looked her up and down. "Yeah. But you'll have to go away. Austin doesn't give a degree in hospital administration. You'll have to go to Galveston or San Antonio."

She dropped her arms and sat on the wrought-iron bench again. "I know."

She searched his face. A mildly curious smile curved his mouth, that was all.

"When would you start?" he asked. "Next semester? January?"

January was only a month away. She felt excitement, yet a strange pang, as well. "Yes. If they'll have me."

"They'll have you," he said with a nod. "They'll be lucky. Believe me."

She leaned toward him eagerly. "You think so?"

"I think so," he said. "Yes."

"I'm applying to Galveston," she said. "I'll try to be home on weekends."

"Good," he said. His smile faded. He seemed completely expressionless.

She looked about, taking in the gazebo, the lagoon, the ducks. "It might do me good to get away from here for a while," she said. "Too many memories. What I'll miss most is—is you, I guess."

"Yeah," he said. "Well."

They sat in silence. She realized she didn't want to look at him because she suddenly had the strange urge to cry.

For a moment his image swam in her mind. Sonny, in his jeans and James Dean jacket, tall, his movements deceptively indolent. His dark hair, his golden skin, his even features, his brown eyes.

"Hey," he said, his tone light. "All of a sudden you look sad, Blondie. What's wrong?"

But she could not put a name to what troubled her.

"Nothing," she said.

WHEN SHE'D TOLD HIM she was going, it was as if she'd ripped a hole through his chest. He kept telling himself he'd be leaving soon, too, so it made no difference. The rationalization didn't help. Nothing did.

He supposed he'd do anything for her. He'd even been part of the stupid chili cook-off because she'd wanted him to. Now she wanted him to be happy for her. Fine. He would pretend to be happy.

Too restless to go back his apartment that evening, he stopped by one of the local taverns, Lingle's. Lingle's bar was a dreary, hole-in-the-wall place at the edge of town. Sometimes Sonny would go there for one beer, only one. Lingle's was seldom crowded, which was why he chose it.

When he walked in the door, the only patrons he saw were Tap Hollister and a pretty, brown-haired woman sitting at his side in a booth. Both looked downcast. Tap gave Sonny a cheerless wave and beckoned him to join them.

"Greetings," Sonny said, sitting down across from him. "You don't look happy. Lighten up. Gloom I don't need."

"I can't help it," Tap said, grim-faced. "And if you're happy, leave. We're in a rotten mood and intend to stay that way. If you've got reason to smile, I'll shoot you."

"Then I'll live," Sonny said. He looked at the brown-haired girl. She tried to give him a smile. It was a failure.

He reached across the table and offered the girl his hand. "I'm Sonny Dekker, temporarily serving time at the clinic and hospital."

"Belinda Dugan," she said, shaking hands. "I teach. Today, I feel like I'm serving time, too."

Sonny studied her. She was a lovely woman, extremely petite, but her brown eyes had a troubled expression, and she seemed nervous.

"Dugan and I are drowning our sorrows," Tap said. "We both had the day from hell. Tell him what happened, Dugan."

Belinda Dugan sighed. "Yesterday six members of the football team flunked my history exam. This morning when I woke up, my car was on the porch of my apartment—upside down. It's a little three cylinder compact. I think they came in the night, picked it up and put it there."

"The lunkheads," muttered Tap and sipped his beer.

"It took a whole *crew* of deputies to get my car right side up and off the porch," she said. "Its roof's all dented in. When I finally got to school, somehow everybody knew. They were all talking about it. Two deputies called the boys to the principal's office and squeezed the truth out of them. They all got suspended from school for a week and dropped from the team."

She stopped and squared her shoulders.

"Go on," Tap said morosely. "Tell him all of it."

Belinda gave Tap a shy, sidelong look. He didn't seem to notice. She turned her gaze to Sonny again. "Now everybody hates *me*," she said. "The assistant football coach won't even speak to me. We were supposed to go to the championship tournament next week. Now we've lost a quarterback, the best field goal kicker, and an all-state tackle."

The barmaid came, bringing Sonny a bottle of Lone Star beer and a frosted glass. "Want a refill?" she asked Tap.

"Sure," he said.

"Tap," Belinda said hesitantly, "should you? That'll make three. You said you should never drink more than two beers. That it makes you—crazy. You said not to let you."

"I want to be crazy," Tap said. "Being sane hurts too much. Go on, Dugan. Finish your tale of woe."

She studied him, her expression worried. She seemed to force herself to drag her eyes back to Sonny. "The long and short of it," she said, "is that now the students and Roger Grimes are saying it's *my* fault. That the test was too hard. That the players were just full of nervous energy. That I should never have called the police—although I didn't know who else to call. I've ruined a championship season. Single-handed."

"A big job for such a little squirt," Tap said. "But that's what they're saying. Nice, huh?"

"Rotten," Sonny said.

Tap threw his arm around her shoulders companionably. "This poor kid was driven from her apartment tonight. Phone calls from angry parents. Their darling children wouldn't *really* commit vandalism. Couldn't she take a little joke? She's a lousy sport, they say. I found her wandering the streets. So I dragged her in here. Misery loves company."

Belinda fidgeted. Sonny felt sorry for her. Not only was her story appalling, but he could see she had a crush on Tap, one so hard it was painful. Tap, in turn, didn't even seem to notice she was female.

The barmaid brought Tap another bottle of Budweiser. He poured it into his mug, then clicked it against Belinda's. "Here's to you, Dugan. Scourge of the Crystal Creek Six."

She gave him a shy smile, but he'd already turned away.

"Now when I learn all this," Tap said to Sonny, "it's the assistant coach, Grimes, I overhear. He's ranting about Dugan. I told him to put the blame where it belongs. On those no-neck apes he calls a team. The arrogant bastards think they're above the law. They're always picking on my band kids. Like it's their favorite form of recreation. I'm sick of it. I told him that, too."

"What happened then?" Sonny asked. "He tried to strangle you, and you smote him with a flute?"

"He called me a stupid SOB, so I suggested that he molests his mother. Then he threatened to punch me out, and called both me and Dugan names. I went for him, but the head coach and the shop teacher held me back. I ended up in the principal's office getting chewed out. But then, so did Grimes. The orangutan."

He sighed in angry frustration and took a drink of beer.

"You shouldn't have tried to hit Roger Grimes," Belinda said, her eyes downcast. "He's huge."

"Phooey," Tap sneered and took another drink.

"So you got in trouble defending a lady's honor," Sonny said. "I didn't think you were that chivalrous."

"I'm not," Tap said, unsmiling. "Dugan here's a good guy, that's all. Aren't you, Dugan?" He gave her a fraternal slap on the shoulder.

She smiled feebly.

"But are my troubles over?" Tap asked Sonny. "No. My best drummer informs me his family's moving to Georgia. My second-best drummer falls in PE and breaks his hand. All this in one day. My drum line decimated. I'm clutching my head and going, 'Why me, God? Why me?' "

Sonny narrowed his eyes thoughtfully. "You need something to cheer you up. Like a lobotomy. I could give you a discount."

Tap chugalugged his beer. "This is lobotomy enough. Be polite and listen. I want to complain. I'm not done."

"There's more?" Resigned, Sonny sipped his Lone Star.

Tap's blue eyes flashed with sorrow and despair. "After school, I stop at the grocery store. There I am, in the checkout line, innocently buying peanut butter, and I look at the magazines. Who do I see staring back at me? Guy Heller and Liz, that's who. On the cover of *People*. Look."

He picked up a magazine from the seat of the booth and threw it on the table before Sonny.

A female movie star's vapidly grinning face dominated the cover, but inset into the cover's corner was a smaller photo of a handsome man with his arm around a curly-haired woman with beautiful cheekbones. Her head was nestled on his shoulder. They were smiling, obviously in love.

The cutline beneath the shot said, "Guy Heller— Raising Hell No More."

Sonny opened the magazine to a page that had been dog-eared. There were more photos of Heller with Liz.

The article's text was zingy and brief. Heller had conquered his demons, it said, married his childhood sweetheart and given up touring. He and Liz lived in Tahoe now, where he was part owner of a club, and he had a new album that was a hit on the country charts. He'd been invited to London for a two-week engagement, and he was taking his new wife with him. He said he wanted to make their honeymoon last forever.

Tap finished his beer and his expression was militant. "It's not bad enough I have to hear the bastard every time I turn on the radio. Now his smug face is plastered all over America—with *my* girl."

Belinda Dugan's brown eyes looked stricken. Tap raked his hand through his hair and shook his head.

"Your girl," Sonny said carefully, "is somebody else's wife."

"He stole her," Tap said bitterly. "And now he's flaunting her. He's giving her all the things I couldn't. A house at Lake Tahoe. A trip to London. Fame. Fortune. Did you see the ring on her finger? The diamond's as big as a goddamn bowling ball."

"You were right," Sonny said to Belinda. "He shouldn't have had the third beer."

"He stole my girl," Tap persisted, taking the magazine and staring unhappily at Liz's picture. "He carried her off to a mansion. While I live in a garage behind Minnie Wollenhaupt's house and teach school in this miserable burg. He hobnobs with stars and stripes—"

"Stripes?" Sonny frowned.

"Celebrities," Tap said. "He hobnobs with stars and celebrities. Who do I hobnob with? That moron dimbulb dweeb of a caveman coach. Grimes—I should have wrapped a saxophone around his head."

Sonny shook his head. "The third beer was a very bad idea. I won't let you drive. Let either Belinda or me—"

"You don't understand," Tap said, his voice nearly breaking. "I *loved* this woman. I still love her. I'll love her the rest of my life."

"Tap, shut up," Sonny said. "You're drunk as a skunk. What if somebody tells the school board? Let's leave."

"You don't understand," Tap repeated. "I mean it. I'll never love another woman. I can't. You don't know what it's like."

"Tap, let's go," Belinda said with surprising firmness.

He ignored her. He kept staring at Liz's picture, his face distorted with grief. "I love her," he whispered again. "My God, but she's beautiful."

Then he turned, rather wildly, first to Sonny, then Belinda. "Do either of you know what it's like—unrequited love?" he demanded. "Do you?"

Belinda's eyes grew more stricken, her facial muscles more tense. "No," she said, "I don't. Let's go. You can talk about it in the car."

"Do you?" he persisted, turning to Sonny. "Do you know how it feels to love somebody who doesn't love you back?"

Sonny felt as if he'd taken a punch to the stomach. "I have no idea," he lied.

Together he and Belinda got Tap outside and into Sonny's car. "I'll drive," he told her. "Just in case he gets hard to handle. You bring his car, then I'll take you home."

She nodded mutely and took the car keys Sonny had fished from Tap's pocket.

But Tap's outburst was over. He sat in the passenger seat, his elbows on his knees and his face in his hands. "Oh, God," he said, "I went and made an ass of myself in front of Dugan, didn't I?"

"She'll forgive you," Sonny said sarcastically. He felt sorry for Belinda, sorry as hell.

"She must think I'm a babbling ninny, a nutcase."

"She thinks you're a hero. You stood up to Grimes for her."

"She's a good kid." Tap shook his head miserably.

"She's not a kid," Sonny asserted. "She's a woman. A good-looking woman. She's got great eyes. She seems nice."

"That's what I said," Tap said. "She's a nice kid. Why'd I get so effing maudlin? God, I see two of everything. You're twins. You've got two cars. We're driving down two streets."

"Consider it an interesting neurological experience. And in the future never drink more than two beers. This is a doctor speaking."

Tap faded swiftly. Sonny had to walk him to his garage apartment, supporting him. Belinda opened the door with his keys. Sonny wrestled Tap's sagging body into the bedroom and let go. Tap, without a word, stumbled to his bed, and fell across it.

"Timber," Sonny said; and shook his head.

"Is he all right?" Belinda asked from the doorway. Her whisper was tense.

"He should be fine. Come on. I'll drive you home."

She nodded. She left Tap's keys on his kitchen table and followed Sonny to his car. "It's only two blocks," she said. "I could walk."

"You might meet a football player," Sonny said. "Let's not take the chance."

"Thanks," she said. She cast a longing look back at the garage apartment.

Once in the car she said, "He's usually not like that."

"I know."

"He just can't hold his liquor. He said he hardly ever has more than one beer."

"I know."

"He's actually a wonderful person. Bright and funny and creative. The students would do anything for him."

"I know."

"It's just he's so passionate about everything," she said, gazing sadly out the window. "He's so full of feeling. He has this incredible lust for life, and everything he does, he does a hundred percent."

"He certainly got drunk a hundred percent."

Belinda toyed with a strand of her hair. "He was going to fight Roger Grimes. Tap's big and strong, but Coach Grimes'd make two of him."

Sonny said nothing. *You've got it bad,* he thought.

She shook her head. "I don't think Tap would have ever done this, if it hadn't been for that magazine. He— he really loves her, you know."

"Maybe he'll get over it," Sonny said, hoping to cheer her. "I wish to hell he would."

"So do I." She gave a rueful laugh. "I guess it shows, right? That I like him?"

"A little," Sonny said carefully. "It shows a little, maybe."

"It's stupid. I'm like a junior high kid. Sometimes I get absolutely speechless around him. Sometimes my heart beats so hard it actually hurts. Nothing like this ever happened to me before. Has it ever happened to you?''

"No," Sonny said, staring at the darkness.

"I'm scared to death the students will notice," she said. "So I stay away from him as much as possible. My day is built around strategies for avoiding him. I'd never have gone into that place with him tonight if I hadn't been so upset—God, I'm so stupid."

"Not stupid," Sonny said. "Just human."

He pulled up in front of her apartment, and walked her quickly to her door. The street was dark, and the wind rattled dried leaves. Something in the gusty night made him uneasy, so he hurried to get her to the door and told her good-night and to be careful. He waited until she was safely inside.

He went back to his car. He reached for the handle and just then heard a scuffling sound behind him, like rapid footsteps.

"Get the bastard!" commanded a low voice.

Damn! trouble! he thought in a flash of awareness. Working on sheer instinct, he whirled around, raising his left hand in a defensive position, poising his right to strike.

But hands were all over him, and a blow struck him on the side of the head. His mind exploded into fiery sparks of pain.

CHAPTER FOUR

HIS ATTACKERS were young, only teenagers, but they were tall and brawny, and there were three of them. Even in his pain, he could smell the whiskey on their breath.

Football players, he thought with peculiar detachment, *drunk football players.*

They'd been waiting for Belinda. They'd decided to go for him instead.

He jerked half-free, knocking one attacker away. At the same moment, his elbow flew back, smashing into the stomach of another, who gasped and let go. He struck out, the edge of his hand catching a third across the throat.

But the second recovered quickly, grabbing Sonny from behind and trying to put a stranglehold on him.

Choking, Sonny broke the hold, twisted and drove his fist into the hard body. It was like hitting a cement wall. The attacker staggered, but didn't go down. He lunged at Sonny, grabbing him around the neck again. Then a second kid tackled from behind, throwing both arms around his waist.

"Get him down, get him down," one panted. "Then kick hell out of him."

He kneed one, and the fellow staggered back, but another lunged to take his place. "You're gonna die, you mother—"

Sonny threw a chopping blow at his throat, but missed because the other kid was still trying to pull him down.

"Flatten him!" cried the one clinging to him. The other threw himself at Sonny in a tackling block. The third swung at him wildly.

The blow glanced off Sonny's shoulder, and the attacker lashed out even more crazily. "Hold him still," he ordered angrily. "I'm gonna murder the bastard."

"Yeah," said another, panting. "Kill him."

They mean it, Sonny thought with the same eerie detachment. *They'll kill me.*

He struck out with all the strength and precision he could muster. He hit one in the jaw so hard that the attacker staggered and fell to his knees. He kneed a second in the stomach, then yanked him upright, hitting him hard enough to make his head snap back. He drove another punch into the solar plexus. The kid doubled up and sat down with a thud on the street, dazed, bent and clutching his stomach.

"And you," Sonny snarled at the third player, who clutched him from behind. He twisted and brought his hands down on his opponent's neck in a karate chop. Then he hauled him upright and hurled him against the car so that he smashed into it. The assailant sobbed and bent over, hugging himself.

Sonny stood ready to take him on, breathing hard. He rubbed his knuckles.

Belinda Dugan came running out of her apartment, brandishing a flyswatter. "I saw it all," she cried. "I called the police."

Sonny stared at her in numb amazement. Why was she carrying a flyswatter? A siren sounded in the distance.

She ran to where one of the attackers sat, looking stupefied, on the pavement. "Shame on you, Lester Fletcher," Belinda said, slapping at his head and shoulders with the flyswatter. "Shame, shame, shame!"

The young man put his hands up to protect himself. Sonny moved to Belinda's side. "You don't need that," he said gently and took the swatter from her. He dropped it to the pavement.

Her shoulders sagged. She looked at him, tears in her eyes. "Are you all right?"

He nodded wordlessly and touched his cheekbone. His fingers came away sticky with blood, and he could taste it, warm and salty, in his mouth. He hurt in too many places to count, but he tried to block the pain, to rise above it.

"Oh, Sonny," Belinda said and burst into tears. The sirens sounded more loudly. He put his arm around her. "This happened because of me," she managed to choke out. She sobbed more helplessly.

"Shh," he said, tightening his hold on her. "It's over now. The police are coming."

The young man still standing shifted nervously and started to edge away from the car. "Don't go anywhere," Sonny ordered. "I've seen your face. The police'll get you—sooner or later. You might as well stay put."

"I—I know them," Belinda said angrily, through her tears. "All of them. Lester Fletcher. Chuck Cooper. Barry Armbruster. Oh, God, Sonny, are you all right?"

"Couple ribs cracked, maybe," he said, his teeth gritted. "It's okay. I'm still standing."

Two cars from the sheriff's department squealed around the corner, their sirens splitting the night air. An ambulance followed, keening just as shrilly.

Sonny's disgusted gaze swept over the young men. One still lay on the ground, sniffling and covering his eyes with his hands. Another sat in the street, his eyes bleary, holding his midsection.

The third, the one Belinda had called Chuck Cooper, huddled against the car, and he had the expression of a cornered animal.

The cars halted and four deputies spilled out. The ambulance skidded to a stop. Whirling red and blue lights made the night surreal.

"What happened?" one of the lawmen asked Sonny, looking him up and down.

He held Belinda more tightly, even though it hurt his ribs. "They jumped me."

"You know why?"

Sonny tried to shrug, but it hurt too much. "They're drunk. Are they football players?"

"Yeah," said the deputy sardonically. "They are. The pride of Crystal Creek." Then his expression changed to one of worry. He studied Sonny, holding Belinda so protectively. "I sure hope," he said softly, "that this ain't the start of a *situation*."

"Yeah," Sonny said, wiping blood from his cheek. "I hope so, too."

Belinda Dugan wept harder. He held her. He was worried about her. She had, after all, been the original target.

AT THE HOSPITAL, Nate Purdy patched Sonny's cracked ribs and dressed his cuts. He insisted, to Sonny's disgust, on keeping him in the hospital overnight for observation.

"You took a couple of hits to the head. I want to make sure nothing's wrong," Nate said.

The next morning Nate released him, but ordered him to take the day off. Grudgingly, he obeyed.

Less than an hour later, Beverly, distraught, appeared at the door of his apartment. He hadn't expected her. He answered the door shirtless, in jeans and his stocking feet.

Beverly's eyes widened, moving from the small white bandage on his cheek to the larger ones that bound his ribs. "Oh, Sonny," she said, and tears sprang into her eyes. She stepped inside unasked. Hesitantly, she touched the bandage on his ribs.

He flinched away from her touch. Her hand so near his naked chest filled his mind with forbidden images. "What are you doing here?" he demanded. "You shouldn't be here."

He moved to the straight-backed chair where his white shirt hung. Wincing from the pain, he shrugged into it as quickly as he could. Most of the shirt's buttons had been torn off, so he had to leave it hanging open. Its left shoulder was spattered with dried blood.

"Why shouldn't I be here?" she asked. "I came to see how you are. Nate just told me—"

"It's no big deal," he grumbled, trying to stuff his shirttail into his jeans. He winced again. "And you shouldn't be here. People'll talk."

"Oh, who cares?" she said, tossing her head. "And stop being so modest. Sit down. What were you doing?"

"Reading," he said.

A thick, technical-looking book lay on the couch. The couch looked old and uncomfortable. A pillow was propped against one of its arms.

Her eyes swept about the small, Spartan apartment. Books were everywhere. They filled the shelves to overflowing, were piled on tables and chairs, sat in stacks on the floor. Half opened boxes of them stood in the corners, and opened boxes lined the bare walls.

The place held no other hint of his personality or past, not so much as a snapshot. She turned her gaze to him as he lowered himself painfully to the couch. The open shirt let her glimpse his flat stomach, his muscled chest. She looked away, feeling as if she'd done something wrong.

"What did they do to you?" she asked, staring at a bookcase. "How badly are you hurt?"

"Cracked some ribs, cut on the cheekbone, a couple bruises. Nothing to worry about."

"But why?" she insisted, looking at him again. "Why did they do it?"

He lifted a shoulder, the one where the shirt was stained with blood. "I don't know. They were drunk."

"May I sit down?"

"If you want. Look, Blondie, I'm fine. It's nothing. When I used to play cowboy, I took a lot more knocks than this."

He pulled his shirt shut and held it that way.

She said, "I can't believe it. Barry Armbruster? He used to be the nicest little boy. And Chuck Cooper? Chuck's an Eagle Scout, for heaven's sake."

"Yes," Sonny said dryly. "He certainly seemed prepared to do his duty."

"How can you joke?" she asked. "This makes no sense, none at all. Lester Fletcher? He used to be such a big, flabby mama's boy, afraid of his own shadow, afraid to take a single step out of line. I can't imagine him doing something like this."

"You don't have to imagine it. It's done. Look, you want some coffee or something? I used to have a coffeepot, I think. I'll find it."

He started to rise. "No!" she protested. "Sonny, stay still. Please. I don't want any."

He sank back against the couch. "You've convinced me."

"Do you want me to get you another shirt?"

"No. I like this one. We've been through a lot together. I like it so much I'm naming it. Fred. This is Fred the Shirt."

"Oh, Sonny," she said in despair. She knew he was in pain, a great deal of it. She could remember too clearly.

Jeff had been hurt like this once, in a pickup truck accident with Grandpa Hank. After his release from the hospital, she'd stopped at his place to give him some books, and had ended up spending the night.

It had been perfectly innocent. He'd fallen asleep from his pain pills. She'd meant to stay only late enough to see he took his last dose of medicine, but she'd fallen asleep herself. The next morning he'd made her breakfast and flirted outrageously with her. And after that, it had seemed inevitable that they fall in love....

A shiver rippled through her. *Jeff is kissing me again,* she thought in a tumult of emotion. *I still love you, Jeff. Stay with me. Never go away.*

She tore her mind away from Jeff; she'd come to see her friend, not to feel sorry for herself. "Tell me exactly what happened last night," she said. "Nate was vague. I still can't believe they did this to you."

He grimaced and clutched his shirtfront more tightly shut. "I met Tap Hollister and this other teacher, Belinda Dugan, at Lingle's. Tap—wasn't feeling well. I took him home, then her. Those three lunks were wait-ing in the shadows.''

Beverly said, ''I heard about that silly mess and how those boys turned her car over. But why did they jump you? You never did anything to them.''

''Look,'' he said. ''They were drunk. They weren't thinking at all. I heard that one of them, the Cooper kid, told some of it. They were waiting for Belinda. He said they wanted to scare her, that's all. But I seriously doubt that's all they had in mind.''

''Animals,'' Beverly said in disgust.

''They didn't expect her to show up with a man. That threw them. Then they saw it was me. It set them off somehow.''

''You? How did they even know you?''

He cast her an unsmiling glance. ''In case you haven't noticed, Blondie, I kind of stand out in town. I'm the only Oriental here.''

Apprehension shuddered through her. ''What do you mean?''

He jerked his chin up to a defiant angle. She realized that once more he was fighting back a wave of pain. ''What I mean,'' he said, ''is maybe they thought she'd been out with me. They didn't like it. Maybe they thought they'd get to her through me. They were al-ready mad. I made them madder.''

''Race? My God—no.'' A wave of nausea swept her. She put her hand to her midsection.

''What other reason is there? Otherwise it makes no sense. None.''

''We're not like that in this town,'' she said.

''No?'' he asked, giving her an appraising look. ''You were when we first met. All you saw was that I was different, right?''

His frankness caught her by surprise, and her cheeks blazed with shame. She looked at the floor, unable to meet his eyes.

She remembered the day she'd met him. Two nurses had been talking about the handsome, dark-haired new doctor. She had never imagined that he would be of a different race. His name, S. J. Dekker, gave no indication of it, and Nate had never mentioned it.

Then, when she'd been introduced to him, she'd felt foolish with shock, and fear had unexpectedly gripped her. She'd grown up in her father's house, where all that was Oriental was threatening. To her humiliation, she'd felt unsettled and almost frightened by this Dr. Dekker.

Later she'd complained to one of the nurses. "Why didn't you *say* he was Chinese? The way you talked, I thought we had Antonio Banderas joining us."

"Well," the nurse said innocently, "he's kind of like a Chinese Antonio Banderas. Those eyebrows, that sexy upper lip..."

Now she kept staring unseeing at the floor. "I was different," she told him. "It was how I was brought up. My father couldn't help how he felt, but I've learned from you. You've taught me to—"

He cut her off. "Shh. Stop, Blondie. I didn't mean to make you feel bad. I shouldn't have said that. I'm not in the best of moods. I'm sorry. Honest. I'm sorry."

Slowly, she raised her eyes to meet his. He had an odd expression, almost sad. "I'm sorry, too. But I really can't believe it, Sonny. That any of our kids would do this for that kind of reason. Especially *those* three."

"But they did."

Beverly, sickened, still had trouble accepting it. Barry Armbruster's best friend in grade school had been a little Hispanic boy named Paco. In second grade, Barry'd cried when Paco had moved away.

Chuck Cooper played football, but basketball was his first love. All of his heroes were basketball players, and most of them were black.

Lester Fletcher's late father had been from Oklahoma and had been part Indian and proud of his heritage. None of them, she thought in perplexity, had the makings of a racist.

"What's got into these kids?" she asked. "First the business with Belinda Dugan's car, now this. What's *wrong* with them?"

He shook his head. "I don't know. But there's probably going to be hell to pay."

"What do you mean?"

"Those three kids, Armbruster, Cooper, Fletcher. They weren't in on the car incident. That means there's three more kids off the team. Nine in all. Crystal Creek's had the heart cut out of its team. There's not enough good players left to beat a team of World War One veterans."

Beverly understood and felt sicker than before. "Chuck Cooper was the only decent quarterback left. Lester Fletcher and Barry Armbruster were two of the burliest linemen. With them gone, we might as well not go to the tournament. I mean, it was pretty impossible to win with six of them gone, but it'd take a miracle with nine out."

His mouth took on a bitter crook. "Football's as serious as a heart attack in this town. No. More serious. People are going to hate this. They'll resent me and probably Belinda Dugan, too."

"You and Belinda? But *you* didn't do anything. Those nine kids started the trouble. They brought this on themselves."

He looked at her coolly. "Not everybody'll think that way. Some people will say, 'They're only kids.' 'They were drinking a little.' 'Boys will be boys.' The usual crap."

"Nobody could think that way."

"Wrong," he countered. "They already do. At the hospital, when I was making my statement to the cops, one deputy very quietly advised me not to press charges. 'They're just kids,' he said. 'You gave 'em their licks. They've paid enough.'"

Beverly was appalled. "Who said that?"

He sighed harshly. "Bobby something. I don't know. Later a nurse came up and said the same thing— 'They're just kids. Give them a break.'"

"Which nurse?"

"Freda Fletcher."

"Oh, lawsy," Beverly said miserably. "Lester Fletcher is her cousin's kid."

"Some kid." Sonny muttered. "Lester Fletcher's six feet tall and weighs 230 pounds."

"Exactly," Beverly said. "Those three are as wide as they are tall. That's why nobody could beat our team. We have a lineup of guys as big as refrigerators."

"Wrong," he said. "You used to. Now you don't. I no sooner got back to my place, than I had a phone call from Barry Armbruster's mother. 'Please don't press charges. Don't ruin my son's life and give him a record.'"

"You mean," she said, "some people actually think those boys should get away with it? Go scot-free?"

"That's exactly what I mean." He winced again, his handsome face contorting slightly.

"But they could have hurt you even worse than they did."

He didn't look at her. "I hurt them back. For some people, that squares it."

"They could have beaten you to death."

He nodded. "Yeah. Which is why I'm pressing charges. What if it's not racial? What if they just wanted to hurt somebody, anybody? They were out of control. God knows what they might have done to Belinda."

She felt hollow and fearful. Sonny was right. The attackers might be young, but they shouldn't be let off lightly. What they'd done was too serious.

"I'll be glad to get to Denver," he said. "Away from all this."

"I won't be glad," she said. "I'll miss you."

He started to reply, but no sound came out. Instead, his teeth gritted against pain. He lost his hold on his shirtfront, gripped his injured ribs.

She rose and went to his side. She put her hand on his shoulder. His muscles were knotted with tension beneath her fingers.

"Don't," he gasped, trying to move away.

"You're not taking your pain pills, are you?" she accused. "And you're hurt worse than you're saying."

"Don't," he repeated. "I'm fine."

She gripped his shoulder more tightly. "You're not fine. And you're not taking the pain pills. Are you?"

"Oh, hell," he said, fighting against grimacing, "they make me sleepy. I can't read."

"You need the pills. You need rest."

"I'm wasting time. If I have to stay home, I might as well read, learn something."

"You already know everything," she said sternly. "At least, that's what Nate says. Except how to relax. Physician, heal thyself. Let me see that bandage. Is it coming loose?"

She slid her other hand inside his shirt. His body stiffened. Very carefully, very firmly, he caught her hand and guided it away from his chest. "Don't," he said quietly. His hand was like warm, live steel clamped around her wrist.

She sucked in her breath. She didn't raise her eyes to his. Instead she found herself staring blindly at his smooth, hard chest. "Sonny," she said, surprised to find herself a bit breathless, "I'm your friend. I'm only trying to help."

"My friend?" he asked, his voice strained.

"Yes. Take your pills. And let me check that bandage."

He released her wrist. A strange weariness crossed his face. "The bandage is fine. You can get me the pills. They're next to the kitchen sink."

"Of course," she said. She rose and went to the kitchenette. Her wrist tingled where he'd touched her, and she had an odd sense of déjà vu. She'd gotten Jeff's pills for him when his ribs were bruised. It had happened months ago, yet it seemed to be happening now for the first time.

She had the eerie sensation that if she turned around slowly, carefully, in just the right way, she would see the man she loved. But that, of course, was impossible. She didn't turn.

She opened a cupboard and found it nearly empty. It contained two glasses, two coffee cups, two saucers, one plate, one bowl. She took one of the glasses and filled it, shaking her head at how few things he seemed to possess, other than books.

She brought the glass and pills to him, trying to shake off her feeling of strangeness. "You live like a monk," she said. "You must have made decent money as a resident. Don't you ever spend it?"

He took the pills, then wiped the back of his hand along his mouth. "I always sent what I could to my grandmother. The rest I saved."

"Saved? For what? To buy your share of the partnership in the Denver practice?" She tried to keep her manner brisk and businesslike, as a nurse would.

"Hopkins-Sloane doesn't come cheap, Blondie. Look, I've been good, I've taken my pill. Go home now, okay? So I can sleep?"

She stood by the couch, studying him. He seemed tired out from more than pain. He worried her. "I could stay until you're asleep," she offered. "You know, just in case you needed help with anything."

He shot her a surprisingly sharp look. "If I ever sleep with you, Blondie, let's make it under different circumstances."

She sighed with relief. "Well, you must not be in too bad shape. You can still pretend to flirt."

"It's my duty," he said sardonically. "As your friend. You need your daily fix of flirting. I do my best."

"Do you want a blanket? Do you even own a blanket? Do you want me to help you into bed? You do have a bed, don't you?"

"Do you want to find out? Go away. Stop taunting me."

"I'm not taunting. It just occurs to me that you allow yourself very few pleasures in life. Somebody ought to teach you what fun is."

"She did. She was a masseuse in Singapore."

"You thing," she said in exasperation. "Are you ever going to allow yourself any luxuries?"

He stretched out gingerly on the couch, and his eyelids were starting to flutter sleepily. "Yes. A horse. When I'm settled, I'm going to buy me a damn fine horse. Like your stepfather's."

"That's all?" she asked in dismay.

She resisted the desire to go to him again, to plump up the pillow on which his dark head rested, to smooth the hair from his forehead.

"No," he said drowsily. "I'll get all the encumberments known to man. A flashy car. A big house. A television set. A hot tub. A wife."

"A wife?" she asked.

"Yeah. Maybe the masseuse from Singapore. Or if you don't be good and go away, I'll make it you. It's a terrible thing, being a doctor's wife. But if you don't behave, you'll deserve it."

"You thing," she said.

She held her breath, waiting for an answer. His shirt had fallen open again, and she could see the steady rise and fall of his chest, bronze against the white of the crumpled cloth.

As if hypnotized, she watched his even breathing for a long time before she realized he'd fallen asleep. Once again, she was reminded with a pang of Jeff, lying barechested and bandaged on his bed, his restless spirit drugged into slumber.

Almost against her will, she moved closer to Sonny and gazed down at him. His black hair was tousled and falling across his forehead, just as Jeff's had been. As if she could reach Jeff again, she allowed herself to touch her fingers to Sonny's errant lock, to smooth it back from his brow.

"I love you, Jeff," she whispered. She missed him so much at that moment that her heart constricted in yearning, and her throat felt choked.

Then she turned from Sonny and left him lying alone in his room full of books.

CHAPTER FIVE

IT WAS EARLY MORNING, the day after Sonny's day of enforced rest, and Belinda Dugan was depressed.

"The parents of five different players called me," she said. "How about you?"

"Two," said Sonny, toying with a sugar packet. He sat with Tap and Belinda in the Longhorn. "The Armbruster kid's. Then Lester Fletcher's mother phoned. She says he's 'sorry,' that he was 'misled by his peers.'"

"A lot of people blame me for starting this," Belinda said, shaking her head. "I don't plug in my phone anymore. I guess I'll have to get an unlisted number. Some of those calls made me feel—well—hated."

"Yeah," said Sonny, throwing down the sugar packet. "It stinks."

Tap had his elbows on the table and his face in his hands. "We could shoot ourselves," he suggested with a groan. "Or there's always the river. I've got a gas oven. We could go over to my apartment and gas ourselves."

Belinda looked at Tap in concern. Always intense, he was taking the incident hard.

"What are you moaning about?" Sonny said. "Nobody blames you for anything."

"I *blame* me," Tap said. "If I could hold my liquor like a real Texan, they'd have beaten me up, not you.

Maybe I'm not a real Texan. Maybe my parents adopted me from a wimpy little state like Rhode Island."

"Your solicitude is touching," Sonny muttered. "And I'd just as soon they'd pounded you, not me. But it was a fluke, that's all. Cheer up. You're trespassing on what's rightfully *my* depression."

"I know," Tap said miserably. "And it depresses me."

"Guilt," Sonny said. "Why do Americans make it an art form?"

Tap sighed and raised his head. Comradelike, he threw his arm around Belinda. She tensed, yet a thrill of sheer physical awareness rippled through her.

But he didn't so much as glance at her. He spoke to Sonny instead. "I try to remember that the important thing is that somebody was with Dugan. God knows what those goons would have done if she'd been alone."

"That's what bothers me, too." Sonny gave Belinda a worried look.

She fought down a shudder. She'd had nightmares about the attack. What would have happened if she'd come home alone, as she'd originally planned? The three players all swore they'd meant only to scare her a bit. They'd planned to throw gravel at the windows, ring her doorbell and run off, childish things like that.

They all claimed they'd thought she'd be in her house, safe and sound. None of them had anticipated a confrontation or an attack, they claimed—it had simply happened. Both Lester Fletcher and Barry Armbruster swore they hadn't meant to hurt Sonny, just rough him up a bit. Chuck Cooper didn't want to talk about it.

Wayne Jackson, the sheriff, had told Belinda that Fletcher and Cooper were plenty drunk, all right. But the other, Barry Armbruster, had been blind, out-of-his-mind drunk. He literally hadn't known what he was doing, and he'd been the leader.

"They might have hurt you bad," Wayne had told her somberly. "They could have raped you."

Now he had a car from the sheriff's department passing her house on a regular basis, at least once an hour.

"Don't shiver, little buddy," Tap said, hugging her more tightly. "You've got the two baddest dudes in Crystal Creek here to protect you. You're safe. From now on, anybody who messes with you, messes with me."

His nearness, his promise to protect her made her go almost faint. She wished he'd move farther away, and paradoxically she wished he'd move closer.

"How would you hold somebody off?" Sonny mocked. "Stab him with a piccolo?"

Tap took his arm away from Belinda. She almost sighed with combined relief and regret. He put his elbow on the table and clenched his fist.

"I used to box," he said. "I'm not the harmless music meister you think."

Sonny shook his head and looked derisive. "A boxer," he said. "I thought you were a tutor who tooted a flute."

"I was in Golden Gloves," Tap said. "Middleweight."

"If you boxed, shouldn't your nose be flat?" Sonny asked. "Shouldn't you have cauliflower ears and birds flying around your head saying, 'Tweet'?"

"Nope." Tap put his arm around Belinda again. "Nobody could lay a glove on me. Whereas, one tap of my fist of fury, and my foe was laid low. Hence, the nickname, Tap.''

"God, Hollister," Sonny scoffed. "Don't you have any modesty?"

"I used to," Tap answered. "But I dropped it. So Dugan here knows it's no mere French horn player at her service. I'll take care of ya, Dugan."

Belinda, miserable and pleased at the same time, tried not to blush.

"Do the students know?" Sonny asked. "That you can actually inflict physical harm?"

"Yeah. Since this mess, I've made it my business that they know," Tap said with atypical grimness. "Like I said. I want Dugan to feel safe." He hugged her again, the way a man joshingly hugs an old army buddy.

I'm going to swoon, thought Belinda. *I'll just fall over on him, and then maybe he'll figure it out—I'm a girl.*

Shirley Ditmars came bobbing into the Longhorn, her cheeks pink from the wind. When she saw Sonny, Tap and Belinda in the booth, she paused and gave them a pointed look. Her nephews, Dennis and Clyde Ditmars, had been dropped from the team for turning over Belinda's car.

Shirley sniffed disdainfully. "This town used to have a wonderful football team. It used to have community spirit." She walked past them and sat as far away as possible.

Kasey, the waitress, had been on her way to refill their coffee cups. She stopped in her tracks. "This town used to have kids who behaved themselves," Kasey called after Shirley.

Belinda exchanged glances with Tap and Sonny.

Kasey came to their table with the coffepot. "Don't mind her," she said, cocking her head in Shirley's direction. "Consider the source."

Shirley made a great show of shaking out the morning paper and holding it up so that it screened her view of them.

"How you doing today, gorgeous?" Kasey asked Sonny. "When you take that bandage off your cheek, will you have a cute little scar like Harrison Ford?"

"Cuter," Sonny said. "Much cuter."

When Kasey left, Tap leaned toward Sonny conspiratorially. "I think she likes you."

Sonny didn't buy it. "*This* is the woman we need to have on our minds," he said, nodding at Belinda.

"Right," said Tap, patting her shoulder.

Belinda's heart cartwheeled drunkenly. She'd made herself stay away from Tap because he had this unspeakable effect on her. Now he seemed determined to be at her side as much as possible. She'd come into the Longhorn alone this morning. Sonny had joined her, and then, to her consternation, Tap.

She knew that his arm around her meant nothing. He was warning the town that he meant to protect her, that was all. He had no more personal feeling for her than a policeman did for a bank safe that he guarded.

"The head coach, Bobby Higgins," Sonny said, "has he finally convinced his players to leave her alone? To leave everybody alone?"

"Yeah," Tap answered. "He raked them over the coals. He says if anything else happens, he'll find who did it, he'll skin them, hang them by their thumbs, draw and quarter them and boil them in oil. Then he'll sit down and think of a way to *really* hurt them."

"Good," Sonny said. "I hope they got the message."

"Me, too. But, of course, the assistant coach is a different story. Grimes is moaning and groaning that they all got a raw deal."

Sonny said, "I don't care what Grimes thinks. As long as they leave Belinda alone."

"They will. Or else." Tap glanced at his watch. "We'd better hit the bricks, Dugan. Come on. I'll carry your books to school."

He scooped up her books and helped her from the booth. When he opened the door of the Longhorn for her, the December air felt cool and healing to her hot cheeks. She and Tap started to walk toward the high school.

"I feel rotten," Tap said, serious again. "I'm the reason he took that beating. It should have been me."

"It shouldn't have been anybody," she said.

"I'd still rather it'd been me," Tap said. "It wouldn't have been so damn ugly."

"It would have been ugly no matter who they did it to."

"No," he said. "If it'd been me, it'd only have been drunk kids roughing up a teacher who'd bad-mouthed them. But this is worse. There was no reason for it, none."

She sighed. "Unless it was because of race. But the thought of it makes me sick. This isn't that kind of town. At least, I didn't think it was. Except for a few people like Horace Westerhaus."

He nodded. "I know. I'm worried."

"Me, too. Why did they do it?" She stopped walking, and so did he. She made the mistake of glancing up at him. When his blue eyes were solemn, like now, they shook her to her soul.

Quickly she looked away. "That's another reason you let people know you boxed, right? So anybody'd think twice about taking on Sonny again."

"Yeah," he said. "I don't want anybody hassling either of you. I mean it, Dugan."

My name is Belinda, she wanted to say. *Can't you ever say it? Am I always going to be one of the guys to you?*

He said, "I'm sorry. I hope you can forgive me."

"Forgive you?"

"I do blame myself for what happened," he said, putting his hands on her shoulders, gripping them tightly. "I'm going to watch over you. I promise you that."

She couldn't stop herself. She raised her eyes to his again, those beautiful blue eyes that always, always stole her soul.

I love you, she thought.

He let go of her, gave her back a friendly pat. "Come on, little buddy," he said. "Or we'll be late. Don't ask for whom the bell tolls. It tolls for us."

CRYSTAL CREEK WENT to the state tournament minus nine of its biggest and best players. No miracle occurred. The Cougars suffered the most mortifying loss in their history: 56–0. The team was in disgrace, the school humiliated, and the fans felt betrayed and angry.

No parent came forth to apologize to Belinda, and only one did so to Sonny. Chuck Cooper's father, Jerry, was foreman at the Hole in the Wall Dude Ranch. He came to the clinic to say how shamed and sorry he was.

"I hate like hell that this happened," he said, raking a hand through his graying hair. "But Chuck was gettin' out of hand. I don't know what's got into him. He's not the boy he was."

Sonny studied the weathered, rangy man. Jerry Cooper shook his head as if he was deeply bewildered. He talked of how Chuck had changed over the summer, becoming moody and unpredictable.

"Maybe this trouble'll turn Chuck back around," Cooper said sadly. "I hope so. I just want you to know I don't blame you for anything in any way. I'm sorry for what he done. He broke the law. Now he should face up to it. Fair's fair."

But not all the townspeople were as philosophic as Chuck Cooper's father, nor were they in any mood to be.

Some disgruntled fans argued that the school had been far too hard on the boys. What had the first six done that was so terrible? They'd only played a prank, and a pretty funny one if you thought about it. The problem was that Belinda Dugan couldn't take a joke.

You couldn't blame the other players for being mad. There they were, their team nearly ruined, their chances for a championship pretty well shot. So some of the kids had a drink or two—kids will be kids—and decided to scare her.

They'd seen her come home with Dekker, and for some reason, they decided to give him a little scare instead. Now he was trying to make a federal case of it, give them records. *Criminal records!*

Assistant coach Roger Grimes humbled himself enough to visit Sonny to plead for clemency. He came into Sonny's consulting room unannounced.

Grimes's round face wore a look of wounded piety. The man was not as tall as Sonny, but he was twice as bulky, and his body mass loomed, seeming to overwhelm the little room. He took off his ball cap as if in supplication.

"Look," Grimes said, running his hand over his thinning crewcut. "Don't press charges against those kids. They suffered enough. They had to stand by and see their team get its butt kicked. They took it hard. They blame themselves. Lester Fletcher actually cried."

Sonny's heart was not exactly rent with pity. He said nothing. He imagined tears from someone the size of Lester Fletcher would be large enough to drown mice.

"Those are good boys," Grimes said. "They took a little drink because they were upset. You can't blame 'em for feeling hurt. That Dugan woman got six of their friends kicked off the team."

"Wrong," Sonny said tightly. "They got themselves kicked off. Don't blame her."

Grimes ignored the comment. "You know, you whupped those boys pretty bad that night. You chipped Lester's tooth."

Lester cracked four of my ribs, you jackass, Sonny thought, *and he probably hurt his fist on my face.* But again kept his mouth shut.

"In fact," Grimes said, narrowing his eyes, "Lester and Barry say they were only roughhousing you, fooling around. You were the one who turned it into a full-fledged fight."

"Me?" Sonny asked in scornful disbelief.

"You. Your judo chops and karate kicks. They're only kids, you know."

"Yeah—six hundred pounds of them. I defended myself."

"Well," Grimes said, "they got in their licks, you got in yours. I'd say it's even. It's over. You shouldn't take it so personally."

"They said they'd kill me. I take statements like that personally."

"That was just kid talk," Grimes said placatingly. "Why don't you drop the charges? Come on, be a good guy. They didn't mean it."

"They hit like they meant it. What if they'd jumped somebody who couldn't fight back?"

"All they wanted to do was tussle a little. It got out of hand. Let bygones be bygones. No real harm was done."

Sonny's ribs still felt as if real harm had been done. "Acts have consequences, Grimes. They need to learn that."

"Learn it? Hell, it's engraved on their hearts. They failed their team. They failed their school. There's no greater shame. But now they've learned their lesson. These are good boys, they're *my* boys. Don't do this to them. If they get criminal records, it'll follow them the rest of their lives. Think of the tragedy it might cause."

"Excuse me," Sonny said sarcastically. "Shouldn't they have thought? Like, 'What happens to me if I break this guy's skull?'"

"They're kids," Grimes wheedled. "Why be vindictive?"

"Because they were ready to kill somebody. Maybe just me, maybe anybody. I don't know."

Roger Grimes's tone grew holier-than-thou. "You ask anybody in town about those three boys. Nobody ever had trouble with them. Never. You're blowing this out of proportion. My wife cries herself to sleep every night,

worrying about those kids. Why do you want to go ru-
ining people's lives?"

"I value lives," Sonny said, steel in his voice. "Which
is why I'm pressing charges. What might they have done
to Belinda Dugan? She barely weighs a hundred
pounds."

"Maybe you don't understand how we do things in
this country," Grimes said. "You know, folks are saying exactly that. You just don't understand our ways.
They're saying, 'What's he want? To cane them, like
over in Singapore?' Show some mercy, man. Folks'd
think a lot more of you."

"I don't care what 'folks' think."

"You drag those three kids before a judge, you know
what this town'll think? I'm telling you, for your own
good, let it drop."

Threat, none too subtle, charged the words. Sonny's
eyes met Grimes's in a cool and steady gaze. "I won't
drop it," he said.

ROGER GRIMES was vocal about the meeting. "I tried
to reason with him," he told anyone who'd listen.
"He's cold. He's mean. He wants those kids' heads on
a plate. Don't ask me why. Ask him."

Peggy Sue Grimes took a sweeter and more guileful
approach. Softly, wistfully, she managed to convey her
message to almost everyone she met. She hoped and
prayed that Dr. Dekker would unharden his heart.
Wouldn't it be wonderful to forget this unpleasant
business? Wouldn't it be wonderful to put the trouble
behind and get on with life?

She came to the hospital and asked to speak to Beverly in private. Apprehensively, Beverly led her to the
coffee room. She knew Peggy Sue was turning people

against Sonny, and she heartily disliked her for it. She wondered what the woman had up her lacy sleeve now.

Peggy Sue was small and trimly built, and she favored frilly clothing. She wore her brown hair swept up in curls atop her head and fastened in place with combs. It gave her a delicately Victorian air. "May I buy you some coffee?" she asked in her proper, little-girl voice.

"No, thanks," Beverly said. "I've got patients to tend. What is it that you want?"

Peggy Sue's large, expressive eyes were as green as a cat's. They filled with tears. "I want peace," she said with a catch in her voice. "I want harmony. I want us all to love each other again, like before."

She put her hand over Beverly's and clutched it pleadingly. "Won't you help heal the wounds and make us whole again? That's all Roger and I want, is peace."

Beverly fought the urge to jerk her hand away. She said, "For someone who wants peace, you and your husband sure go around setting people against other people."

Peggy blinked back her tears. "Don't scold me, Beverly, please. Nate Purdy already has. But I have to speak what's in my heart. I couldn't live with myself if I didn't."

Beverly arched an eyebrow cynically. "I've heard that you've already spoken what's in your heart. That you keep speaking it a mile a minute. Even to the patients who come into the clinic. Did Nate tell you to stop? I hope he did."

Peggy's lower lip quivered, and so did her voice. She gripped Beverly's hand more tightly. "He told me not to talk about it in the clinic. He said what I say outside is my own business. This is outside."

"Shouldn't you be at the clinic right now?"

"I have the rest of the day off. I have to go into Austin to see my back specialist. I'm in a lot of pain, but I had to come talk with you. About Dr. Dekker."

"Why don't you talk to Dr. Dekker himself?"

Peggy's tears welled again. "I've tried. He won't listen to me. But he'd listen to you. He thinks the world of you. *Everybody* knows that—how the two of you are."

Beverly's nerve ends tingled in warning. "Exactly what do you mean by that?"

Peggy's expression became righteously innocent. "Why, nothing. Only that the two of you are such good friends. So I know you'd want to help him."

"Help him?"

"Help him forgive and not press charges against those three boys. For his sake as well as theirs. I like Dr. Dekker. I respect him immensely. Oh, excuse me, please."

From her skirt pocket, Peggy Sue took a handkerchief with tatted edging. A tear had spilled to her cheek, and she brushed it away.

"I'm sorry," she said. "I'm not crying to play on your sympathy. It's just that Roger and I love these boys so much. They're like the sons we never had. That maybe we'll never have. Those are *my* boys, Beverly. My pride and joy."

"They're not boys, they're young men," Beverly countered. "They got liquored up and tried to beat a man who'd never done them a bit of wrong."

"It was a mistake," Peggy said, an ache in her voice. "It was the worst mistake they ever made. But they've paid for it. Being thrown off the team, losing the tournament—"

"What if there'd been no tournament to lose?" Beverly challenged. "What if they hadn't been Roger's players? What if three just plain boys got just plain drunk and just plain tried to kill someone? Would you be here then?"

"Yes—I told you. All I want is peace and forgiveness and love. Why should those boys carry a black mark for the rest of their lives? They can't repent any more than they already have. Anything more you do to them is just plain cruelty. And it'll just make people hate Dr. Dekker more."

"Hate him *more?*" Beverly said, appalled. "Why should anybody hate him at all?"

"For turning that scuffle into a full-fledged fight," Peggy said earnestly. "For trying to give three misled boys criminal records. Why should he be so bitter? If we can forgive, can't he?"

"You're twisting everything around," Beverly accused. "Why are you saying all this to me?"

Peggy gripped Beverly's hand so hard it hurt. "Because you can influence him. You could make him see the light. People would think the world of you. You could—"

Beverly yanked her hand from Peggy's grasp. She stood and stared in irritation at the other woman. "I'm sorry, Peggy, but I won't let you maneuver my emotions like—"

"Beverly, you *know* those boys," Peggy said, folding her hands together as if in prayer. "You've known them all their lives. You *know* they're not bad. Ever since we've come to this town, Roger and I have devoted our lives to these kids. Help Dr. Dekker not to hurt them any more. That's all I ask. He's a doctor. He's supposed to stop pain, not inflict it."

"Stop talking about them as if they're the victims," Beverly snapped. "And stop acting as if Sonny is Public Enemy Number One. I won't listen to any more of this."

She stalked toward the door.

"Maybe he doesn't care what people think, but you should," Peggy's teary voice called after her. "People are talking about you two, Beverly."

Let them talk, Beverly thought rebelliously.

AT THE END of that week, in the late afternoon, Sonny sat in the hospital coffee room, trying to recover from emergency duty. Beverly waltzed into the room, a vision in a powder-blue skirt and sweater. In spite of his weariness, his heart quickened.

"Nate said you were over here on another emergency," she said. "You look frazzled. A tough day?"

He looked her up and down. There ought to be a law against this woman wearing a sweater; her breasts curved too enticingly. And it should be a criminal offense for her to wear that gardenia perfume. It filled him with the painful desire to nuzzle and kiss all her pulse points.

He kept his voice controlled and sardonic. "I had a busy shift. There was a tractor accident, a motorcycle accident, a horse-back riding accident, a hunting accident, a stroke, an angina case, a cut foot, a ruptured appendix and a tendon injury."

She looked so sympathetic that it filled his stomach with drunken butterflies. "Poor thing. Is your shift finally over?"

"Yes. Thank God."

She settled down beside him on the plastic-covered couch. Her perfume made the butterflies get drunker. "You're more than tired," she said. "Something's bothering you. I can tell from your expression."

He shrugged and stared into his cup at the cold coffee. "The kid with the tendon injury didn't want me to treat him," he said in disgust. "Joe Bob Westerhaus. He was one of the guys who turned over Belinda's car. I told him, 'You take me or you've got nobody, friend.'"

"So he let you treat him?" she asked.

"What choice did he have? And the ruptured appendix belonged to Barry Armbruster's sister. The family wasn't exactly ecstatic that I was on duty. Mr. Popularity I'm not. Oh, well. To hell with it."

He knew people were turning against him. All three families, Coopers, Armbrusters and Fletchers, had friends and relatives eager to pretend nothing had ever happened.

Peggy Sue Grimes kept deftly stirring up sympathy for the offenders, and Roger Grimes boldly shifted the onus from the three players to Sonny.

"This is crazy," Beverly finally said. "I never realized how manipulative Peggy Sue really is."

"She's good, all right. And she managed to miss a day and a half of work this week. I don't know why Nate puts up with her."

Beverly rose and fed some coins into the coffee machine. He drank in the way her hips curved beneath the blue skirt, the sleekness of her legs.

"First," she said, "she plays shamelessly on Nate's sympathies. And Rose's, too. They're both pushovers for that 'we want a baby so badly' routine of hers. The Purdys couldn't have children of their own, you know."

She moved back to the plastic-covered couch and handed him a fresh cup of coffee. "Here," she said, taking the other cup from him. "Drink this. You need refueling."

Don't be so thoughtful. It kills me when you're thoughtful. "Thanks," he said, and pretended to stifle a yawn. "Something strange happened yesterday."

"Where? Here?"

"No. The clinic. Peggy Sue was leaving for home. She dropped her purse. It spilled. Guess what I saw."

She sat beside him, curling her legs beneath her. He had the stupid desire to draw her near, have her lay her head on his shoulder, lean his cheek against her hair. He thrust the thought away and forced himself to think of Peggy instead.

Beverly said, "I can't guess. What?"

"Birth control pills. I'm a hundred percent sure."

She sat up straighter and stared at him. *"What?"*

He nodded. He knew his eyes were intent on her, but he kept his gaze cool, analytical. "Birth control pills. MenoSurex from the Upshaw Company. In the green and white package. Still in the box. I saw the name, the logo."

Beverly was astonished. "Birth control pills? Why? And why would she be carrying them around?"

"Why does she have them? Good question. Why was she carrying them around? It looked like a new prescription. She'd had another appointment with her specialist that morning. She could have picked them up in Austin."

"Peggy Sue, who wants a baby so much? It makes no sense. Maybe she picked them up for somebody else," Beverly said, trying to be fair.

"Maybe. Maybe not."

Beverly frowned. Even frowning, he thought, she was beautiful. "Maybe it's part of a treatment for infertility," she said. "Did I read that somewhere? When a woman goes off the pill, she has more chance of getting pregnant?''

"Maybe that's it," he said skeptically. "Maybe not."

She shook her head. "Sonny, this gets stranger and stranger. She and Roger have lived here three years. She's always talked about how they want a baby. If she's seeing a fertility expert like she says, wouldn't he prescribe something a little more sophisticated than regular birth control pills?''

That was his suspicion exactly, but he couldn't prove it. He shrugged. "You'd think so. There's something weird here. I keep asking myself why she and Roger are so anxious to keep those three guys out of court. Is it just compassion, like they say?''

She made a helpless gesture. "I don't know. Maybe they really just want to protect them. It could be. Peggy Sue said one thing I can't get out of my mind.''

"What?''

"I *have* known those boys all their lives. They really were nice kids. Until this. What got into them? What on earth got into them?''

The words jogged something in his mind, and suddenly an idea struck him. It was one that he should have thought of long ago. It had taken Beverly's chance remark to make it spark into life. Maybe because his mind was far too often on Beverly herself.

"Blondie, you're something, you know that?'' he said in a soft growl.

"Me?'' she said innocently. "You're teasing me. Why?''

"Being a genius doesn't mean having all the answers. It means asking the right questions. And you just asked a great one.''

"What do you mean?'' she asked.

But the PA system announced his name. "Dr. Dekker, report to emergency. Dr. Dekker to emergency, right away."

He groaned. "What do they want me for? My shift's over."

But he rose, tossed away the paper coffee cup and gave her a rueful smile. "See you," he said, and he left.

It was best he'd been called away, he thought. He was almost too tired to resist her.

Beverly sat alone in the coffee room, looking after him. Her heart thudded swiftly and hard, and she didn't understand why.

But she understood why they'd summoned him to emergency yet again. It was simple. A difficult case must have arrived, and they'd called for him because he was the best and brightest.

She felt a little surge of pride that was almost, but not quite, possessive. And her heart kept beating hard, for no reason at all.

CHAPTER SIX

CAROLYN KNOCKED at Beverly's open door.

"Hi, Mama," Beverly said. She sat at her dressing table, putting on her makeup. "Come in."

Carolyn stepped inside the room. She was a tall woman, trim but voluptuous, and clearly Beverly had inherited much of her beauty from her. Carolyn was forty-six, with the first traces of silver threading her blond hair. The set of her mouth was serious.

"Going out with Sonny again?" she asked. She crossed her arms and leaned against the frame of the door.

Beverly sensed tension in the air. She knew what Carolyn was about to say, and she'd been dreading it.

"We're going riding," she said, picking up her eyeliner. "That's all."

"You were just out with him last night," Carolyn observed.

"We checked out that new restaurant in Fredericksburg. He'd never eaten sauerkraut. I had to raise his consciousness."

"You're seeing a lot of him lately," Carolyn said. Her voice seemed overly casual.

"We're just friends," Beverly said, and made a fine line along one upper eyelid.

Carolyn's expression didn't change. "You always say that. But you go on a lot of dates with him."

Beverly drew a perfect line along her other lid. "They're not dates. We're just together."

"They *look* like dates," Carolyn said. "People *think* they're dates."

"Oh, poop," Beverly said inelegantly. "I don't care what people think."

"That's not like you," Carolyn said. Her face was stern, but worry clouded her eyes.

"All my life," Beverly said, picking up her mascara, "I've bent over backwards to make a good impression. As if all life was a beauty event. And that I had to look pretty and be Miss Congeniality and have talent and have all the politically correct opinions. Phooey."

Carolyn regarded her daughter, frowning slightly. "Beverly, people are talking about the two of you."

"I don't care," said Beverly.

"You haven't been yourself. Not since that man came along."

Beverly set down the mascara wand and looked at her mother. "Maybe I've only been myself *since* he came along. I don't have to pretend with him."

Carolyn sighed and crossed her arms more tightly. "Darling, I don't understand what's going on between you two. Frankly, I don't think anybody does."

"There's nothing to understand. We keep each other company, that's all."

Carolyn moved behind Beverly and put her hands on her daughter's shoulders. Complex emotions played across her face. "I'm worried about you." She paused a moment, pressing her lips together. "All right, I'll be honest. I'm afraid you're depending on this man too much."

"I can talk to him, that's all. He makes me laugh. He's stuck here for the next few months. I don't feel like really going out with anyone, so we kill time together."

"You're sure of this?" Carolyn asked.

"Of course, I'm sure. Why do you care?"

Carolyn swallowed. A strained look crossed her face. "I was afraid you might be falling in love with him."

Beverly blinked in surprise. "In love? I mean, Jeff's only been—gone—four months. How could I be in love?"

"Your father," Carolyn said hesitantly, "had a great problem dealing with people like Sonny."

"I know," Beverly said, bowing her head so she wouldn't have to look at the mirror images of her mother and herself.

"I supposed you'd have to say he was prejudiced," Carolyn said.

Beverly took a deep breath and held it. Her father *had* been strongly prejudiced. There was no denying it.

"He was a wonderful man," Carolyn said. "And he wasn't a bigot by nature. He had strong reasons for feeling the way he did. He couldn't help it."

"I know," Beverly said, but she kept her gaze averted, feeling conflicted. Her father had volunteered for the war in Vietnam during its earliest years. His platoon had been caught in an ambush.

Frank Townsend had been one of two men injured and captured. His companion had died a long and terrible death, while Frank could only look on, locked in the same small prison hut. Five months later, he was traded in return for two Vietcong prisoners. Emaciated, diseased, his wounds still unhealed, he was sent home.

Carolyn squeezed Beverly's shoulders more tightly. "He was haunted. I can't count the times he woke up in the night, sweating, his muscles in knots, trying not to scream. I had to hold him in my arms..."

Beverly felt as if she couldn't get her breath. "You're saying that Daddy wouldn't like me seeing Sonny."

"He would have hated it. Every time I see you two together I think of how he would have hated it. I can't help it."

Beverly tensed with shock and resentment. "*You* don't want me to see Sonny?"

"Beverly, Vern was over there, too, in that ghastly business. He was missing in action. He won't even talk about it. Both the men I've loved went through it. Really, Beverly, how else would I feel?"

"You don't even want me to be friends with him?" Beverly asked in disbelief.

"If it's only a friendship, I'll cope with it. The other—that's different. I couldn't. I don't believe in mixed marriages. It's not fair to the children."

Beverly had an unsettling mental flash. With startling clarity she imagined a child. He was a beautiful child with black hair and mischievous tilted dark eyes. She drew in her breath sharply.

"Just because I'm friends with a man doesn't mean I'm going to have his children. I—I don't have those kinds of feelings about him. I'm sick of saying it—we're friends."

"Friends can become lovers," Carolyn said. "That's how it started with you and Jeff. The next thing you knew, you were madly in love with him."

Beverly gripped her mascara wand more tightly. She still loved Jeff and mourned him. There was no comparison between her feelings for him and her friendship with Sonny. "That was different."

"Was it?" Carolyn asked. "Was it really?"

"Yes," insisted Beverly. But once again she had a fleeting mental glimpse of that lovely, dark-eyed child.

Then she shuddered. It was the memory of Jeff again, making her shiver with her need for him. *Remember me,* he seemed to whisper. *You're mine.*

SONNY SUPPOSED Beverly would be amazed if she knew how he felt about her. She was like a drug in his system, tormenting him with desire.

But all she wanted was a friend, so that was what he pretended to be. He had thought, until he met Beverly, that he had become thoroughly Americanized. But now he knew that a deep, central part of him was still Oriental. He could hide his feelings well, and he refused to embarrass either himself or her by revealing them.

But he came close to losing his control that afternoon, when she decided to teach him the joys of the hayloft. They had just put up the horses after riding. "It's fun," she said with a laugh. "Come on. I'll show you."

She started up the wooden ladder to the loft. "Come *on,*" she teased.

He hesitated a moment. Her hips, sweetly curved, were at his eye level. She filled out her jeans gloriously.

His heart hammered, his groin tightened, and he gritted his teeth. He put his hands on the ladder and climbed up behind her.

At the top, she stepped out on the loft floor and stood there, slightly breathless. She wore a soft white sweater and an unbuttoned denim jacket. Her white broadbrimmed hat was tipped back at a perky angle. Her golden hair gleamed in the sunlight that fell through the open window of the loft.

He stood beside her. It would be so easy, he thought, to draw her into his arms, to lower his lips to the softness of hers. His blood pounded harder.

If you touch her that way, you'll lose her, he told himself. She wasn't yet ready to face a physical relationship. A muscle twitched in his jaw.

She walked to the edge of the floor, where the hay was pitched down to the ground floor. The loft was full of bales, and the air was aromatic with their scent and that of the horses below.

She turned and gave him that smile that shook him through. "It's easy," she said, holding out her arms and spreading her fingers. Jeff Harris's diamond still glittered on her left hand.

He held his breath, watching her. She stood smiling at him and balancing on the floor's edge. Then she took a graceful little hop and fell down into the heap of hay below.

"Come on," she called, looking up at him mischievously. Her hat had fallen off. She lay in a delectable sprawl, half-covered by hay, with a stalk of it clinging to her hair.

His heart, he decided, had already fallen down there with her. The rest of him might as well follow. He stepped off the edge of the floor and let his black cowboy boots lead him into space.

"Oof!" he said as he struck the hay. He was half-buried in it, and its dust tickled his nostrils.

"Oh," Beverly said, alarm in her breathy voice. "Your ribs. I forgot. Are you all right?"

Suddenly her fingertips were touching his midsection. His red windbreaker had fallen open, and he felt her warmth through the thinness of his T-shirt.

"Don't," he said, tight-lipped.

She bent above him, her face concerned. She kept her hand lightly on his rib cage. "Does it hurt?"

He could put his arm around her, pull her down to him and kiss her there in their fragrant bed of hay. He ached with lust, but her face was as innocent as an angel's.

"No," he said. " But don't touch me like that."

"Oh," she said. He never let her touch him if he could help it.

It drove him too crazy.

She took her hand away, and she fell back into the hay. "I didn't mean to get personal," she said.

"It's okay."

"God, I love this place," she said, sticking a stalk of hay between her teeth. "Cal and I used to play here for hours, pushing each other off."

He didn't turn to face her. He stared up at the beams of the loft. "You and Cal," he said. "Your good-looking cousin. You were closest to him?"

"In a way," she answered. "I mean, my cousin Lynn was my best friend back then, but Cal and I were most alike. And we both loved to fall. Isn't that goofy? We'd go catapulting through space like crazy people. He always loved taking chances."

"What about you?" he asked, careful to lie very still, not to move toward her.

"I had a secret wild streak. I was supposed to be my daddy's little lady, but Cal could tease me out of it. He's a terrible tease. I had an awful crush on him one summer."

He felt a futile rush of jealousy for her lucky cousin during that long-ago summer. "Did he reciprocate?"

"No. He started fooling around with Billie Jo Dumont. When he took her into the hayloft, all they jumped was each other."

"He fooled around with the mayor's wife?"

"She wasn't the mayor's wife then. She and Martin were a long way in each other's future. She was a wild thing back then."

"And you weren't?"

"I told you. I had to be Daddy's good girl."

He took a deep breath. "Nate Purdy told me about your father. About him being a prisoner of war."

"Oh," she said in a little voice.

"Your mother. I see the way she looks at me. She doesn't approve," he said casually. "Is that why? Because of your father?"

He heard the hay rustle and sensed she was turning toward him. He kept staring at the beams of the loft.

She propped herself on one elbow so she could look into his face. "Daddy was prejudiced. It rubbed off on Mama. I mean, my stepfather was in Vietnam, too. He doesn't talk about it, but he's not uptight about it, the way Daddy was. Still, I think it's all mixed together in Mama's mind. Try not to take it personally."

He didn't look at her. He gave a scoffing little laugh. "Yeah. Don't take it personally."

"She's worried, that's all. She thinks you and I might get serious about each other."

"What did you tell her?"

"That I wasn't over Jeff and that you and I were just killing time together."

"Yeah," he said.

"Sonny?" she said. He could feel the flutter of her breath against his cheek.

"What?"

"Come on. Let's go up and jump again."

"What is this?" he asked. "Your second childhood?"

"Absolutely. Are you coming or not?"

"Not. I'm conserving my strength."

She stood, dusting off the seat of her jeans. The movement gave him pleasure and pain at the same time.

"What are you conserving it for?" She picked up her hat and knocked it against her jeaned thigh.

"Go jump again," he said casually. "I'll tell you when you get back down."

He sat up, leaning his back against the boards and dusting off his red jacket. He waited, his heart still thudding, while she climbed the ladder again. He heard her boot steps above him, then saw her poised there.

She gave him a grin. "Geronimo!" she cried and leapt out into space.

She landed with a soft thud beside him. "Now tell," she said, rolling over, lying on her stomach and looking at him. "Why are you saving energy?"

He leaned farther back, just so he wouldn't be so close to her. "I think I'm going to get into more trouble."

Her blue eyes widened. "What do you mean?"

He couldn't help himself. He reached out and flicked a stem of hay from her hair. "Hayseed," he said gruffly.

"What do you mean, more trouble?" she asked.

"I'm thinking of cutting a deal with those kids. Not taking them to court."

She sat up straight and stared at him. "You can't do that. What they did is unforgivable. They were dangerous, out of control. Wayne Jackson said so himself. Belinda Dugan says she still has nightmares."

"I've thought a lot about what happened that night," he said. "And what could have happened to her. I think of her crying. I had to hold her, like she was a kid."

"You're very good at being cried on," she said ruefully.

He tried not to remember holding Beverly, having her cheek rest against his chest, feeling her hair soft against his face.

"I kept wondering why," he said. "Why would they do such a thing, even drunk?"

Beverly shook her head. "I can't understand. Especially Chuck Cooper and Barry. Chuck was always a straight arrow. And Barry used to be such a nice little boy."

"Lots of people say that. They say exactly that. A nice *little* boy. I went to the library. I looked at old yearbooks. He used to be a pudgy little guy, soft. But he's built like a truck now. Half those kids on the team are."

"They're big. They were formidable."

"They're major big," he said. "And I think this town's got a major problem."

"Problem?" she said, wide-eyed again. "What?"

"I think those kids are abusing steroids. I'm going to offer to drop the charges if they'll be tested."

Her face went blank. "Steroids?"

Restless, he stood, brushed off his clothes. She, too, rose, the stunned look still on her face. *"Steroids?"* she repeated.

"Think about it," he said, moving to the aisle between the stalls. "None of this ever made sense, right? That night they jumped me—why? Then you asked, 'What got into them?' And it hit me. I started putting things together."

She clutched at his jacket sleeve. "Do you have proof of this?"

He stared down at her hand. "I can't prove anything unless they're tested. But I think I'm right. I know it. And it's more than just those three. I'll lay money on it."

"Sonny, that's a serious charge. Why do you think so?"

He shook his head. "Everybody emphasizes those kids were never in trouble before. They've undergone a personality change. It's probably chemical."

"Steroids change your personality?"

"Damn straight, if you overdo them. These kids are at an age when their hormones are going crazy anyway. Load them up on extra testosterone, and they're going to get aggressive. Real aggressive."

"My God," she breathed. "It makes sense. I mean, look at Lester Fletcher. He used to be a butterball, and now his muscles have muscles. I just thought he'd been working out."

"A lot of them have been working out. Think about it. Have you ever seen a bunch of kids as bulked up as they are? It's no accident this school has the biggest, baddest team around. Everything points to it."

"How?"

He sighed and leaned against a stall, crossing his arms. "I started asking questions. Last summer Barry came to Nate for an acne problem. So did Lester Fletcher. Chuck Cooper's mother brought him in two months ago. He had a hell of a case of hypertension. Hypertension? At his age?"

"You're right. That's not normal."

"Then Joe Bob Westerhaus came into emergency with that tendon injury. He said he'd done it in the weight room. The tendon had snapped, and his muscle rolled up like a window shade. I never saw anything like it. But when you said what you did, it hit me that I'd read about something exactly like that. In a book on steroids."

"Tendon injuries?"

"Exactly. I asked Nate if the team had a lot of tendon injuries. He said yes. These are all signs."

"Good grief, have you told Nate this?"

"Not yet. So far I've just asked questions. I had Tap ask around, to see how many of those kids were working out. When they started getting bulked up."

"How many? When?"

"There may be as many as ten or twelve. The seniors have been working out for at least three years. That's when Roger Grimes came here. Three years ago."

She stared at him in horror. "Roger Grimes? You think *he's* wound up in this?"

"Could be. You've seen him. He looks like he's spent his life pumping iron."

"Sonny, this is serious. Steroids are illegal."

"In the U.S. But not in some countries. There's a black market. A big one."

"And you think they're not just doing steroids, they're *over*doing them?"

He nodded. "It's the nature of the drug. None of these kids believe they'll be hurt by it. Plenty of people will tell them that, too. If you're a skinny little guy, and you want to put on thirty pounds of muscle in three months, steroids sound irresistible. But they can be physically and emotionally addictive.''

Beverly's expression was bewildered. "How?"

"Abusers can develop a condition called megorexia. They fixate on their bodies. They can never get muscular enough. They keep striving for more."

"It sounds like the reverse of anorexia," she said. "Like the girls who can't get thin enough."

"Exactly. And they can't stop doing the drug. They've got to keep up with the competition at any cost. And the cost is that they screw up their body chemistry, in some cases badly. And that can screw up the mind. Aggression is a common side effect when that happens."

She went to him, put her hand on his arm. "If you think this is true, you've got to tell their parents. These kids could hurt themselves badly."

"Yeah," he said. "Steroids have serious side effects. Hypertension. Liver problems. Sexual dysfunctions. Personality disorders."

She gripped him more tightly. "Sonny, go tell Nate. Right away."

He said, "All I have are suspicions. I'd rather wait."

"Wait? Why? You can't."

He was conscious of her touch on his arm, and found himself putting his hand over hers. It seemed impossibly smooth and soft. He swallowed, finding it hard to speak.

"If it's true, I'm not going to be a popular guy. I'd rather wait until January. When you're gone to Galveston. I don't want somebody taking anything out on you because of me. It's not that long. Just a couple of weeks."

"You can't do that," she said, her gaze holding his. "I won't let you."

"Look," he said, "it could get ugly. What if it turns out that half the team's been on steroids all this time? If that's how they got two championships in a row? Those championships could be revoked. This town could really get a black eye."

"Who cares?" she said. "These are kids' lives we're talking about. You've got to do the right thing."

She grasped his hand and held on tight.

He stared at their joined hands. "Do the right thing," he said. "Yeah."

"I'll help you," she said.

"No. I want you to stay out of it. Completely. Don't get involved."

He drew his hand away even though she tried to keep it. He couldn't touch her without wanting her in his arms.

"I'll go talk to Nate," he said.

"I'll go with you."

"No. I mean it. You stay out of it."

WHEN HE LEFT, she stood on the porch and stared moodily after his car. She felt empty and sick with worry.

Even more people will resent him after this. If anybody hurts him, I'll die. I'd die without him.

The realization struck her so forcibly she could not speak. How could she think such a thing? What was happening to her? She was suddenly frightened.

Carolyn stepped out on the porch. "Beverly, what's the matter? Is something wrong?"

"Nothing," Beverly lied. "Nothing's wrong at all."

CHAPTER SEVEN

NATE PURDY was alarmed by Sonny's suspicions. The two men sat in Nate's study.

"I feel like somebody punched me in the stomach," Nate said. "How could I not catch on? Did I think such a thing could never happen here?"

Sonny rose and began to pace. "The book I brought you. It says that anywhere from five to eleven percent of high school males are using or have used steroids."

"My God," said Nate in disgust. "Don't they know the side effects?"

"They're kids. They think they're immortal. The bad stuff only happens to other guys. In the meantime, instant muscle. Winning season."

"Damn!" said Nate. "Where are they getting it?"

"I don't know. But there's plenty out there. Kids get in deep when they keep upping their doses. You can get behavior changes, big time."

"And I'd never see needle marks 'cause they take it in the butt," Nate said. "Hell's bells."

"The question is," Sonny said, "when and how did this start? And how can it be stopped?"

Nate massaged the bridge of his nose. "I have to wonder about Roger Grimes. He's built like Arnold Schwarzenegger. For all we know, he could have encouraged them to do it. I hope not, for Peggy's sake. He's all she's got in the world. She thinks he's a god."

Sonny kept his reservations about Peggy Grimes to himself. "Grimes wouldn't be the first coach who did."

"You've told nobody about this except Beverly?"

"Beverly and you."

Nate exhaled a long sigh. "So your idea is to say you'll drop charges if the kid agrees to be tested."

"Right. I want the guy to be there with his parents when I tell them. I want to see his reaction. And the parents to see it."

Nate shook his head. "Steroid testing's expensive. And it's not always accurate."

"I know. But maybe we can scare them into telling the truth. Then we're halfway home."

"You'd really drop the charges?"

"Yes. The important thing is to get them off the damned stuff and to find the source."

"We're not going to win any popularity contests if this is true," Nate said.

"If," Sonny said. "I may be completely wrong."

"You're not wrong," Nate said. "Why didn't I see it? I could kick myself."

"Don't feel that way," Sonny said.

"Let's start right now. With the Armbrusters," said Nate. "I'll get on the phone and set up an appointment. I'll go with you to see them."

Sonny nodded. He would need Nate's support. Nobody might believe him alone. They could see him as the outsider, the man with a chip on his shoulder.

But nobody would doubt Nate Purdy. Would they?

BARRY ARMBRUSTER SAT at the dining room table, looking sullen and scared. He wore a T-shirt that conformed to his muscularity, and his biceps looked as hard as cobblestones.

Barry's father was a stout man of medium height, and his mother was thin, almost fragile-looking. They sat on either side of Barry.

Barry's jaw had a militant jut. In the kid's eyes, Sonny saw what he thought he'd see: a trapped expression.

"I don't have to take any test," Barry said belligerently. "It's against my constitutional rights."

To hell with your constitutional rights, Sonny thought. *I'm trying to save your health, you musclehead.*

"What's the matter, Barry?" he asked. "Afraid that you'll flunk?"

"I don't have to take any test," Barry repeated. He shifted uneasily.

Charlotte Armbruster was stunned. "You're accusing my son of doing drugs?"

"I want him to take a test," Sonny said. "That's all."

"You're saying he does drugs," she accused. "What are you trying to do? Haven't you done enough to him?"

Robert Armbruster frowned. "He's only in high school. He wouldn't take steroids."

"Good," Nate said. "Then he'll take the test. He has nothing to hide."

"My son isn't taking any drug test," Charlotte snapped. "He's not a drug addict. Are you insane, Nate Purdy?"

"No, Charlotte, I'm not. And if you're so sure he's innocent, what's your objection? I've got test tubes in my bag. Barry can take a little whiz, with witnesses, and we can cork up a specimen and send it to be analyzed."

"I'm not taking steroids," Barry said, "and I'm not taking your lousy test, neither."

His father scowled at him. "If you're not using, you shouldn't be afraid of the test."

"Robert!" Charlotte cried angrily. "Surely you're not encouraging him to—"

"Better he takes a leak in a bottle than ends up in court. Barry, get in the bathroom and unzip."

"I'm not taking any test," Barry said defiantly.

"No, Robert," Charlotte said. "What if word gets out? I won't have my child subjected to the humiliation of—"

"Court isn't humiliating?" Robert countered.

Nate held up his hand for silence. "Dr. Dekker's made his offer. We don't want to listen to you argue. Give us a phone call when you've made up your minds."

"I'm not taking any test," Barry said. "It's against my principles. If he wants to take me to court for stickin' to my principles, he can do it."

"Let's go," Nate said in disgust. "Let 'em thrash it out. Good night, everybody."

Robert Armbruster rose and walked Nate and Sonny to the door. "I'll be in touch," he said.

"Robert," Charlotte called, "you come back—right now!"

"She's high-strung," Robert Armbruster said from between his teeth. "Like her mother."

"Robert!"

Once the door was shut behind them, Nate shook his head. "Sure seems like a lot of work to go through for about twenty cc's of warm pee."

Sonny allowed himself a sardonic smile.

The scene was worse at Lester Fletcher's household. Lois Fletcher would not even let them in the house.

"Charlotte Armbruster called to warn me. What is this, the gestapo? You just descend on my house and demand my child take a drug test?"

"Just anabolic steroids, Mrs. Fletcher," Sonny said. "They're a sort of occupational hazard for young athletes."

"My son is not a drug fiend. And he doesn't lie. He's given me his word of honor that he's never used steroids."

Sonny thought darkly that Lester Fletcher's word of honor should be worth about the same as his urine specimen.

"If he's telling the truth, then he shouldn't mind taking the test," Nate reasoned.

"No. You will not charge into my house demanding that my child urinate on command. While you watch. What are you, Nate Purdy, a pervert?"

"Lois, calm down. It's a simple test, and Dr. Dekker will drop the charges if Lester takes it. Do you want the boy to have a record? A probation officer?"

"If Dr. Dekker was a gentleman, he'd drop the charges. Go away and stop these police-state tactics. Or I'll sue you for defamation of character."

She slammed the door in their faces.

"Do you think we made her mad?" asked Sonny.

JERRY COOPER and his wife sat in the modest living room of the foreman's house at the Hole in the Wall Dude Ranch. Jerry's long, kindly face was troubled.

Luellen, his wife, was plump and plainly dressed. She wore a solemn expression. She and her husband sat on either side of their son, Chuck, on the sofa.

Jerry Cooper kept staring at the floor, a faraway look in his eyes. From time to time he would shake his head.

"We know why you're here," Luellen said. "Charlotte Armbruster called."

"I have the same thing to say to you," Sonny said. "I'll drop the charges if Chuck agrees to take a test."

Luellen folded her hands together in her lap, a gesture that seemed full of resignation. "You can drop the charges. But he doesn't have to take the test. Tell them, Chuck."

She looked sadly at her handsome, muscular son. A look of despair crossed his face. "I take the juice," he said. He put his hand over his eyes and bent his head.

"Things keep happening to me," he said brokenly. "Sometimes I feel my footsteps shake the earth. I get rushes of power I can't control. I try to be good, but I get these feelings. I tried to stop taking the stuff, and I c-c-can't. I'm scared."

Sonny rose, went to him, put his hand on the weeping boy's shoulder. "It's okay, kid," he said gruffly. "We're here to help."

Chuck Cooper told a long, rambling, and incomplete story. He had been taking anabolic steroids for two and a half years, since he was fourteen. He'd started "stacking" drugs during spring training, taking two sorts orally and doubling his usual dose. Last summer he'd also started injecting himself with testosterone cypionate.

He would not say if other team members were using the drugs. He would not tell his source or sources.

Sonny knew that the boy was trying to be loyal, but that the kid was also afraid of informing, probably rightfully so.

Still, he needed to know more. "You have drugs now, Chuck? If you want us to help, you need to turn them over. Otherwise the police might come with a search warrant."

The boy looked up in alarm.

Nate spoke. "The police won't arrest you if they don't find you buying or selling or holding. If you want your health back, turn the stuff over, Chuck. All of it."

The boy looked both dubious and scared. But he arose wordlessly and led them to his bedroom. His father followed. His mother went into the kitchen, crying quietly.

The three men watched as the boy moved a dresser a few feet from the wall. He pulled up two loose tiles and lifted a floorboard. His father, watching, stiffened.

The kid's got an effing drugstore down there, Sonny thought. Bottles of pills, vials of liquid, a half-empty box of syringes filled the little cache.

"Is this all?" Nate demanded.

"No," Chuck Cooper said in a small voice. "I got more in my car."

"Lord help us," Sonny heard Nate say under his breath.

None of the bottles or vials was labeled. There was no way to tell where they had come from.

BEVERLY SAT on her bed, staring at the pictures on her dressing table. There was a photo of her father, a tall, striking man with a full head of white hair. The photo was framed in real gold.

Next to that was a portrait of Jeff in an identical gold frame. He looked heartbreakingly handsome, his mouth curved in a slightly pouty smile. His white Stetson was pulled down at a sexy angle, and his blue eyes stared out from beneath its brim.

Reluctantly, she raised her gaze from his picture and looked at a small snapshot thrust carelessly into the corner of the mirror.

The photo had been taken back in November after the chili cook-off. Beverly and Sonny sat on a rail fence, and she was laughing.

He wore, of course, his red windbreaker, his tight, faded jeans, his black boots. He was offering her a stem of what looked like a flower, but was actually loco-weed.

He'd said something so outrageous, he'd reduced her to helpless laughter. She couldn't even remember exactly what it was, because he was always saying something outrageous.

He had his roguish look, his crooked grin flashing. One dark eyebrow was cocked, his dimples showed, and his dark hair fell over his forehead. She'd always known he was good-looking, but for the first time, she realized how exotically handsome he was.

Why, in his way, he's every bit as handsome as Jeff, she thought. Then she looked away in confusion, feeling strangely disloyal to Jeff's memory.

The phone rang. She moved back to the bedside table, picked up the receiver. "Hello?" she said.

"Hi, Blondie," said Sonny's husky, slightly accented voice. "Did I wake you?"

"Not at all. What happened? Did you see Nate? I tried to call but you didn't answer."

"Yeah. I saw him. We went to all three houses."

"How'd it go?" She was tense with concern for him.

"Not so great," he said and told her about Barry Armbruster's parents and Lois Fletcher.

When he related what had happened at the Coopers', however, she found herself almost in tears. "Oh,

Sonny, poor Chuck. And his poor parents. What'll they do?''

"It took a hell of a lot of talking, but we got them to agree to put him in an in-patient drug withdrawal center. He's starting to have psychotic episodes. He's also going to have withdrawal symptoms—headache, nausea, chills and sweats, rapid pulse—the whole nine yards."

Beverly shook her head. "That's terrible."

"We phoned Austin from the Cooper house. They said to bring him right in. Nate's going along for support. He's a good old guy."

"But what about Barry Armbruster and Lester Fletcher?"

"Nate hopes that Barry's father wins the day. He doesn't think Lois Fletcher will budge."

"Do you know how many kids are involved in this?"

"No. If I went by looks alone, I'd say ten or twelve."

"Do you have any idea where they're getting the stuff?"

"Very little. We're going to have a talk with the coach tomorrow, then the principal."

"Poor Coach Higgins. It's going to break his heart. This is his last year before he retires. And he hasn't been well. To have all this happen!"

"Yeah, but he's got to face facts. These kids are probably going to have to be randomly screened from now on. It may be the only way to discourage them. Which is going to cost money and make a lot of people mad."

"Oh, it's going to be awful," Beverly said miserably. "I was starting to believe the whole thing was going to blow over. It's not, is it? It'll just get worse, won't it?"

"Yeah," Sonny said. "It will."

THE NEXT DAY Barry Armbruster's father phoned Nate Purdy. He said that Barry had admitted the truth. He had been taking steroids, and like Chuck, he'd been stacking since spring, taking megadoses.

Barry would not say who else was involved. He would not tell where he was getting the stuff.

Nate said he wanted the boy brought to the clinic within the hour; he wanted to check him out and talk to him. But it was impossible to get more information from Barry. He claimed he didn't need help to give up the steroids; he could do it on his own.

Later, Nate and Sonny went to the high school to talk to the principal, Dr. Mongon, and head coach Bobby Higgins. It was a long, disturbing afternoon.

By the time Sonny got back to his apartment, it was dusk. He phoned Beverly. She'd been anxiously waiting to hear from him.

"You're telling me so much, my head is spinning," she said. "Can't we talk face-to-face?" Somehow, she thought, things would seem less upsetting if she was with him. "I'll drive into town and meet you."

He hesitated for a long moment. "I'll come see you instead," he said. "Give me half an hour."

She was too restless to wait inside for him. She slipped on a sweater, went out and sat on the porch swing, rocking nervously. The evening was warm and quiet.

She was relieved when she saw his battered Ford coming up the lane, and her heart gave an unexpected little jump when he got out of the car. He wore his usual jeans, T-shirt, and red windbreaker.

Beverly had turned on the Christmas lights. She had trimmed all the front windows and the front door with blinking colored lights, and when Sonny climbed the stairs, their rainbow hues flickered across his face and body.

He sat down, not next to her, but on the porch railing across from her. He gave her only the faintest of smiles, then looked out at the night sky, which was thick with stars.

"Well," Beverly said, "you told me about the coach. What about Dr. Mongan? The principal?"

"We didn't make him a happy man," he said.

"What's he going to do?"

He sighed, sounding tired. "He'll talk to the school board. He and Higgins are going to ask for random steroid testing. If a kid's name comes up, and he won't submit to the test, he's off the team. If the board'll agree."

"Will they?"

He looked at her, his face solemn. "I don't know. There are some people on the board who'll fight this kind of thing tooth and nail."

Beverly nodded worriedly. She knew exactly who would fight it: Horace Westerhaus, the most hidebound man in town.

"What about the police?" Beverly asked.

"Nate talked to the sheriff. He told him we think there's a problem. But he hasn't given any names. The names will get around soon enough."

She rose and came to sit on the railing beside him. Was it her imagination, or did he edge away slightly? A small, sickly knot formed in her stomach. She tried to ignore it.

"What about Lester and Lois Fletcher?" she asked.

He shook his head. "They're hanging tough. If I don't drop the charges, his arraignment's in two weeks. I figure he'll sit tight as long as he can. He's hoping if he stays off the steroids, they'll be out of his system. At the last minute, he'll agree to the test and pray he passes."

A cool breeze came up and she wrapped her arms around herself to keep from shivering. "Could he? Pass the test?"

Sonny tossed his head, a weary gesture. "It's possible. We don't know how sophisticated these kids are. Or their supplier."

She looked at him in concern. "Have you got any idea who the source is?"

He shook his head. "There's probably more than one."

"What about Roger Grimes?"

Sonny's lip curled. "He looks like a good bet. But there's no real evidence against him. Not a shred."

Beverly stared at the blinking Christmas lights. They created an atmosphere that seemed too innocent and too merry for this to be happening. "But why would he do such a thing? Just to win? He'd endanger these kids just to win?"

He stared out at the stars. "Maybe it hasn't hurt him or anybody he knows—till now. That's why he wanted the charges dropped. So there wouldn't be any chance it would come out."

"But he knows it's illegal, Sonny. That it's wrong."

"Maybe he doesn't think it's wrong. Hell, Blondie, for years the stuff was legal. Health clubs were pushing it. Who expects a health club to steer you wrong?"

"This makes me all nervous and twitchy," Beverly said. "Let's take a walk. Down to the pecan grove."

"Yeah," he said. "Sure."

In silence they descended the stairs. They walked toward the little pecan grove that her great-grandfather had planted almost a century ago. The breeze stirred her hair, rippled Sonny's jacket.

She glanced back at her house. The lights twinkled cheerfully across the darkness. "Peace on earth, goodwill toward men," she said with unhappy irony.

"Not the season to be jolly," he said. "This thing's going to keep me busy. I've got to go into Austin. Talk to people. Go to the medical library."

She looked up at his profile, dark against the starlight. The knot returned to her stomach. "I hope you'll save some time for me," she said with a lightness she didn't feel. "I have to leave soon."

"That's okay," he said, as if it didn't matter. "You'll be home some weekends. We'll see each other then."

"Sure," she said with the same false lightness. He nodded, but said nothing.

She shivered slightly in the increasing cold. "For a while, we'll be changing places. You'll have to tell me what's going on in Crystal Creek."

"Yeah."

They walked the rest of the way in silence. She sensed he was shutting her out, and she was hurt. Was he trying to break off their friendship before they had to part? Just so her name wouldn't be drawn into his next controversy? She didn't care about the controversy. She wanted his company more, much more.

When they reached the pecan grove, Beverly stopped and gazed up at the stars through the bare branches. "We're having a big family get-together at my uncle's place at Christmas. I want you to come. To be my—escort."

"Sorry," he said. "I volunteered for emergency duty. So Sinclair can go home and Nate can have the day off. I can't be out of town."

"Oh," she said. "I see." She swallowed with difficulty. "How about New Year's? Mama and Vern are having a supper. Vern said I could ask you."

"Same thing. I'll be on call. I can't party."

"Oh…tomorrow night I was thinking of coming into town. My cousin Cal and his wife are coming in from Austin. They and some friends of theirs, Hutch and Betsy, are going dancing. You'd like Hutch. He's like you in a way. Independent. He's very intelligent, and—"

"I'm going to Austin. To the med library."

Looking up into all those stars was making her dizzy. She lowered her head, blinking fast, and gazed at the ground. The cool breeze made her shiver.

"Are you cold?" he asked.

"Not really," she said. She didn't want to turn back. She had the terrible intuition that something was ending between them, and she wasn't ready.

"Yes, you are. Here. Take my jacket."

She protested, but he shouldered out of his jacket and made her put it on.

"You'll freeze in only that T-shirt," she said. The fabric settled about her warmly, as if alive from the heat of his body.

"No, I won't. Zip up," he said. His sure hands locked the base of the zipper, and he fastened it all the way up. His hand, hard yet gentle, brushed her chin. A feeling like electricity swarmed through her.

She looked up into his eyes. Neither of them spoke. Her lips parted slightly. Almost timidly, she raised her hand and touched his arm. His bare biceps felt hot against her cold fingertips. The stars seem to dance around his head like an aura, and they made her dizzy again.

Abruptly he stepped away from her, and her fingers touched only empty air.

"Let's go back," he said almost roughly. He jammed his hands into his back pockets and started toward the house. The way he carried himself was determined, almost angry.

She hurried to keep pace with him. Again, neither of them spoke.

I won't let you cut me out of your life just because you think there might be trouble, she thought fiercely. *I won't. I'm not afraid.*

Yet, she was frightened, deeply so. But of precisely what, she couldn't say.

THE NEWS of Chuck Cooper and Barry Armbruster spread through the town, slowly and in whispers at first, then more quickly and boldly, like a fire catching and growing.

Some were stunned with surprise; others were angry and disbelieving. Horace Westerhaus's weekly paper carried a scathing editorial saying that two admitted cases of steroid abuse did not make an epidemic.

Crystal Creek High School, the voice of the paper seethed, had always stood for sportsmanship and valor. To suggest such winning spirit came from a pill or needle was blasphemy.

Horace also made a recorded statement that he ran hourly on his radio station. He said that any story of substance abuse by the team was slanderous twaddle.

The head coach, ailing Bobby Higgins, worried that his team had fallen into deep trouble. But Roger Grimes was righteously indignant. And he was vocal about his anger.

Roger said he would stake his reputation on the strength of his boys' characters. He had been invited to speak at the monthly Rotary Club lunch meeting, and he used the opportunity to lash out, full strength.

He said that steroid testing was an insult to the boys, the teachers, the school system and the good citizens of Crystal Creek.

He spoke with great emotion. "People are trying to tarnish our championship spirit. They are trying to tarnish the names of your sons, your friends' and neighbors' sons.

"I will be frank. These allegations spring from someone who is an outsider, who has no idea of what these boys are like. Someone who doesn't understand their brave, winning spirit, that Crystal Creek spirit.

"Now you can listen to mudslinging rumors. Or you can listen to your hearts."

Roger went on to deliver a passionate conclusion. "If such a test is approved, I will leave this school system in protest. Because to me, Crystal Creek is part of an American dream. Don't, I pray you, let the dream be destroyed."

He worked himself into such distress that he had to dab his eyes at the end of his speech. "Excuse me," he said in a broken voice.

Nate Purdy rose from the luncheon table. He'd been the only doctor in attendance. "No," he said. "Excuse *me*." He stalked from the room in disgust.

Later he told Sonny, "I never heard such crap. Sheer theatrics. My God, he gave me heartburn to kill a cow."

"I'll be in Denver in February," Sonny said. "I don't give a damn what he says."

"Sure," Nate grumbled. "Stir everything up, then leave me here alone to face it."

"You'll come out smelling like a rose," Sonny said with a cynical smile. "Everybody thinks you're great. Kindly old Nate Purdy. I'm the villain of the piece."

Nate's anger seemed to recede, and his expression sobered. "It's not right. But I'm afraid there's some truth to it. I'm sorry, Sonny. Damn, but I'm sorry."

Sonny clapped the older man on the shoulder. "It doesn't bother me. Like I say, two months, and I'm gone."

"It could be a long two months," said Nate.

THE NEXT MONDAY, Peggy Sue Grimes came late to work at the clinic. Her eyes were red with weeping. Her hands trembled; her chin quivered; she kept biting her lower lip. The other women workers gathered around her, begging her to tell them what was wrong.

Peggy burst into tears. She folded her arms over her desk, bent forward and buried her face in them.

"I finally got pregnant," she sobbed. "I was only four weeks along. But this weekend, I—I lost it. It's because of these terrible steroid lies. Oh, what an awful thing to say about our boys. It breaks my heart. Roger's, too. Maybe I'll never have a real family again."

She wept so hysterically that Nate had to give her a shot to tranquilize her and send her home. "Damn," he said, looking worn, "she's the innocent victim in all this. I hate it."

Sonny's face was hard. He didn't believe there'd been a pregnancy, not for a moment. But he couldn't prove it, so he said nothing.

He knew that as soon as the news got around, people would not look on him merely as the damnable accuser of the football team. He was now also the ogre who'd made Peggy Sue Grimes lose her yearned-for baby.

What do I do for an encore? he thought grimly. *Shoot Santa Claus?*

EMOTION IN TOWN was high and growing higher. Beverly knew that Sonny was avoiding her, trying to protect her from any fallout that might occur. She, in turn, felt fiercely protective toward him.

She was surprised to discover how feisty she could be. She had spent her life being pretty, sweet and agreeable. She had been trained never to voice controversial opinions or to argue.

But she defended Sonny hotly at every opportunity she got, and even had angry words with the august Horace Westerhaus, right in front of the Longhorn Coffee Shop.

"How dare you say the doctors in this town have no civic pride?" she challenged. "How dare you say they're troublemakers? I'm ashamed of you. These kids need help."

"Beverly?" Horace bristled. "What in thunder's got into you?"

"What got into *you?*" Beverly demanded. "I'm sorry you're on the school board. I'll fight to see you're never there again. If I have to, I'll run against you myself."

"You?" he snarled in disbelief. "On the school board?"

"Yes," she said with conviction. "Me."

"Your job is to look pretty and keep your mouth shut," Horace snapped. "You're not doing so great on the mouth shut part."

"And I don't intend to. I'm going to call you up and complain every time I hear that disgusting editorial," she said, and she kept her word.

Horace Westerhaus went about saying that he believed Beverly Townsend had gone crazy. "That foreigner's poisoned her mind," he said darkly.

When Sonny kept making excuses not to see her, she turned the tables and went to see him. She drove to the clinic, marched in and said she had to see Dr. Dekker immediately, it was an emergency.

Peggy Sue Grimes was not there, of course. She had taken to her bed and was staying there on sick leave. She regularly issued brave statements that she was managing to cope, that she blamed nobody and forgave everyone.

A moment later a nurse called for Beverly to come into a waiting room. Once there, Beverly was too upset to sit. Her heart drummed.

The door opened and Sonny stepped inside. He had a stethoscope around his neck. He frowned in concern. "Blondie? What's wrong?"

He'd never looked better to her. Gratefully, she drank in his features: the sculpted cheekbones, the square jaw, the fine nose, the piercing brown eyes.

"You've been avoiding me for a week," she said. "I'm hurt."

He looked wary, even disapproving. "I've been busy," he said without emotion.

She'd seen him use that screen of coolness before to close himself off from another person. She wouldn't allow him to use it against her, not at a time like this.

"You're staying away from me," she said. "Why?"

"I don't want you touched by this mess."

"Is that all?"

"No." He looked away.

"Then what?"

He squared his jaw and stared out the window. "The day we went to talk to the principal and Bobby Higgins, Nate told me something. He said I should know. People are talking about us. Some of it's ugly. I don't want that happening to you."

"I know they're talking," she retorted. "I don't care. It's nothing but lies. Lies can't hurt me."

"This is your home. You have to live here. I don't give a damn what they say about me. You, it's different."

"*I* should have a choice in this. You shouldn't decide for me. It's not right, and you know it. And I choose to be with you—if you'll have me."

He didn't meet her gaze. A frown line appeared between his eyebrows. He shook his head. "If I'll have you? Beverly—"

"I won't let you shut me out this way," she said. "I'm not afraid of what people say, and I'm not afraid of what they might do. I'm not a child, and I don't want to be protected. I don't like it. You can't go on treating me like this."

He turned and looked into her eyes. "No," he said. "I suppose I can't."

She was unaccountably shaken. She said, "Until I go to Galveston, I want things just the way they were."

His smile seemed mocking, almost bitter. "Just the way they were."

Her throat felt choked. "I said, a long time ago, that I needed a friend. You said you'd be one. You stood by me. Now I intend to stand by you."

"You shouldn't say that. Let Tammy Wynette sing it."

"I'm serious," she said. "And I don't want to hide it from people. The staff Christmas party, the one Nate and Rose are giving. You're going. I'm going. Why can't we go together?"

It occurred to her, in a rush of embarrassment, that he might have asked someone else. But he gave her his slow, sideways smile. "You hang on like a bad head cold, don't you, Blondie?"

"Yes," she said, lifting her chin. "I do."

AND SO, SOMEHOW, they made their way through a tense Christmas season. People talked about them. She didn't care. Some people said cruel things to her. She didn't care. A few people stopped speaking to her. She didn't care.

Soon she would be in Galveston, and shortly after, Sonny would be in Denver, gone for good. What did it matter if people gossiped? She let them gossip, and she held her head high.

CHAPTER EIGHT

DR. MONGAN, the high school principal, gave an informal New Year's party for the teachers. Neither football coach showed up.

Even without the coaches, the party had a stiff and stilted air. Nobody wanted to mention the football team, but everyone was thinking of it.

Tap escorted Belinda, although it wasn't a date. He'd called, asking for a ride. His car was in the shop yet again, he said. It had thrown a rod.

How romantic, Belinda thought when they walked into the party. *He's with me because his car threw a rod.*

She'd worn her best dress, a little black number with a plunging back. She'd had her hair done, and it was swept up elegantly, with little tendrils artfully curling at her nape and ears. Her earrings were long and dangly, and her black shoes had spike heels.

He'd looked at her and said, "Hey, you look nice, kid." He still treated her as if she was his little sister, or worse, his little brother.

He looked incredibly handsome. For once he wore a sport coat and tie, even if the tie did have a picture of Marvin the Martian on it. His black dress slacks made him look long-legged and lean-hipped.

He was jaunty and mercurial as always. Once he bent to whisper something in her ear, and the nearness of his lips, the warm flutter of his breath almost made her shudder with desire.

But she'd become so used to hiding her feelings that it was second nature to her. Now Tap was talking animatedly to Bellva Ryan, another teacher. Belinda realized that once Tap left, the party would lose what little life it had.

Her glass was empty, and so was his. "Here," she said. "I'll get you a refill." Her fingers barely brushed against his, but even that slight contact shook her.

This is ridiculous, I'm ridiculous, everything's ridiculous, she thought as she moved toward the refreshments.

There were two punch bowls of pressed glass, and each held grapefruit concoctions that looked identical. But one bore a hand-lettered sign that said Alcoholic, the other a similar sign that said Nonalcoholic.

Tap, of course, had been drinking plain punch, and so had she. But now she hesitated. She looked across the room at Tap, smiling and charming Bellva. A thought suddenly popped into Belinda's mind, a bold and shameless thought.

Almost numbly she reached for the ladle of the punch that contained vodka. She filled both glasses to the brim.

The devil made me do it, she told herself.

She carried the glasses back to where Tap stood. He must have just reached the punch line of his story, because Bellva dissolved into helpless laughter.

"You've got to tell that again," Bellva said, wiping her eyes. "I want Rex and Judy to hear. I'll get them."

She set off, still giggling to herself.

"Thanks, Dugan," Tap said, taking a glass from her. He took a long drink, half emptying it. Then he wrinkled his nose. "This tastes funny."

"Mrs. Mongan just poured in some more ginger ale," Belinda said, lying with an ease that amazed her.

"Well," he said, cocking one dark gold eyebrow, "it's not bad." He reached for a handful of mixed nuts from a bowl sitting on the piano.

"Wow," he said. "Salty." He drained the glass. "I'm going to get another."

"I'll get it," she said quickly. "Here's Bellva with Rex and Judy. You need to tell your story again."

Belinda whisked Tap's glass away and went back to the punch bowls. She set her mouth in a determined line and filled the glasses again.

I'm madly in love with this man, and I'm slipping him a mickey, she thought grimly. *I have no scruples. None.*

The party began breaking up at ten o'clock. The couples would go home and celebrate the New Year together. Some of the single teachers were going out for pizza. Tap and Belinda were invited. She held her breath.

Tap shook his head. "No, thanks. I'm going to drop by and see Dekker. He's on call tonight."

Belinda let out a long, silent sigh of relief. "I need to get home," she said. "I've got a little headache."

Tap seemed fine until Dr. Mongan saw them to the door. "It was a nice party," Tap said blithely. "Thank you, Dr. Mongoose."

Dr. Mongan's expression became at once startled and stony. His wife, at his side, burst into laughter. "I know they call him that behind his back," she said. "But you're the first one with the nerve to say it to his face."

"Say what?" Tap asked innocently.

"You called me Dr. Mongoose," Dr. Mongan said.

"Oh, my God—I'm sorry," Tap said, horrified.

Slowly Dr. Mongan smiled. "It's all right, Hollister. They've been saying it for years. Good night."

Tap managed to contain himself until they got into the car. Then he doubled over in mirth. "Oh, God, I called him Mongoose. Oh, yow!"

He kept laughing as she switched on the ignition and put the car in gear. He laughed for four straight blocks. At last, he subsided and sagged back against the seat. "Jeez," he said, "I don't know what got into me. I feel weird."

"Maybe you're allergic to cashews," Belinda said and gave him a furtive glance.

"I'm sort of light-headed," he said. "Maybe I should walk to Sonny's."

"You can walk from my house," she said. "It's not far."

"Right," he said. "And I should see you inside. I don't trust our fearless fighting Cougars. Odds are a couple of them are getting plastered tonight."

"You never drank in high school?" she asked carefully.

"Me? No. You've seen why. Once in junior high, a friend swiped a six-pack from his dad. I chugalugged three beers and then stood up. Something hit me, really hard. It was the floor. And I couldn't get off it."

"Gee," she said, wondering how two cups of punch compared to three beers.

"I was disgusting," he said. "And like fools, we tried it again the next week. Same thing. Nope. I gotta stay away from it."

"Hmmm," she said. "So how would you and Sonny celebrate the New Year?"

He laughed. He had a truly contagious chuckle, and it always made her smile. "We've got this gin rummy game. I'm down eighteen thousand points. But my luck'll change. I know it."

"What if he's not in?"

Tap shrugged. "He may not be. If anybody's going to wrap a car around a tree, tonight's the night."

"What then?"

"I go home to my lonely bachelor pad."

"Won't you come in and have a cup of coffee with me?" she asked. "It's going to be lonely for me, too."

"Sure, Dugan," he said. "When do your folks get back from the Caribbean?"

"Not for a week. This is the first New Year's I've ever spent away from home. It feels strange."

"You get used to it. I don't go home much since my dad remarried. His new wife didn't like our old house. She said she felt like she was competing with all the memories. He's got a whole different life now. Everything's different."

She stole another glance at him. His mother had died when he was in high school. He didn't like to talk about it. She pulled into her driveway. "Come on in," she said, wondering if he heard the strain in her voice.

Her apartment was small, but her decorations gave it a cozy air. An afghan her grandmother had crocheted draped the back of the couch, and she'd hung the walls with framed, brightly colored posters.

"Have a seat," she said, gesturing toward the couch. "I'll put on the coffee."

And soft music, she thought, *and keep the lights dim. Oh, how do people do this all the time?*

"Nice place," he said. "You said you have a headache? Sure you're okay?"

"It's gone," she said and put the "Bolero" album on the CD player. She went into the kitchen and filled the teakettle, then set it on the range and turned on the burner.

"I hope instant's okay," she called. Her voice shook slightly, and she hated herself for it.

"All I ever make myself," he replied.

She went to the kitchen door and gave him a smile. "Excuse me," she said, "while I change into something more comfortable." *I can't believe I said that,* she told herself.

"Yeah," he said. "Those shoes must kill you."

Once she was in her bedroom, her knees felt shaky. She had one negligee, a gift from her sister. She seldom wore it because it was too fancy. It had a matching peignoir.

She gritted her teeth and took the set from the closet. She stripped down and slipped into the negligee. It was filmy and white, with a low-cut lacy top that showed what cleavage she had. She put on the peignoir but didn't fasten its pearl buttons.

"Oh, Lord," she said in despair. Her only bedroom slippers were large and fuzzy and shaped like rabbits. She would have to go barefoot. She spritzed a little perfume behind her ears.

Then she forced herself to boldly reenter the living room. The teakettle was whistling. "Is everything all right?" she asked brightly.

Tap was reading a magazine and didn't look up. "Did you know some penguins can fly?" he asked. "I didn't."

She sighed and padded into the kitchen. She made two cups of instant coffee, the fancy chocolate-almond flavored kind. Then she opened a cabinet door and took out a small bottle of brandy. Her father liked brandy in his supper coffee. She'd bought it for her parents' visits.

Again she hesitated. Then she splashed a few drops into his cup. *When this is over,* she thought, *I'll repent then.*

She picked up the cups and waltzed into the living room, her gown and peignoir flowing around her. She sat beside him and handed him his cup. "To the New Year," she said cheerfully, as if she did this sort of thing all the time.

He looked at her and blinked in surprise. He set aside the magazine. "To the New Year," he echoed.

She clicked her cup against his. They both drank. Tap kept staring at her. "It tastes—good," he said. "Different."

"It's a new flavor," she said and took another sip.

"Really?" he said, and he, too, took another sip. His eyes fell to her breasts.

"Bolero" throbbed seductively from the CD player. She took a deep breath, not knowing what to say. Perhaps the truth was best.

"Tap," she said shakily, "I know you're in love with somebody else. It—doesn't matter."

"That's quite an outfit," he said, meeting her eyes. "I never imagined you in something like that."

"Do you like it?" she asked. "This part comes off." She set down her cup. Boldly, almost desperately, she slipped out of the peignoir. She sat very straight, her arms bare, her hands clasped tightly in her lap.

His blue eyes ran over her in disbelief. "Dugan..." he began, his voice dubious.

"My name is Belinda," she said.

He nodded. "Belinda," he breathed.

He set down his cup. He looked into her eyes again.

"Belinda," he repeated softly. He reached out and touched one of the tendrils that curled by her ear.

A shudder ran through her that quaked her to the heart. "I mean, I know," she said. "That you love somebody else."

She leaned toward him slightly. He touched her throat, her shoulder, her throat again. "She's far away," he said. "But you're right here."

"Yes. I am." Her heart pounded.

"Her eyes are blue," he said, bringing his face closer to hers. "But yours are brown. Beautiful brown."

He took a curl between his fingers, leaning nearer still. "Her hair is curly. But yours is—like silk."

His hand fell to her shoulder, clasping it, then stroking down her arm. "You're like silk all over," he said.

She touched his face. "Tap," she said and raised her lips to him.

He drew her into his arms, lowered his mouth to hers and kissed her. No one had ever kissed her so, with such hunger and ardor. His lips were hot and sure and questing against hers. He kissed her cheek, her temple, her ear, the curve of her throat, her mouth again. His hands moved over her back, her bare arms.

Every touch seemed to heighten her desire for him, her love of him. There could not be enough of his kissing, not in a hundred lifetimes.

"Belinda," he said against her lips, his voice breathless, "I want you. Do you want me?"

"Yes," she managed to say. *I've wanted you from the first time I looked into your eyes.*

He kissed her again, then cupped her chin in his hand. His voice was low and gentle. "Can we go into your bedroom?"

"Yes," she whispered.

He stood and drew her to her feet. She leaned against him, her arms around his waist. "You've made my knees weak," she said against his chest. "I didn't think that really happened to people. I'm not sure I can walk."

"That's sweet of you," he said. "That's so sweet."

He picked her up as easily as if she were a child. She put her arms around his neck, laid her face against his shoulder. *This can't be happening,* she thought. *Not really. Not to me.*

He carried her into the bedroom.

WHILE TAP HOLLISTER was making mad, sweet love to Belinda, Sonny Dekker was trying to calm Lois Fletcher. Her son, Lester, had attacked her with a croquet mallet.

The ambulance attendants had brought her into the emergency ward in hysterics. Even after a sedative she was tearful and shaky.

"Try to get hold of yourself, Mrs. Fletcher. Everything's going to be fine. But you've got to talk to me so we can help Lester."

She wept afresh at the mention of her son's name. "He was like an animal," she said. "Like a beast, a stranger."

She had a bruise on her shin, another on the inside of her arm. Lester had hit her twice with the croquet mallet before she escaped.

"He *was* a stranger," Sonny told her. "He wasn't himself. Now tell me what happened. From the beginning."

She took a deep breath. "I wouldn't let him go out with his football friends anymore. They were a bad influence. Lester got sulky—resentful."

Sonny nodded. She seemed so forlorn that he took her hand in his.

She said, "He wanted to go out for New Year's Eve. I said no. I didn't trust those boys. Lester's too impressionable."

"I understand. Go on."

"I wanted us just to have a nice evening at home together. Milk and cookies. I checked out a video movie. *Bambi.* He used to love it so when he was younger."

Sonny repressed a sigh. A New Year's Eve of milk, cookies and talking bunny rabbits might drive a stronger man than Lester Fletcher to the brink.

"Lester's been as grumpy as a bear with a sore head lately," Lois said, wiping her eyes. "He wanted to watch that music video channel. You know the one. Women flaunting their bodies. Men grabbing themselves. It's disgusting."

Sonny squeezed her hand reassuringly. "So you had a disagreement?"

"I walked over to that set and shut it off. They were running a special on that person who struts around singing she's a 'material girl.' I can't stand her."

"What did he do?"

"It was like this change came over him. He got this— this look on his face. He stood up so fast he knocked over his chair. Cookies fell all over."

"And then?"

Lois Fletcher's chin quivered. "He stalked off to the garage. A minute later I heard this terrible banging."

"And then?"

Fresh tears rose in her eyes. "I went to the kitchen. I opened the door to the garage. And there was Lester, trying to smash the hood of the car with a croquet mallet."

"He was beating on the car?"

"Like a deranged person. I marched up to him and said, 'Young man, stop that right now!'"

"That's when he turned on you?"

"Like an animal. The look in his eyes wasn't sane. He swung at my head. I dodged and ran. I got away. I locked the door. I called the police. Oh, my poor baby—what happened to him? It's like he's possessed."

"Mrs. Fletcher," Sonny said, "the police said they found a half-empty vial of methandrosterone in his room. That's a steroid. I'm sorry."

"Why?" she begged him tearfully. "Why *my* child? I've devoted my life to him."

Sonny couldn't answer. His guess was that Lester Fletcher had gone off steroids, hoping he could pass a screening test. Withdrawal had occurred. Lester, depressed, frustrated and crawling with physical cravings, had gone back to the drug, taken too much and flipped out.

"Your son isn't the only one," he said. "We'll help him. But we need to find out where this junk is coming from. We'll need your full cooperation."

She sat slumped, weeping anew, and could not reply. Later Sonny called Nate at Reverend Howard Blake's. The Purdys and Blakes were seeing in the New Year together.

"I think we've got our case," he told Nate. "Lester Fletcher lost control tonight. His mother had to call the police. It's steroids. The police found them."

Nate groaned. "You know, nobody will believe this, but I'd rather have been wrong about this whole damn mess."

"Yeah. Me, too."

"What happened?"

Sonny told him.

Nate sounded cynical and resigned. "Well, Lois Fletcher could drive anybody around the bend. They'll need counseling, both of them."

"I let her know that."

"Where's Lester?"

"They took him to a psychiatric unit in Austin. I'm going to call about getting him into rehab as soon as possible. I'll need your help. You're his regular physician."

"You've got it," said Nate. "Where's Lois?"

"Staying with a neighbor. She couldn't face going home. Lester pretty well tore up the garage. She was lucky to get off as easily as she did."

Nate swore softly. "One kid going psycho, one halfway there. What happened to this town?"

"It wanted another championship season," said Sonny.

BELINDA AWOKE, feeling dozy and warm. She lay in Tap's arms, her cheek pressed against his naked chest. She sighed, snuggling closer to him.

He had been everything she'd dreamed he would be: passionate, generous, tender, yet with an exciting wildness in him. He made love the way he did everything, with an exuberance that left her breathless.

She touched his chest. It was hard and warm and dusted with golden hair that tickled her cheek. He had a beautiful masculine body, long, lean and sculpted with muscle.

But more than his body, it was his mercurial soul and quick mind she loved. There was no one else like him, laughing and careless on the surface, but beneath, hot-blooded and fervent. She could not imagine *not* loving him. It did not seem possible.

He stirred uneasily. He drew her more closely against him. He murmured a name, but it wasn't hers. Her heart shriveled.

His hand rose to stroke her long, loosened hair. "Liz?" he said softly. She felt his body tense. He was awakening, and she didn't know what to say to him.

His hand roamed to her arm, closed around it. He drew back from her. "Dugan?" he whispered incredulously. "You?"

"I'm Belinda," she said helplessly.

"My God, Belinda," he said, clearly horrified. "What have I done to you?"

"What I wanted done," she said, gazing at his shadowy face.

He shook his head. He let go of her arm. "This was wrong," he said.

"It didn't seem wrong," she said.

"You came out wearing that filmy thing. My head felt funny. I just—lost control."

"It's all right," she said, reaching to touch his chest again.

But he pulled back, avoiding her touch. He got out of bed. "Good grief," he said. "Where are my pants?"

"You threw them across the room. I think they landed in the bathroom."

"Good grief," he said again.

He disappeared into the bathroom and came out, zipping up his slacks. "Belinda," he said earnestly, "this shouldn't have happened."

"I wanted it to happen."

"I didn't know that."

"No," she said, sitting up and pulling up the sheet to hide her nakedness. "You never noticed."

He raked his hand through his hair in frustration. "Where's my T-shirt?"

"I think it landed on the dresser."

He stalked to the dresser, fumbled for the T-shirt and put it on. He came to the bed and sat down, but he didn't touch her. "I can't even see you," he said.

She reached and switched on the bedside lamp. She looked into his face, which was stern and troubled. *Now he hates me,* she thought and looked away, tears in her eyes.

"Belinda," he said solemnly, "I shouldn't have done this. I mean, it was like using you. I hate that. I don't know how it happened." He paused. "And I've got a hell of a headache," he muttered. "My God, it feels like the Russian army is marching in there."

"I gave you punch with vodka in it," she said miserably. "Two glasses. And I put brandy in your coffee. Not much."

"Dugan—why? Look at me." He took her by the shoulders and made her face him.

"I wanted your resistance down," she said. "It was a terrible thing to do. But you never look at me. You treat me like one of the guys."

He swore softly and shook his head. "I never treated any of the guys like *that*. Forgive me. I feel rotten."

"Don't. I told you. I wanted it to happen."

"Dugan, I never guessed. I'm really sorry. Really."

"Don't call me Dugan," she said sharply, turning her face away again. "And don't call me kid. I'm a woman."

"You're a lovely woman," he said. "But I don't want you to feel that way about me."

"I can't help it. I do. I didn't mean to, but I do."

"Put some clothes on. I feel like a rat, talking to you naked. Have you got a bathrobe or something? I'll get it."

"Yes," she said. "Hanging on the bathroom door."

He let go of her, rose and got the robe. He thrust it at her and didn't watch as she slipped it on. Then he sat down again and took her by the shoulders. "Look. What I did with you, it wasn't love. I've got to tell you that."

"I know." She blinked back tears. She couldn't cry. She'd used every other trick she knew. She knew she mustn't use tears, as well. She had been unfair enough.

"I like you," he said earnestly. "I respect you. But I don't love you. This can't be the start of that sort of relationship."

She didn't answer. She'd felt as if she had finally come alive when he'd taken her in his arms. Now she was dying, fading back into some lifeless, puppetlike existence.

"Dugan—Belinda, please look at me," he begged.

"I can't."

"We'll pretend this never happened. And I'll stay away from you. I didn't understand."

"You love Liz," she said, still not meeting his gaze. "You can't have her. But you could have me."

He squeezed her shoulders. His voice was kind. "I don't do things that way. It wouldn't be fair. This didn't happen. It's that simple."

It did happen, and it's not simple, she wanted to cry out, but she was too ashamed.

"I'm going to get dressed and try to get out of here without anybody seeing me," he said. "Nobody has to know. Are you all right? Are you going to be all right?"

She nodded. But she thought, *I'm anything but all right. I've made a perfect fool of myself.*

She watched him furtively. He'd flung his clothing every which way. His tie was hanging from the other bedside lamp. He tied it and shrugged into his sport coat.

Then he sat down beside her again. He took her hands in his. "I'm flattered—Belinda. You were very sweet. Incredibly sweet."

He bent his head and kissed her on the lips, all too briefly. She wanted him to keep holding her hands, but he dropped them and stood. "I've got to go," he said, sadness in his handsome face. "Thank you."

He left the bedroom. She heard the front door open, then close. She no longer had to control herself. She fell back to a lying position, clutched her pillow and wept bitterly into it.

He didn't love her, he didn't even want to have an affair with her. She'd tricked him into trying her, and he'd found her wanting.

That he had been kind and honest about it somehow made it worse. She hadn't been honest, and she'd been shameless into the bargain.

At least there should be no consequences. He probably thought she was awful for having condoms in her medicine closet. He probably thought she'd planned this for weeks.

Her brother-in-law had put them there when her family helped her move into the apartment. He'd left them beside a little note with a happy face on it. "Housewarming present," the note had said. "Just in case. Love, Dave."

She'd almost thrown them away. But then she'd met Tap, and been so infatuated she couldn't stop dreaming that some night he might show up on her doorstep declaring, "I love you. Be mine."

It hadn't happened that way. She could feel nothing except humiliation and knew the fault was hers alone.

Happy New Year, she thought darkly. *I certainly got it off to a great start.*

And she wept harder.

CHAPTER NINE

NOW TWO MEMBERS of the football team languished in detox centers. The school board, after a hot debate, voted for random screening of the team. Any player might be tested at any time.

"It's a desperate measure," Mayor Martin Avery said. "But these seem to be desperate times."

Assistant coach Roger Grimes resigned in protest, and nine players dropped from the team rather than submit to tests. Peggy Grimes wept that the only family she had was being destroyed.

Scandal tore the town into warring camps. Some angrily denounced Nate, Sonny and the school board. They rallied in support of the departing Roger Grimes. They attacked and decried the notion that the team's members could engage in such wholesale wrongdoing.

So what if Chuck Cooper and Lester Fletcher had stupidly got themselves in trouble? That didn't prove a thing about other players. Why lynch the whole team? Testing? The thought was abominable. What was this, a police state?

As for Sonny, everybody knew he had a grudge. He wasn't content to persecute the three misguided boys who'd hassled him. No, he wanted to throw suspicion on the entire team. He'd somehow suckered in Nate Purdy, who should know better.

But other people, equally irate, took the opposite side. There was a problem—why weren't the police doing something? If drugs circulated among the kids, why didn't the sheriff find the source and cut it off?

Sheriff Wayne Jackson was doing the best he could. But he had no clue as to the source of the steroids, and nobody was admitting anything.

The town's factions included cynics. Among them was Dr. Greg Sinclair. "They'll never get this stuff out of the schools," he declared. "They'll never get it out of sports. It's too entrenched. Hell, in some places, athletes in junior high do it."

"I've been reading about it," Nate countered. "It's a goddamn plague. High school kids do it to get on the college teams. College kids do it to get drafted by the pros. The pros do it to keep their edge. It's madness."

"If they're careful, they won't get hurt," Greg argued. "Come on. What happened here is extreme. Face it. Thousands of people do it. They don't all flip out or snap."

"I despise that attitude," Nate retorted. "Anabolic steroids are illegal. That's the bottom line—they're against the law."

"It's a law nobody can enforce," Greg said with a scoff. "A test costs a hundred bucks. Are you going to test every third-string seventh-grader in the country? Every high school kid? It'd cost a fortune. And the tests can be beat. Forget it."

"I won't forget," Nate vowed. "People can throw eggs at my house. They can tar and feather me. I won't stop. I intend to fight. And if I ever find out who's behind this mess, God have pity on him. Because I won't."

THE DIVISIVENESS that rent the town colored the little time remaining to Sonny and Beverly. They went for a long, last ride before she went to Galveston. She was to leave in two days.

The January sky was blue, the air mild and still. They rode their horses along the edge of the creek.

Tonight, Beverly's aunt and uncle were having a party for her at the Double C. Tomorrow night her mother and Vern would host a smaller, more intimate farewell dinner. Beverly would see Sonny at both places, of course. But this would be the last time she could be alone with him.

She looked about at the rugged Hill Country that she'd always loved so deeply. It was dull with winter, but still beautiful to her. The hills hunched like brown, sleeping giants beneath the empty sky.

She'd put on her plainest jacket, one of well-worn leather, and an old dark blue Stetson. The hat went back to her teen days as a rodeo queen. She'd meant to dress up more for Sonny, but somehow, it had seemed wrong, false.

Tonight and tomorrow night she would wear fashionable, glittery things. Today she wanted to be only herself, plain and unadorned.

Sonny wore his usual faded jeans and cowboy boots. His heavy denim jacket emphasized the width of his shoulders. For Christmas Beverly had given him a black Stetson.

He'd grumbled that he'd look like an idiot in it, but he'd worn it anyway. Beverly thought it suited him perfectly. He'd tilted the brim at a rakish angle that captured his blend of nonchalance and intensity.

How odd, she thought, that Sonny looked more natural on a horse than Jeff ever had. Jeff had hated admitting it, but horses made him nervous; he'd been more at home in the oil field than on the range. Beverly could ride rings around him. But Sonny kept up with her with ease.

She cast him a sidelong look, thinking again how right he looked in the saddle, his back straight, his hat brim cocked just so, his profile clean and even against the Texas sky.

Peculiar emotions twisted in her chest. She knew that this ride was the beginning of the end. From now until Sonny departed for Denver, their relationship would be one long, drawn-out goodbye, much of it done by long distance.

She guided Dandi around a patch of prickly pear. "I feel bad about leaving," she said. "Like I'm deserting you."

Sonny gave her a sardonic look. "You think I need you to protect me?"

"Of course not," she said, looking away. "I just mean that some people are being pretty rotten to you. I feel like I'm running out."

"I'll be glad you're out of it," he said. "It's stupid. It's a—what-do-you-call-it? A tempest in a teapot."

Beverly shrugged sadly and patted Dandi's neck. "I've always loved this town. I never thought I'd have to apologize for it. I'm disappointed. Bitterly."

"Hey, Blondie. Cheer up."

"I can't. This whole, ugly mess, it's the sort of thing you read about. But you think, 'It can't happen here.'"

"Beverly," he said, "it happens everywhere. Humans are only human. That's their virtue. That's their vice."

She said nothing. She listened to the clink of their bridles and the creak of saddle leather.

"It's good you're going," he said in a flat, quiet voice. "People talk about you. Because of me. I don't like it, having your name dragged through the mud."

"Oh, who cares what they say?" she asked with passion. "I don't."

But about some of it she had to care. In private, her mother had grown even cooler toward Sonny. "Some people say you're sleeping with him," Carolyn had told her.

"Well, I'm not," Beverly had retorted. "I've never so much as kissed him. We've never even held hands."

"That's not what they think. Be careful. Once a reputation's gone, you can't get it back."

"Reputation," Beverly had said with disdain. What good was reputation if it was only the opinion of nasty gossips?

She gave Sonny a troubled, sidelong look. "I'll worry about you."

The corner of his mouth turned up slightly. "Don't. They won't hurt me. They might burn a cross or two on the lawn, but what the hell? I'm leaving. But you're different. This is your home."

"Home," she said ironically.

"Home," he repeated. "You belong here. I don't. I can't. And I don't want to."

Moodily she smoothed Dandi's silver mane. "You'll be glad to leave us all behind, won't you?"

There was a beat of silence. "No. Not all of you."

A breeze came up, bearing a chill. She buttoned the collar of her jacket and stared down at her saddle horn. "It'll be strange without you. When I'm in Galveston."

It was true. Nothing could change that fact: of everyone in Crystal Creek, she would miss him most.

He shrugged carelessly. "You'll be home on weekends. After you get settled."

"I know," she said, still staring at the horn. "But you'll be gone at the end of February. That's not far off."

"Thank God," he said with maximum sarcasm.

She shot him a questioning glance. He frowned, shook his head. "I didn't mean it that way. It'll be— strange not having you around, too."

His gaze, steady and dark, held hers for an instant, then she quickly looked away. She raised her chin. "It's hard for me to tell you what you've meant to me."

"Then don't." His voice was half teasing, half-gruff.

No, she thought. *I suppose I shouldn't.*

She nodded, forcing herself to smile. "All right. We'll switch subjects. How's Lois Fletcher?"

"A changed woman. She's realized that Lester doesn't have a halo, and neither does she. The two of them are going into counseling when he gets out. That's good."

"And Chuck Cooper?"

"He's doing well. He'll be home this week."

The breeze grew stronger and cooler. Beverly turned up her jacket collar and shivered slightly. "I can understand about Lester," she mused. "He was never attractive, he never fit in, and his mother fussed over him like a hen with one chick. I can see how he got sucked into this thing, how he wanted to belong...."

Her voice trailed off. Sonny nodded, his expression somber. "Right. But why Chuck Cooper? Why Barry Armbruster?"

"Exactly," she said. "Barry was so sweet. And Chuck? Chuck always seemed almost perfect."

He sighed. "Chuck's a sensitive kid, talented, smart. He wanted to go to a good college. He thought his ticket was an athletic scholarship. He liked basketball, but he wasn't tall enough. So he did the juice. He didn't handle it well."

"And Barry?" she asked.

"His family's not completely messed up. But it's not perfect, either. They've got their problems. I think they've always put pressure on him to succeed. And the drugs are a chemical thing. Some people can't handle them. It's like Tap and alcohol. Only this stuff's a lot more insidious."

Clouds had appeared on the horizon, moving toward them swiftly. Beverly urged Dandi to a faster walk. "I wish Wayne Jackson could catch who's supplying this stuff," she said. "Then people'd *have* to admit what's going on. Do you have any idea where it's coming from?"

He studied the approaching clouds. "I have my guesses."

"Who? Where?"

"One source might be Grimes. But I think he's too slick. Still, he could give them a damn good hint about where to get it. I imagine he has."

"Austin? It's the closest city."

"Probably. And it could be anywhere in Austin. A gym. A college kid. Even another coach. Anybody."

She looked at him in concern. "Have you told all this to Wayne Jackson?"

Sonny nodded. "He thinks the same. But suspecting something and proving it are two different things."

Beverly's frown grew more troubled. "But can it ever be stopped, if nobody talks?"

"Somebody's got to be caught red-handed with the goods," Sonny said. "Or confess. That's not likely."

She shuddered. "All these boys, so young. And they don't even know what they're doing."

"You're cold," Sonny said. "Take my gloves."

He dug into his jacket pocket and offered a pair of black leather gloves.

"No," she said, shaking her head. "They'll be too big. You keep them."

"Take them," he said in a tone that brooked no argument. "I've never liked blondes with blue skin. Too gaudy."

Gratefully she took the gloves, and as she did so, her cold fingers brushed his warm ones. She ducked her head and slipped on his gloves. They were, indeed, too large, but they warmed her and gave her an odd sense of security.

"A cold spell's coming," he said in his low voice. "Let's give these horses a run, then head back."

"Fine," she said.

They kicked the horses into a gallop. Outlaw's Arabian blood gave him speed, and Beverly knew that Sonny was reining the big horse in, giving her a chance to keep up.

But the terrain was rough, and there were so many obstacles to dodge, she found it difficult to stay by his side. Patches of prickly pear and scrub and briar, outcroppings of limestone and broken rock, the uneven earth itself seemed designed to keep them apart.

TWO NIGHTS LATER, Sonny departed early from the small dinner party at Beverly's. She went with him as far as the porch, so they could be alone a moment. He expected no more than a moment. Her mother had watched her jealously as she'd walked him out the door.

The night was dark and moonless, unseasonably warm, and the cloudless sky was full of stars. Beverly wore a pale blue silky dress, dusted with sparkling things across the top. They glittered, reflecting the starlight off the seductive curves of her breasts. He ached to touch her.

"I wish you wouldn't go so soon," she said. Her hair, looking smooth as silk, gleamed in the starshine. Her perfume tingled in his nostrils.

"It's your last night with your family," he said. "They shouldn't have to share you."

He and the Purdys had been the only nonfamily members there, and Nate and Rose had just departed. That had left Sonny and Beverly with only her mother, stepfather, and her McKinney relatives.

Sonny had sensed that Carolyn hoped he would leave early so that she could have her family, especially her daughter, to herself. Carolyn was polite, almost cordial. But deep in her blue eyes, he saw ice, and he knew why.

He also knew that now he should shake Beverly's hand, bid her a flippant and brotherly goodbye and get the hell away.

Then it would be done. He'd see her, perhaps, during a coming weekend or two. Then he'd be gone for good. It would be over.

But he couldn't make himself move away from her. He was too transfixed by the gleam of starlight on her hair.

She put her hand up tentatively, as if she were going to touch his arm. He drew in his breath. But she let her hand fall away and only gazed at him.

"I won't say goodbye," she said. "I don't want it to be goodbye. So I'll just say good-night."

"Sure. Good night. Let me know your phone number when you get one. Maybe I'll call you up, give you a tough time."

"You've always given me a tough time," she said. "But good times, too. Yes. Of course, I'll call. First thing."

"Good."

They stood, looking at each other for a moment that seemed both immeasurably long and short to him. He thought he saw something different in her eyes, something new, but he told himself scornfully that this was wishful thinking.

"Would you kiss me goodbye?" she asked, almost shyly. "For luck?"

If I start to kiss you, I won't stop, he thought. But he put his hands on her upper arms. For a moment he could only savor the softness and warmth of her beneath his fingers.

He bent his face to hers. His heart drummed.

She moved almost imperceptibly closer, raising her face to his. Her lips parted slightly, inviting him.

Oh, God, he thought drunkenly. *I shouldn't do this.* But he was swept away, helpless as a man in a flash flood. Slowly, unwillingly, he drew her closer, bent nearer.

"Beverly!" Carolyn's voice pierced the night. "What are you doing out there? You'll freeze."

Beverly jerked back guiltily. But Sonny still held her possessively by the upper arms, his hands tense and burning from touching her. He stared at Carolyn's silhouette in the doorway. For an insane and blissful moment, he'd forgotten her existence, forgotten everything but Beverly.

"Oh—" Beverly said, embarrassment in her voice.

"Excuse me," Carolyn said shortly. "But you shouldn't be out there without a wrap of some sort."

"I'll be right in," Beverly promised. Sonny watched as the door closed. But he could still feel Carolyn's disapproving presence. And so could Beverly, he could tell.

"This is stupid," she said. "I feel like I'm twelve years old again."

She shook her head so that her smooth hair swung.

Reluctantly, he let go of her. He gave her a companionable chuck under the chin, then forced himself to touch her no more. "So long, Blondie," he said in a low voice. "Knock 'em dead in Galveston."

She stared up at him again, and once more he sensed something new in her gaze.

"Good luck," she said softly, her eyes fastened on his.

Then, suddenly, she rose on her tiptoes and brushed a kiss on a corner of his mouth. It was a light kiss, but it lingered half a second longer than it might have. In that split second, his blood blazed and the whole universe seemed to quake around him. *Oh, God,* he thought. *Oh, my God.*

"Good night," she said in a shaky voice, and spun away from him. She opened the door and disappeared inside her house.

He looked after her, wasted by desire. He felt undone, ruined. For five months he'd pursued her in the only way he could. He'd offered her friendship because that was all she would accept. He'd played the brother because she would not let him be a lover.

After all these months, she'd given him one kiss—of goodbye. It was a quick kiss, innocent, self-conscious, almost childish. Yet it had made his mind burn like a shooting star, and had set his veins on fire.

One small kiss. That was all.

He turned away from her door, hurried down the steps and across the shadowy yard.

His blood beat in his ears like a mocking mantra. *Fool,* it said. *Fool, fool, fool.*

CHAPTER TEN

BEVERLY LEFT for Galveston, pretending to be upbeat and happy. Sonny pretended to be unconcerned. Carolyn was sincerely happy there were now so many miles between the two.

In the meantime, Belinda Dugan met the new semester with her head held high and her chin set at a determined angle. She meant to get on with life.

She would act with as much dignity as she could. She would look forward, not back. And when the school year was over, she would head for someplace as far as possible from Tap Hollister—Borneo, perhaps.

For two miserable days and nights she'd wallowed in shame over her wanton seduction of him. She'd felt as if she'd descended into the deepest pit of hell and was damned to stay there. She'd wept until she was sick.

Then a peculiar thing happened. It was as if she cried herself through the worst. Then a healing breeze seemed to sweep through her soul, cleansing away the self-pity, the self-loathing, the self-absorption.

She'd made a mistake. She wouldn't let it ruin her life. She'd stolen one night with Tap and paid dearly for it. She would have the rest of her life to decide if it had been worth it . . .

But, oh, she thought, *his strong, naked arms enfolding her, his hands upon her skin. His warm mouth drinking hers. His bare body upon her own in the sensuous tangle of the sheets...*

At school she avoided him because he was so sweet, so tactful, so concerned and so unattainable. He was too pure a soul to understand his kindness was a form of cruelty.

He'd stopped joining her and Sonny for morning coffee. He no longer hovered protectively about her. She'd heard his explanation was that the football players were now in such trouble that none of them dared to misbehave further.

Today she'd stayed after school because she was trying to master a new video camera the school had purchased for the fine arts department. It was an expensive piece of equipment, and she wanted to use it well.

The hall was shadowy and her footsteps echoed as she neared the office she shared with three other teachers.

She was not prepared for what happened next. As she rounded the corner, she nearly stumbled over a figure crouching before her door. She gasped in alarm.

Chuck Cooper was hunkered down by the locked office. He had a wire from a coat hanger thrust under the door. He looked as startled as Belinda felt. Hastily, he raked a yellow envelope from under the door, then accidentally pushed it back again.

"Chuck! What are you doing?" Belinda demanded.

Chuck stared up like a trapped animal. "I—I wrote a note to Mrs. Weisen. I changed my mind." With desperation, he began to poke beneath the door with the wire again.

"Stop that," Belinda said. "I'll open the door. Stand up and explain to me."

He stood, but wouldn't meet her eyes. "Now," Belinda said in her most authoritative voice, "what's going on?"

Chuck stared at the floor. "I thought Mrs. Weisen gave me an unfair grade in geometry. I wrote a note. I slid it under the door. Then I changed my mind."

"You scared me half to death," Belinda said, unlocking the door. "You looked like a safecracker."

The door swung open, and Chuck snatched up the envelope. But before he did, Belinda clearly saw the writing on it. Anonymous-looking block letters said "MISS DUGAN."

How odd, Belinda thought with a start. *Chuck's not even one of my students. Why would he write to me?*

Chuck tucked the envelope inside his letter jacket. "I'm sorry I scared you. Thanks," he said, backing out the door.

Belinda, mystified, tried to halt him. "Stop," she ordered. Chuck went still, but looked ready to bolt.

She said, "That's not Mrs. Weisen's name on the envelope. It's mine. Why did you write me a note, then take it back? May I see it, please?"

"No," Chuck said, shaking his head. "You must have seen wrong. I got to go."

"Chuck—" Belinda tried to sound as stern as she could. It didn't work. He turned and sprinted down the hall. "Chuck!" Belinda cried after him.

He didn't stop. He disappeared around the far corner. Belinda threw her books to her desk and set off after him. But by the time she reached the corner and looked down the hall, Chuck was gone.

She stared at the door through which he must have escaped. What in the world was he up to? And what was in the note?

She was ready to push open the door when Tap entered, nearly crashing into her. He caught her to keep from colliding with her. She stared into his unbelievably blue eyes.

He held her, gazing down with concern. Her cheeks burned, and she felt half-faint. "Belinda," he said. "What's wrong? Chuck Cooper ran out of here like the devil himself was after him."

"Not the devil," she said, trying to marshal her thoughts. "Me. Which way did he go?"

"Toward the front. What's wrong?"

"I don't know," she said, wresting away from him. "But I want to find out."

She set out at a run toward the front of the building. She didn't know if she was trying to find Chuck or to escape Tap. But Tap came with her. She careered around the corner of the building, Tap at her side. Then they both stopped.

The front of the school was deserted except for Chuck. He stood near the motorcycle racks by a trash can. He was tearing up the envelope and stuffing it into the trash.

He turned, looking over his shoulder. When he caught sight of Tap and Belinda, alarm crossed his face. Immediately, he turned back to the trash can, rummaging. He pulled out the pieces of the note and stuffed them into his jacket pockets.

"What the hell?" Tap asked.

"That note," she said. "He was going to give it to me. Then he didn't want me to see it. He ran."

"A note? Is he your student?"

"No. I don't understand. But something's bothering him. I want to talk to him."

But Chuck was already struggling with the safety lock on his motorcycle. In a moment he would be speeding away.

Tap drew himself up to his full height. He cupped his hands to his mouth like a megaphone. "Yo!" he called. "Chuck! We're friendly forces. Let's talk, my man."

But the cycle was unchained, and Chuck leapt astride it. Hunched over the handlebars, he gunned it down the drive, and when he reached the street, roared off.

Belinda's spirits sank, and she was all too conscious of Tap beside her. Her heart thudded.

"Come on," he said, nodding toward the trash can. "Let's check. Maybe he didn't get it all."

She nodded numbly. Together they went and poked among the papers, cast-off wrappers and soft drink cans. *In the merry mid of January,* Belinda thought darkly, *my true love and I rummaged through the garbage together. How symbolic of our relationship.*

"Ha!" Tap said with satisfaction. "Is this a piece?" He drew out the ragged corner of a yellow envelope. In it was a scrap of paper with block letters in blue ink.

"I think so." Then she found another piece, and Tap found a third.

"Let's go inside," he said. "So nothing blows away."

"Okay," she said, keeping her eyes averted.

She felt, rather than saw, that he was gazing down at her. "You look cold," he said.

For a moment she was swept by the fear that he was going to wrap his arm around her the way he used to. "I'm fine," she said stiffly.

They walked together in awkward silence. "Is everything—well—okay with you?" he asked at last. "I mean, I haven't talked to you in private."

You could have called, she thought bitterly.

"I should have called," he said. "I didn't want to embarrass you or anything. But if there were any—consequences, you'd let me know, wouldn't you? I couldn't let you go through something like that alone. I couldn't stand that."

She blinked hard and struggled to keep her chin from trembling. He was asking if she was pregnant. Worse, he was asking kindly. Why, she asked herself miserably, did he have to be such a damned gentleman?

"You don't have to worry," she said in the same stiff voice. "Everything's fine."

"You're sure?"

"I'm sure."

"Good," he said. "Good."

He opened the outer door for her. They walked down the shadowy hall. They seemed to have nothing to say to each other. Or perhaps there was now too much to say, and silence was the only safe course.

She stole a glance at him. He looked so somber it broke her heart. She—and what she had so stupidly done—had made him this way. She wanted him back the way he used to be, laughing, joking, supercharged with life.

"Tell me exactly what happened with Chuck," he said.

She was grateful for any topic other than themselves. Haltingly she told him of finding Chuck crouched by her door, trying to retrieve the envelope. They reached her office. The straightened coat hanger still lay before the door.

She cleared a place on her desk, and together they arranged the pieces of the note. The scraps spelled out an incomplete and cryptic message.

"ELL DR DEK," said one scrap. "RIME," said another. A third bore what seemed to be another fragment of a word, "TRICENT."

Tap frowned. "That doesn't cast any light on things."

Belinda stared at the torn pieces of paper so she wouldn't have to look at Tap's handsome face. His nearness created a smothering pain in her chest.

"This 'DR DEK' has to mean Dr. Dekker," she said. "Maybe 'ELL DR DEK' means 'Tell Dr. Dekker.' Maybe he wants him to know something. But why give it to me, not him?"

Tap shook his head. "Maybe wanted to cover his trail."

"But why me? He could have left it for you. Everybody knows you two are friends."

He was quiet a moment, as if musing. "The three of us were friends," he said. "Maybe he chose you because you're the least logical choice. Again, to throw us off his trail."

She nodded, trying to concentrate. "Do you think this has something to do with the steroid business?"

"Yeah," he said. "I'd bet good money. He was trying to leak some information, probably on impulse. But he got scared, changed his mind."

"I don't blame him. If the others found out, God knows what they'd do."

"Right," Tap said, his face grim. "Look. I can't make head or tail of this. Suppose I give it to Sonny? Maybe he can come up with something."

"Sure," she agreed in almost a whisper. "Take it."

He scooped up the scraps and stuffed them into the pocket of his leather jacket. She couldn't help noticing how lean and strong his hand was. She remembered his touch and shivered slightly.

"You're sure you're okay?" he said in that chivalrous tone that drove her crazy. "Belinda? Are you okay?"

She refused to look at him. "Call me Dugan," she said, hating the bitterness in her voice.

BEVERLY'S FINGERS trembled slightly as she dialed Sonny's number. It was late Saturday afternoon, and her new phone in Galveston had just been connected.

She hadn't even called her mother yet, but she hungered to hear Sonny's voice. She hadn't talked to him for a full week. Twice she had tried to call from a pay phone, but couldn't reach him, and he had no way to reach her.

Her heart gave a little leap when she heard the receiver lifted on the other end.

"Hello," he said. "Dr. Dekker here."

She almost sighed with happiness and relief. She curled up on her bed, leaning her elbow on her pillow. "I've got a phone again," she said. "Consider me armed and dangerous."

"I've always considered you dangerous," he joked.

"You don't even sound surprised to hear from me," she said, disappointed.

"It's not like you went to Antarctica, Blondie."

"Well, it feels that far. Don't you miss me?"

"Don't flirt, Gert. I might miss you a little. What are you? Homesick already?"

She smiled. She had been flirting with him a bit, harmlessly, of course. She liked the familiar sound of his voice; it tickled her ear deliciously. "Homesick. Yes and no. Classes start Monday. I'm scared to death. But excited, too. I miss everything and everybody. So tell me all that's happened."

"Nobody's shot me yet. Or Nate. We're getting optimistic."

"Umm," she said. "Don't get cocky."

"I was born cocky. You want news? Okay. The new chili place finally opened. Hutch's."

"How's the chili?"

"It gives your tastebuds orgasms. And Mrs. Hutch? What's her name?"

"Betsy?"

"Betsy. She's decided to get a realtor's license. Hutch said he talked her into it. That she's too damn smart to work for that rinky-dink radio station."

"Good," Beverly said, smiling. "Nobody should have to work for Horace Westerhaus. She'll be wonderful at real estate. What else is happening?"

"Peggy Sue Grimes's chin quivers every time she looks at me. But she's being very brave. She's universally admired."

"Ugh," said Beverly. "What else?"

There was a beat of silence. "We've got another little mystery on our hands."

Her smile died, and she frowned. "Mystery?"

"Yeah. Get a pencil. Help me out."

Beverly reached for the pen and notebook on her night table. "We're going to be Holmes and Watson?"

"Exactly."

He told her succinctly of Chuck Cooper and the shredded note. She wrote down the fragmented words and frowned harder. They were a teasing riddle: TRI-CENT, ELL DR DEK, RIME.

"Lawsy, Sonny, it's alphabet soup. Can't somebody just go to Chuck and squeeze it out of him?"

"No. It could be dangerous for him. So don't tell anybody else about this note. Not even your best friend."

"*You're* my best friend," she objected.

"Fine. Now, help me decode this mess."

"Well, the 'DR DEK' part obviously means you."

"Right. So then does 'RIME' mean Grimes? As in good old Roger Grimes?"

Beverly thought. "It could. But it could be a part of *crime*. And *rime* is a word itself. So's *rimester* and *Crimea*. There's *prime*. And *primer*. And *prime rate* and *primeval*—"

"Slow down, slow down," Sonny said in mock disgust. "What are you, a walking dictionary? The only ones I thought of were 'crime' and 'prime.' Okay. I'm caught up."

"All the 'prime' phrases. *Prime minister, prime number, prime time.* How about *prime offender?*— maybe he was trying to sound grown-up."

"Some professor is going to carry you off and marry you," he grumbled. "You're too damn smart. Anything else?"

"There's *trimeter* and *trimester.*"

"If you get any brighter, I'll have to wear shades. I would have thought of these, but English is only my second language."

"Oh, pooh, it's your sixth or seventh," she teased back.

"So marry me," he said. "We'll have incredibly brilliant children."

He was only joking, yet his words jolted her. Once more she envisioned a black-haired baby not like herself at all.

"Don't be silly," she said, forcing the image of the child from her mind.

"Okay," he said. "Don't marry me. I'll catch you in my next life. In the meantime, what can you make of TRICENT? All I can come up with is *tricentennial,* which makes no sense."

Beverly stared at the letters thoughtfully. "Maybe it's a name."

"I've thought of that. There's a drug with the brand name Tricentolene. But it's an eyewash. I'm going crazy with this. It'd be easier if you were here to help."

I wish I was there, she thought, full of vague longing. But she made herself stick to business. TRICENT. The letters teased her.

"It's strange," she said, shaking her head, "I'm usually good at word games. This looks like it should be easy, but I can't come up with anything. Still, something nags me. Like it's there, but I can't reach it."

"Okay," he said. "Don't try to force it. If it comes to you, call. I don't care about the time or anything else."

"I will," she promised.

"Good," he said. "I wish I could figure it out. I still think that Roger Grimes is mixed up in this. But he's going to walk away, and nobody's going to touch him. It burns me."

"I know," she said. "Me, too."

"Oops," he said. "My beeper just beeped. Somebody's got a heart attack—or a hangnail. I've got to go. Take care, Blondie."

But we've barely talked, Beverly thought, empty with disappointment. *I'm not ready to let you go.*

But she had to. There was no choice.

That night, she had trouble falling asleep. She tried to drug herself by reading a boring book of travel memoirs. The ploy almost worked. Over a detailed account of the life cycle of the coconut rat, Beverly's eyelids grew irresistibly heavy.

She nestled back into the pillow, letting the book lie open on her chest, and her lashes fluttered shut. She started to sink into a warm doze.

Suddenly, just as her world was turning to a pleasant, welcoming darkness, a picture flashed across her mind with startling vividness. She saw a white sign with red letters.

Her eyes snapped open, and she sat up. A funny, excited feeling pounded in her stomach. She snatched her notebook and pen from the night table. She scribbled down a string of words. She glanced at the clock; it was past midnight.

Sonny had said to call him any time. She didn't hesitate. She took the phone and once again dialed his number.

The phone rang three times. Then she heard his voice, sleepy but professional. "Dr. Dekker. Yes?"

"Sonny," she said breathlessly, "did I wake you?"

He gave a low, sensuous groan. "Beverly?"

"Yes. Sonny, listen. It could be important."

"Ummmp," he said.

She pictured him sinking back against his pillow, his dark eyes falling shut. He slept naked. She knew because he'd let it slip once that he refused to complicate his life with nightclothes in any form.

She imagined his wide shoulders bare and warm against the sheets, his chest uncovered. It was a totally unbidden image, and she thrust it from her mind.

"Sonny? Are you listening?"

"I'm listening. Which is a good trick when you're not conscious. Ummph."

She sat up straighter, clutched the receiver more tightly. "Those letters? TRICENT? I was falling sleep when all of a sudden I remembered this sign in north Austin. It's on Fetrow Street. It's got a picture of this creature, half man, half horse. And it says, NUTRI-CENTAUR. It's got the TRICENT letters right in the middle."

Silence pulsed between them for the space of two heartbeats, then three. When he spoke, he no longer sounded sleepy. "Nutricentaur? You could be right. What is it?"

She took a deep breath. "It's a health food store. The kind of place that bodybuilders go to. But it's also got a pharmacy. It's a weird combination. A lot of my girl-friends used to go there. You could get diet pills. Maybe if they supply diet pills, they'd do the same with ster-oids, too."

There was another moment of silence. "Blondie, that's twisted. It's beautiful. It's perfect. I think I love you."

Beverly smiled, her heart raced, and she felt unac-countably happy at his joking words.

"You *thing*," she said.

BEVERLY WAS absolutely certain her intuition about Nutricentaur was right.

The idea had flown up from her unconsciousness like some glorious bird soaring into the light of day. It took Sheriff Wayne Jackson only four days to shoot it down and leave it dead in the dust.

"I'm sorry," Sonny told her over the phone. "It sounded great. A health food store would be a good front. But Wayne had it checked out. It's a straight outfit.''

"But then why would Chuck name it in his note?"

"Maybe he didn't," Sonny answered. "Maybe TRI-CENT means something else."

"But what?" Beverly asked. She had stubborn faith in her hunch. "I've thought about it. It *has* to be Nutricentaur. I can feel it."

Sonny's tone was skeptical. "What can I tell you? Big Wayne says, 'No way.' ''

"Maybe Big Wayne's wrong," she countered.

"Maybe, Sherlock. But proving it's something else."

He was right, of course, but her sense of disappointment was deep. Then she brightened. "I'm pretty well settled in here. I'm driving home early Saturday morning. Maybe I could meet you at the Longhorn for a late breakfast?"

"Sorry," he said in his husky voice. "I'm on emergency call until noon."

Her heart sank again. "Oh. What about afternoon? Will you be free? I'm tied up Saturday night. It's Mama's birthday. She wants a private celebration."

Carolyn had said firmly that she wanted to go to supper with only Beverly and Vern, then spend a cozy evening at home. Her request shut out all outsiders—including Sonny.

"Saturday afternoon?" Beverly asked hopefully.

"Saturday afternoon?" he said, no emotion in his voice. "Sure. If it'll make you happy."

The thought of seeing him again filled her with restless excitement. "Yes," she said softly. "It'll make me happy."

Very happy, she thought.

SATURDAY AFTERNOON, when Sonny drove down the lane that led to the Circle T, he was filled with uneasy expectation. She was back, and here he was, dancing attendance on her. What a fool he was. But he couldn't stop himself.

He pulled up to the imposing house and parked between Beverly's brand-new Cadillac and her mother's Jaguar. The January breeze stirred his red windbreaker as he mounted the steps of the house. His blood raced, pounding in his temples.

He didn't even reach the doorbell. Beverly seemed to swirl out the door like a movie star, even though she wasn't wearing anything that could actually swirl. She was dressed plainly in jeans, a white turtleneck and a suede jacket.

She was smiling, her head was uncovered, and her gold hair glinted in the sunlight. For an insane moment he thought she was going to fling herself into his arms. Unthinking, he took a step toward her.

But she stopped short. So did he. This left them standing too close to each other, looking too deeply into each other's eyes, breathing too hard. His heart beat so fast that his pulses drummed.

She stared up, lips parted, as if she felt as helpless and wary as he did. He was swept by the pleasant, yet frightening sensation that he might drown in her blue eyes.

Carolyn appeared, unsmiling, at the door. Her expression was stony. "Beverly," she said, "please remember you have to be back by five. We've made reservations."

"I'll remember," Beverly murmured, but she didn't look at her mother. She kept gazing at Sonny.

"Hello, Sonny," Carolyn said rather shortly. "Please have her back by five. She has a commitment. It's family."

He summoned all his willpower and dragged his eyes from Beverly. He flashed Carolyn his most innocent smile. "Yes, ma'am. I will. Happy birthday," he said.

She smiled stiffly. "Thank you."

He'd wrestled his expression under control, so he tossed Beverly a sardonic glance. "What happens if I don't get you back by five? You turn into a pumpkin?"

"Bumpkin is more like it," she said, smiling. "I'm just a little old country girl, you know?" She took his arm.

"I know," he said dryly. "Just like Scarlett O'Hara."

THE AFTERNOON sped by too quickly. They drove to Enchanted Rock, then simply walked and talked.

Beverly was surprised at how happy she was simply to be with him. The coolest, most rational part of her mind asked why she should feel such euphoria. After all, it was only Sonny, and they were friends, that was all.

He kept the conversation on neutral topics. As always, the subject of the steroids loomed large.

"I've been thinking about Peggy Sue," Beverly said, her forehead furrowing.

"Sweet little Peggy Sue," he said ironically. "Yeah. I've been thinking of her, too."

"She phones in prescriptions for all three of you at the clinic," Beverly said. "Has it occurred to you that she could call in false ones? That she could counterfeit steroid prescriptions? Phone them in to some druggist who was less than scrupulous? Let's pretend it might be Nutricentaur. It's possible, isn't it?''

He exhaled a harsh sigh. "It's possible, and I've thought of it. But I haven't said anything to Nate. He's a little soured on Peggy. But not enough to think she's capable of that.''

"So theoretically she could do it?''

"Sure. Each doctor has a Drug Enforcement Administration number for identification. So pharmacists know we're legit. She's literally got our numbers.''

"She could have been doing it ever since she got here.''

"Right,'' he said grimly.

Beverly shook her head. "If she did, all the steroids were top quality. And the prescriptions would look legal on the records.''

"The drug log would have to be doctored, but it could be done. Neat little piece of business.''

"But we can't prove it,'' she said. "It's all circumstantial.''

"I'll tell Wayne. Let him check it out. Maybe they can figure out if it's true. They'll have to. We can't.''

They were silent for a moment. Without looking at her, he said, "What time is it? I should be getting you home.''

"But it seems we just got here,'' Beverly protested. "We haven't had a chance to talk about anything except this.''

He flicked her a challenging glance. "Can you think of anything more important to talk about?''

She bit her lip. He was right, yet there *were* other things to speak of, and she wanted the sheer pleasure of being with him. She said nothing.

"What I can't figure," he said, "is how you came up with the name Nutricentaur. And why you believe so hard that it's mixed up in this. Is that what they mean by women's intuition?"

She smiled sheepishly. "Call it beauty-pageant bimbo intuition. The word was out about the diet pills. The name was down there in the old subconscious. Like an old tire sunk in the swamp."

"Please. You're speaking of the human brain. My specialty of study. A more elegant comparison, please."

"Okay, a whitewall tire in the swamp. Now, look—will we have another chance to talk? If I skipped church tomorrow, we could have breakfast together. How about it?"

His frown softened but didn't disappear. "I can't."

"What about tomorrow afternoon?"

"No," he said. "Not that either."

The statement stunned her. Was this all she was going to see of him? These few stolen hours spent trying to sort out a sordid drug mess?

"Sinclair's feeling down," Sonny said curtly. "I'll have to fill in for him on emergency. Nate can't. He's worn out as it is."

"Greg Sinclair?" she asked in surprise. "Feeling down? What's wrong?"

A muscle twitched in his cheek. "Sounds like Epstein-Barr virus. He's exhausted. Nate's worried about him. We've got to give him time off."

Alarm shot through her. Impulsively she seized his hand. "But with Greg gone, there's only you and Nate to hold down the fort. How will you manage, just the two of you? And you're right—Nate shouldn't push himself any harder."

"Don't look so scared," Sonny said gruffly. "I'll watch out for him. I promise you."

She studied his face. The afternoon sunshine highlighted his high cheekbones, the strong line of his jaw.

His fingers tightened around hers. "Trust me," he said.

His hand felt warm and strong in hers, as vital as life itself. She resisted an impulse to lay her cheek against his chest, the sudden desire to be comforted in his arms.

"I do trust you," she said in a tight voice.

An almost sad smile turned up the corners of his mouth. "Come on. I've got to get you home to Mama. Then maybe I'll go talk to Wayne again. I wish we could tie up this mess before I leave for Denver."

I don't want you to leave, she thought, holding his hand more tightly. *Something's changing here. Something's happening between you and me.*

CHAPTER ELEVEN

WHEN BEVERLY was a little girl, she had confidentially thought her life would be like a fairy tale.

Ultimately all good people would be rewarded, all bad people punished, and she would ride into the sunset with a prince who looked like a young Robert Redford.

Real life was proving less neat and satisfying than a fairy tale. It wouldn't even imitate a good detective story.

Sheriff Wayne Jackson listened to the theory that Peggy Sue Grimes might phone in false prescriptions, but said a more sophisticated agency than his would have to check it out. He would turn it over to the state police.

Sonny said he didn't know if the state police were doing anything about it, but if they were, they were taking their own sweet time.

Nobody good was being rewarded. Nobody bad was being punished. No loose ends were being tied. Instead there were new troubles. The worst was that Greg Sinclair was still ailing. Sonny phoned to say Sinclair would need at least two months off.

Concern pierced her. "How can he take off that long? You told me so yourself—three doctors aren't enough. Who'll take his caseload? His emergency shifts?"

"I'm taking his shifts. Nate and I'll split his case-load. What else can we do?"

"Sonny, you'll end up doing twice as much work as Nate, just to spare him. I know you."

"We'll get by, Blondie. Don't worry."

"What about the new doctor? The one replacing you? Have they even found one yet? Could he come early, help?"

"They've found one. He'll be here at the end of February."

The end of February. Her heart sank. Sonny would be gone at the end of February.

"Who is he?" she asked mechanically, not really caring. She was too overwhelmed by worry for Nate and Sonny, as well as concern for Greg Sinclair.

"His name's Womesh Godbole. He's a specialist in family practice, and Nate's lucky to get him."

Beverly's low spirits skidded even lower. "Womesh Godbole? What kind of name is that?"

"Hindu."

"A Hindu? From India?"

"Right." She heard the irony in Sonny's voice.

"A new ethnic type to pick on," Beverly said miserably.

"Cheer up. They'll be so glad to get rid of me they'll welcome him with open arms."

"I'm sorry," she said. "I can never tell you how sorry I am."

"Don't waste energy on sorry. I've got a job for you."

"What?"

"I've been looking through the files. Peggy Grimes went to school at Galveston. Five years ago. See if you can dig anything up on her, will you?"

"Me? I'm not a detective."

"Sure you are, Blondie. You came up with Nutricentaur. Her maiden name was Burns. Can you check it out?"

She sighed. She would do it, of course. For him. "Yes. I'll try."

"Good girl. How are classes?"

"Hard. I've written my hand off taking notes and read my eyes out studying. I want sympathy. How about it?"

"Wimp," he said, but with affection in his voice.

"I am a wimp," she said. "I feel like I'm in exile. I miss Crystal Creek."

I miss you, was what she meant. Oh, certainly she missed her mother, Vern, Amanda, and Nate Purdy and Rose, too, but she did not truly yearn to see anyone else. Her cousin Lynn had once been her best friend, but now Lynn had her own family and different interests altogether. It was as if Beverly were weaning herself from Crystal Creek, even though she had nowhere else to go.

Sonny was joking, teasing her, but his words hardly registered. All she felt was a sense of impending loss.

"And when I was your age," he said, "I walked eighteen miles to school in the freezing dark, and it was uphill both ways. I had nothing to eat but sleet and gravel, but did I complain? No. I was *thankful*, by God—"

"Sonny," she said, trying to keep her voice from shaking, "with you covering for Greg, I'll hardly get to see you before you go. Will I?"

His comic monologue came to an abrupt halt. He was silent a moment. "Not much," he said at last. "I'm sorry."

She tried to compute how he could handle both his and Nate's emergency shifts.

"If I came home next weekend," she began. "If I got there Saturday by noon—"

"I'm on call Saturday noon to Sunday noon."

"If I got there Friday night?" she asked.

"I'm on call till midnight."

She gritted her teeth. "I can't come the weekend after that. I have two midterms that Monday. I'll have to study all weekend."

"The weekend after that, I've got the same schedule. We could have Saturday morning. That's about it."

Her eyes burned and her throat tightened. "And the weekend after that?"

"I leave," he said, his voice even. "I go to Denver on the 27th."

For a moment she couldn't speak.

Two stolen mornings at best—that's all they had left. It wasn't enough. It wasn't nearly enough.

THE NEXT MORNING before class, Beverly phoned the alumni office to ask for information about Peggy Grimes. A man answered. He sounded bored.

"This is Beverly Townsend," she said sweetly. "I'm at my wit's end. I was in a beauty event five years ago with a girl who went to school here. A bunch of us want to have a reunion. But it's like this one girl disappeared. The last address we have for her is Crystal Creek. She's not there. Her name was Peggy Sue Burns. Could you help me? Give me some background? Her hometown, anything?"

The man became flirtatious. He said from the sound of Beverly's voice, he'd bet she'd had won the beauty contest.

She was coy, she was coquettish, she was teasing. But she did not lose sight of her goal. "If I could only find our friend," she said, with just the right touch of pathos.

"Okay, okay." He surrendered. "I'm going to pull her up on the computer screen. You married, sexy-sounding Bev?"

"Engaged," she lied blithely.

"Too bad," he said. "Okay. Here we go. Peggy Sue Burns. We got her, all right. You got a pencil?"

"Yes," she said.

"That Crystal Creek address is three years old. If she's moved lately, it'll take us a while to catch up. You want her parents' address?"

Beverly froze. Peggy was supposed to have lost both her mother and father in a car accident when she was still in high school. "Her parents?" she echoed.

"Mr. and Mrs. Ronald J. Burns, Sr. You want it?"

"Yes," Beverly said, scribbling madly. "Please."

"Okay. It's 5257 Strobel Avenue, Dallas, 75204."

"You're darling," she said. "I can't thank you enough."

"You could send me a picture of yourself," he said.

"You're a terrible tease," she said. "But you're sweet as can be. Goodbye now."

"Wait—" he said urgently.

But she hung up and stared at the name and address. So Peggy wasn't an orphan after all? "Peggy Sue," she whispered, "just what have you been up to?"

She picked up the phone again and dialed information. She asked for Dallas, the Ronald J. Burns residence.

She got the number, then dialed, fighting down a nervous feeling in the pit of her stomach. She planned on what she would say if either of Peggy's parents should pick up the phone.

But all she got was a woman's voice on an answering machine: "This is Bernice Burns. I'm unable to take your call right now. If you wish to leave a message, please wait for the signal. You will have four minutes."

Beverly hung up in frustration.

Her exasperation grew. Almost every hour on the hour she tried to reach Bernice Burns. Each time, she got the same recorded message. It told her only one thing: Peggy Sue Burns had a mother who was very much alive.

TAP HOLLISTER had taken a vow never to touch another drop of liquor as long as he lived.

He and Sonny sat in Hutch's Place, Sonny nursing a beer and Tap finishing a bowl of chili.

"So Peggy Grimes might have parents?" Tap said. "That's weird. Why would she lie?"

Sonny shrugged. "I don't know. Sympathy, maybe. Or maybe she's got something to hide."

Tap examined his friend's face. Sonny's mouth was set in the stubborn line of a man wrestling fatigue.

"Did you tell the police?" Tap asked.

Sonny arched one dark brow in disgust. "Yeah. We've got it down to a science. I tell Wayne Jackson. Wayne tells the state police. The state police do nothing."

Tap shrugged. "Sometimes when they take their time, it means they're on to something big."

Sonny's lip curled. "And sometimes it means they got more important things. When's the last time you read about a steroid bust?"

Tap considered. "Never."

"Right," Sonny said acidly. "And I doubt if you will—around here. The police have bigger fish to fry."

"They don't care if Peggy Grimes is lying?"

"So she lies. That doesn't make her guilty of anything. I don't think they'll even check it out."

"But Beverly is?"

Sonny's mouth drew up in a begrudging, one-cornered smile. "Yeah. She is."

"But she's not coming home this weekend?"

The smile disappeared. "No. Her mother's going there instead. Dragging cousins along. Bev can't get out of it."

Tap studied the other man through narrowed eyes. "You and Beverly..." he began, but the question died off, unfinished.

Sonny gave him a quick, cold glance. "I won't be seeing much of her. No big deal. I'll be in Denver soon. Finally. It feels like I've spent a lifetime in this burg."

"Yeah," Tap muttered. "Well."

"What?" Sonny asked cynically. "You're not rising to the town's defense? You, the eternal optimist?"

Tap shook his head. Memories of the past seven months gave him a bad taste in the back of his mouth. The worst of it was what had happened with Belinda.

The painful part was that he *liked* Dugan. She was a nice kid, and heartbreakingly sweet in bed. He'd thought often of that night.

He didn't blame himself for going to bed with her. That had been her doing. What he blamed himself for was that he couldn't care more for her. His heart was engaged elsewhere. That was that.

I'm sorry, Dugan, he thought moodily. Then, chagrined, he amended it: *No. I'm sorry, Belinda. I should have loved you instead. But I didn't.*

"Your little buddy," Sonny said, as if reading his mind. "Belinda. You're avoiding her. I don't ask her why. And she doesn't say. Something happened?"

Tap had his faults, but he was a gentleman to the marrow. "New Year's. I made a pass at her," he lied. "I was pretty crude, I guess. I don't blame her."

"Oh." Sonny took an idle drink of beer. He didn't believe the story, Tap could tell, but he didn't pry.

"She mentioned looking for another job," Sonny said.

Tap's heart felt a pinch that he recognized as guilt.

"Yeah," he said, trying to sound casual. "I figured she would."

He hated that she was leaving because of him. She was a good teacher, and in spite of the football incident, she was developing a devoted following among the smarter students.

"Too bad," said Sonny.

"Yeah," Tap agreed, the bitter taste in his mouth again. "Too bad."

The two men were silent for a moment. Sonny rubbed his fingers wearily across his brow. "How's Chuck Cooper? Can you tell what's happening on that front?"

Tap shook his head. "He looks unhappy, worried. This business has changed him."

"But he hasn't said anything to you?"

"Nothing."

"Have you ever asked him—"

"Hell, yes," Tap said, cutting him off. "Give me some credit. Of course, I asked. I asked him twice about that torn-up note."

"Damn—I'm sorry. I'm not thinking straight."

"Go home and go to bed, will you?" Tap said. "I'm getting tired just looking at you."

"Yeah," Sonny said. He drained his beer and set down the mug. At three o'clock that morning, two drunks had run their car into a telephone pole. Sonny had spent the wee hours picking windshield glass out of them, and monitoring the driver for a spinal injury that could be serious.

He zipped up his red windbreaker and gave Tap a wry look. "Say a prayer for me. That nobody has twins tonight."

Tap nodded. "You got it."

He left. As the door shut behind him, Tap heard somebody say, "That troublemaker's leavin' soon. Good riddance. I'd die before that SOB got his hands on me."

Damn! Tap thought, sickened. His life was a mess, the school was a mess, the town was a mess. When he'd come here, people couldn't say enough about how great Crystal Creek was, how lucky he was to be here.

Now the town was a rat's nest of strife and unsolved problems. What would it take to put the place right again? A miracle?

DR. GREG SINCLAIR went home to Dallas to put himself in the care of specialists. His absence meant a stint of slave labor for Sonny and Nate. To make matters worse, a new flu strain swept Crystal Creek, and both men were swamped with patients.

Nate, weakened by the long hours, finally fell prey to the flu himself. Sonny phoned Beverly to tell her not to make the drive to Crystal Creek for his sake. It would be his last full weekend in town, and with Nate sick, it would be like a madhouse.

"Womesh Godbole's coming, too," he said. "And I've got to show him the ropes. Then this mess is his problem."

Was it his imagination, or did her voice tremble when she answered? "All right," she said. "I'll stay here and study like the drudge I am. But next Sunday I'm coming home. I'm driving you to the airport. I insist."

"Sure," he said, keeping any emotion from his voice. "It's a deal."

When he hung up, he thought, *That's it*. It would be good that he would be near her as little as possible. Each time he saw her was like a stab to the heart. He wanted her so much it was like a sickness, and he was tired of pretending he didn't.

Yes, it would be good to have a thousand miles between himself and Beverly, to let his memories of her grow stale and powerless. As for the town, he could not leave soon enough.

When Nate fell sick, Sonny ended up with all the town's patients. A sulky parade of flu victims had slumped through his office, dislike in their eyes.

Selected Westerhauses, Fletchers, Armbrusters, Ditmarses—they came to the clinic and glared sickly at him, letting him him know they had turned to him only in desperation. Their sons had been heroes once. He had ruined that for them. They would not forget, and they would not forgive.

When he finally left for Denver, he hoped Crystal Creek would seem like a bad dream. With luck, Beverly would seem equally unreal.

Between patients he managed to set his affairs in order for leaving. He'd sold his rusting car to a high school student with a bent for mechanics. The kid would pick it up the day Sonny left.

His last Saturday was a haze of hectic events. There were emergencies he had to treat and Dr. Womesh Godbole to brief. Sunday arrived, and with it, the last time he would probably ever see Beverly.

She drove him to the Austin airport and waited there in a crowded restaurant with him until twenty minutes before his plane was due to depart.

Then he'd stood, shouldered his carry-on, and she'd stood, too. Together they walked out of the restaurant and back into the teeming concourse.

He looked down at her, struggling to keep his face expressionless. "I guess this is it. Take care of yourself. We'll stay in touch."

Suddenly her small hand was on his arm, tightening on the sleeve of his windbreaker, as if she didn't want him to go. She raised her face to him, her lower lip trembling.

"I'll never be able to thank you enough," she said, her voice shaky. "Or tell you what you've meant to me."

His heart had become leaden, an insufferable, painful weight in his chest. "Yeah. Same here," he said.

Then he couldn't help himself. He bent and kissed her. He'd meant it to be a short kiss, disguised as one of friendship. He failed.

Once his mouth was on the pliant warmth of hers, she gave a small sound like a little whimper deep in her throat, and it made him slightly crazy. Her hand tightened spasmodically on his sleeve as if she really didn't mean to let him go.

He had only one free arm, and he wound it around her, pulling her close. She came willingly, almost eagerly, he thought, dazed, and he drew her nearer still.

He drank her lips with kissing, as if he could draw out her soul and make it one with his. He felt her arm around his neck, clinging tightly to him, and it drove him crazier still.

Dimly he heard a wolf whistle and knew it was meant for them. *She's only letting this happen because it's goodbye,* he told himself. *Stop. You're letting her know too much. Stop, you damn fool.*

He drew back abruptly, breaking the kiss. She stared at him with misty, confused eyes. But she kept her arm wound around his neck, and her lips were parted as if she wanted to say something, but could not.

Helpless, he bent and kissed her again, but briefly, as he'd meant to the first time. Then he broke the kiss and stepped backward, putting space between them. She let go and stood with her hands clasped in front of her breast, like a woman watching something terrible happen.

The look on her face half broke his heart, because it made him hopeful when he refused to believe there was any hope. He shook his head, as if to tell her that he understood anything other than this was impossible between them.

"Goodbye, Blondie," he said.

Then he turned, hitching his carry-on more firmly over his shoulder, and left her. He didn't look back.

CHAPTER TWELVE

HE'D KISSED her goodbye. And with that kiss, everything changed for her. Everything—herself, Sonny, the day, the world, the universe, everything.

As his lips took hers, a wild elation soared within her. Her heart turned over; a fluttering feeling possessed her soul, and desire, all the more powerful because it was so strongly mixed with affection, flew through her veins like electric shock.

It was as if she had been waiting through a hundred years of numb slumber for this moment, this touch, this man. She clung to him, hungry for more of this sweet, new madness.

His mouth fit hers perfectly, his arm went around her perfectly, his body fit against hers perfectly. It was as if she and he were pieces of a puzzle, joined at last.

She was stunned when he drew back and stepped away from her. He looked at her with something like regret, and a corner of his lip twitched in a rueful smile.

Then he said goodbye in his careless way, and turned, walking out of her life. She stared after him, devastated.

She wanted to run after him, but pride and fear kept her rooted where she stood. "Sonny?" she said so softly that no one could hear her. "Sonny?"

Shakily, she put her fingertips to her lips, astonished at her own emotions. *My God,* she thought. *I've fallen in love with my best friend. What do I do now?*

Stunned, she did nothing, said nothing. She saw him check through the metal detector, then disappear down the concourse. He was gone.

She resisted the impulse to run after him or have him paged. If she did such a thing, how might her life change? She did not have the courage to find out.

She hurried to the parking lot, pretending that nothing had altered, but it had, profoundly. She wondered how she could have been such a fool, blind to him for so long.

He'd always joked that he desired her, that he was even a bit in love with her, but he'd never acted on it. She had no idea if he meant a word of it.

He'd kissed as if he desired her, but desire wasn't love. She might never know how he really felt.

Oh, they had made the usual promises to phone and write. They would stay in touch—for a while. But she had sensed a terrible finality in their parting.

She knew that he'd never come back to Crystal Creek. He disliked it and with good reason. And if she went to him, what would happen? She'd seen how people had reacted merely to the *idea* of her loving him.

She drove back to her Galveston apartment, grateful that she wasn't going home to Crystal Creek to face her mother. Her mother would take one look at her and know, Beverly was sure. But what was she going to do? What?

THE SCHOOL WEEK crawled by with maddening slowness. Before Sonny had left, Beverly's apartment had seemed cozy and homelike. Now it echoed with emptiness, which made no sense. He had never been there, not once. Yet loneliness seemed to fill its rooms and suffocate her.

She had to go home for the next weekend; there was no choice. It was her uncle J.T.'s birthday on Saturday. Carolyn was throwing a mammoth party, the sort Beverly used to love. Now it didn't interest her. She had other things on her mind.

Throughout the week, to distract herself, Beverly kept trying to call Peggy Grimes's parents. It had become a stultifying game. Five or six times a day she would dial the number. Always the phone would ring six times, then the answering machine would drone its unchanging message.

On Friday when she got back from class, she steeled herself to try one more call, then she would head to Crystal Creek for the weekend and J.T.'s party. First, however, she switched on her own answering machine. She'd been waiting in vain to hear from Sonny, hoping for such a call and fearing what it might make her feel.

But it was her mother's voice that first greeted her from the machine. Carolyn told her to drive carefully, that tornado warnings had been issued for the Austin area.

Then there was a message from Sonny. Delight flooded her.

"Hi, Blondie," the recording said. "I'm in the mile-high city. Actually it's a mile and three and a half feet. The three and a half feet's solid snow.

"I start at the clinic Monday. One of the partners is into sleep disorders—weird stuff. He says if I find any narcoleptics fallen over in the hall not to mind. Just to step over them.

"I'd hoped to catch you home. Any luck tracking down Peggy Grimes's folks? I was thinking about that mess today. Thinking of everything back there. Guess I was in a Lone Star state of mind.

"I got a phone finally. The guy who installed it had to mush in by dogsled. My number's 303 555-3637. Give me a call sometime. If a polar bear answers, hang up."

She played the message twice, her heart beating hard. Then she dialed his number. Her heart pounded even more wildly when he answered.

She said she'd called to wish him luck. She told him she hadn't been able to reach Peggy Grimes's parents. After that, he and she chatted, rather aimlessly. He made her laugh, as usual. It seemed to take them a long time to say goodbye. She didn't want to hang up.

HE SAT in a bland, characterless apartment in Denver. On Monday he would officially join the staff at Hopkins-Sloane. He'd finally achieved his life's ambition—and all he could think about was a blonde in Texas.

"Good luck," she had said when she'd phoned. Her voice still echoed, whispery and warm, in his ear. Hearing her had sent threads of fire and yearning stitching through him.

"That's all, I guess," she'd said in her slightly breathy drawl. "I just wanted to wish you luck."

"I thought you were going to say you wanted me," he'd joked. "That if I came back, I could be your love slave. You'd tie me to a futon and cover me with maple syrup."

"You outrageous *thing*," she'd said, laughing. She always called him "thing" when he teased her, and he'd teased her often, because he loved to make her laugh.

"I hope you like Denver," she'd said. Did he detect loneliness in her voice, regret? Or was it only wishful thinking on his part?

"I'll like it fine," he'd said. "Any place is home to me. You know me."

"Is it cold there?" she'd asked. He'd glanced out his window. All he saw was snow. He'd never seen so much snow in his life.

"Yeah, it's cold," he'd said, thinking of her. *If she'd say, I wish you'd come back for me, he'd turn around and go. Damn Hopkins-Sloan, damn Denver, damn everything. He'd go back for her.*

Instead she'd said, "So now you belong to Colorado. It's Texas's loss."

He'd hesitated, picturing her with such clarity it hurt, her hair like sunlight, her eyes the deep blue-violet of bluebonnets. He replied with false carelessness, "I've done Texas."

And Texas has done me, he'd thought. *Or undone me.*

"Oh," she'd said. Again he wondered if he imagined disappointment in her voice. But then they went on making small talk, joking, not saying anything really.

When she hung up, his apartment room felt impossibly empty and isolated. He could have been at an outpost in the wastes of the planet Pluto instead of downtown Denver.

He shook his head in frustration. He was disciplined to a fault; he kept his emotions under strict control, and he hadn't allowed himself to feel anything approaching loneliness since he'd been eleven years old. But that was how he felt, dammit—lonely.

He kept telling himself that he should have been glad to shake the dust of that one-horse town from his feet.

He had no business pining over a Texas beauty queen. It was only by a fluke that he'd ended up in the town, only by mistake that he'd gotten involved with her.

Now the mistake was rectified; his career was back on track, and his fate was back in his own hands. He should forget that fractious town. And the woman, too.

Most especially he should forget the woman.

TALKING TO SONNY left Beverly so agitated that she forgot to try to call Peggy Grimes's parents again. She packed hastily for the weekend, loaded her car and headed west toward Claro County.

She switched on the radio to distract herself with music. Did she want Sonny to ask her to come to him? Would she go if he asked? Was she that brave?

All her life she'd labored for approval—could she live without it? What would her mother say? And what of her father, if he were still alive? Would he have disowned her?

Everything she thought conflicted with what she felt, and everything she felt so perplexed her that her head ached and her chest hurt. The radio played love songs, but she didn't really hear them.

Neither did the weather reports register on her consciousness. A tornado watch was on in Travis, Blanco, and Claro counties. The airwaves were full of storm warnings. She ignored them.

SONNY PACED the confines of his apartment. He looked out on the Arctic landscape. The sky was dark. It had been almost four hours since Beverly had called.

He remembered all too vividly how she had returned his kiss in the airport. He remembered the tiny, maddeningly sweet moan she'd made when his lips first touched hers, and how she'd wound her arm around his neck.

My God, could she have kissed him like that if she didn't care? Maybe he should try to get back to see her when her school term was over. Make it seem casual. Like he was coming back to do research in Austin.

Research, hell, you jerk, he told himself angrily. *What do you want from her? An engraved invitation? A signed note that everything would be nice and safe, your pride, your hope, your goddamn sense of saving face?*

For six long months he'd pretended he cared for her less than he did. After all, she'd been in mourning for her blue-eyed all-American boyfriend.

Then, finally, with approximately a thousand people looking on, he'd kissed her. He'd meant it to be friendly, but his body was tired of lying, even if his mind wasn't.

She'd kissed him back in a way that eclipsed the concept of "friendly." She'd no longer seemed like a woman in mourning. She'd kissed like a woman on the edge of love.

He loved her. She might—just possibly—love him back. So why wasn't he going after her? Why wasn't he fighting for her? There were obstacles, sure. So what?

He paced back to the table, and opened the bottle of Napa Valley wine that a nurse back in Crystal Creek had given him for a goodbye present.

He poured himself a shot, downed it like whiskey, then walked to the phone. He dialed Beverly's Crystal Creek number. She'd said she was driving to her mother's tonight. She should be there by now.

Carolyn answered in her brisk, no-nonsense way. He thought, *Someday, if I get this girl, I'm going to have to charm your hand-tooled boots off, Dragon Lady.*

"Hello, Mrs. Trent," he said as pleasantly as he could. "This is Sunarjo Dekker. Is Beverly there?"

"She's taking a bath," Carolyn said shortly. "I just came into her room to turn down the bed."

"Would you tell her I'd like to talk to her?"

"It'd be better if you'd call back tomorrow. She's getting ready for bed."

He refused to back off. "I have to talk to her now. It's important," he said.

Carolyn finally relented, not altogether graciously. Sonny tried not to think of Beverly rising naked from her bubble bath, wrapping her still-damp body in a towel.

There was a long, nearly eternal, silence before he heard her voice. "Sonny?" she said in her breathless way.

He wondered if Carolyn was still in the room and supposed she was. What the hell. "I miss you," he said. "I missed you even before I left. What do you say?"

"I—don't understand," she answered hesitantly.

He took a deep breath and got more reckless. "For months I tried to resist you. But I conquered my goddamn willpower. What do you say?"

There pulsed a space of three heartbeats. "I don't know what to say."

"If I turned up on your doorstep, would you kiss me hello the way you kissed me goodbye?"

"I—I don't know."

"Would you like to find out?"

Another silence, longer than the first. "Yes," she said at last. "Oh, yes. Yes, I would."

"I'll fly back tomorrow. I'll rent a car in Austin. I'll be there as soon as I can."

"Yes," she said, more eagerly than he could have prayed for. "Come back. Please do."

He wanted to say, "I love you," but the words stuck in his throat. He could say nothing at all.

"Sonny?" she asked, her voice nervous.

"Yes?" he managed to say.

"I'm afraid," she whispered.

He swallowed. She had every reason to be afraid. He envisioned Crystal Creek raising a thousand objections against him, erecting a thousand obstacles between them.

But he didn't voice his thoughts. All he said was, "I'll be there, Blondie. Come hell or high water."

SATURDAY DAWNED, warm, humid and windless. Tap Hollister awoke, sweating in his rumpled sheets. He'd been having another sexy dream about Belinda. The dreams haunted him lately, and they were always rated X.

In them she did wonderfully lascivious things to him, and he did them back. They frolicked like a pair of libidinous minks. Shirtless, he sat up and groaned.

God, he thought, he had to see her today, to work with her. He had to take the concert band to the regional contest in Fredericksburg. The band boosters wanted videotapes, and Belinda was the school's only video camera expert.

How was he going to look her in the eye when he'd been having these crazed, oversexed dreams about her all week? And why was he having them? Why her, instead of Liz? Couldn't he have Liz even in his dreams?

He sighed harshly and got up. He was wearing only a wrinkled pair of boxer shorts with yellow smiley faces printed on them. "Chill out," he said to the smiley faces. "You got nothing to be happy about."

He padded barefoot to his bedroom window and looked out. The morning sun stained the sky fiery red, and the birds twittered restlessly.

He gazed across the yard at Liz Babcock's house. It stood untenanted now, empty.

Liz, he thought, staring at her house. He tried to conjure up her face in his imagination and found it surprisingly vague. He struggled to envision her beautiful blue-gray eyes. He couldn't.

He put his hands on the windowsill and thought, guiltily, of Belinda Dugan. He could see *her* all too clearly in his mind's eye. Why shouldn't he? After all, he'd spent the morning fondling her naked body in his dreams.

He shook his head to clear it, then stared at the fiery sky again. Four times this week Belinda Dugan had starred in his nighttime fantasies. Four times.

Belinda? he asked himself dubiously. Why? And why could he no longer picture Liz?

He raked his hand through his tousled hair. He knew why, and it embarrassed him. It was something that Sonny had said one night at Hutch's Place.

He recalled the conversation all too vividly. "Why are you obsessed with her?" Sonny had asked flippantly. "Have you got a mother fixation?"

A mother fixation. Suddenly Tap had no longer seen himself as the hot-blooded lover of an unattainable beauty. He saw himself as still trying to come to terms with the loss of his mother and seeking the comfort of an older woman.

The thought dogged him relentlessly. And the dreams about Belinda had begun. Belinda was pretty and sweet and smart and young and appealing. But he'd hurt her terribly. He didn't know if she would ever forgive him. How could she?

She would hate this day of forced contact with him. He didn't blame her. He dreaded it himself. Things were such a mess between them that nothing could put them right.

BEVERLY WATCHED the blood-red dawn. She'd awakened early and been unable to go back to sleep. Now she sat at the kitchen table, nursing a cup of coffee.

He's coming back, she thought. *What will I feel? What's going to happen?*

Her heart beat hard in combined fear and anticipation. He wouldn't arrive for hours, not until one o'clock, at least. She tried to imagine his rented car drawing up in the drive, him getting out. He would walk toward the porch, and she would be inside, waiting for his knock.

No, she couldn't stand waiting. She would be out the door, flying into his arms, kissing him hello.

No, no, no. That was too emotional, too rash. There were so many problems, so many questions, so many reasons to be careful. She couldn't just rush into his arms as if there was no tomorrow. Or was that precisely what she *should* do?

She heard the soft rustle of her mother's satin robe and straightened in her chair. Nervously she touched her lips, as if wiping away the traces of imaginary guilty kisses.

Carolyn entered the kitchen. She looked at Beverly but didn't smile. "You're up early," she said.

"I couldn't sleep."

"Thinking about *him*, I suppose," Carolyn said, her voice cool. She walked to the counter and poured herself a cup of coffee. Last night she had said little, but she hadn't been able to hide her displeasure that Sonny was coming back.

"Yes," Beverly said, raising her eyes to meet Carolyn's disapproving gaze. "I am."

"Then think hard," Carolyn said. "All your life you've had things easy. I warn you. This will *not* be easy."

Beverly set her jaw. "He's coming back to see me, that's all. That doesn't mean I'm going to marry him."

"But you're thinking about it, aren't you? You can't hide the truth from me. I know you too well." Carolyn sat down across from Beverly, challenge in her eyes.

Beverly chose her words carefully. "If I've found someone I care for, I'd think you'd be happy."

Carolyn's expression didn't change. "You promised me this wasn't going to happen."

"I—didn't think it would. It caught me by surprise."

"I couldn't sleep all night, wondering what your father might think."

"That's not fair, Mama."

Carolyn ignored the statement. "Thank God your father didn't live to see this. It would break his heart."

"Mama!" Tears sprang to Beverly's eyes, but furious, she blinked them back.

"Frank Townsend's grandchildren," Carolyn said. "Not white, but yellow. It would have broken his heart."

Beverly could bear no more. She pushed away from the table and stood. "You've got no right to say such things. You'll regret this."

"No, Beverly," Carolyn said fervently. "What I'd regret is *not* saying it. Because if you're about to do what I suspect, you'd better face the reality of it."

"You should be ashamed to talk like this."

"I'm talking like this, and I love you," Carolyn shot back. "I'm your mother. Think of what other people will say. Your whole life long, they'll say it. Again and again."

"I refuse to listen to this," Beverly said, with a toss of her head. "I'm ashamed for you."

She stalked from the kitchen and back to her room. She'd always loved and admired her mother, but now love was mixed inextricably with resentment.

She slammed her door shut, not caring if she woke up Vern. Her temples throbbed and her chest ached. What hurt and frightened her most was Carolyn's brutal honesty.

I'm talking like this and I love you.... Think of what other people will say.

Her mother wasn't simply berating her. She was warning her, as well.

There's a price to loving this man, was what Carolyn had meant. *Can you pay it? Can you really?*

CHAPTER THIRTEEN

SONNY WAS DELAYED in the Dallas airport. Cold, heavy rains poured down, and lightning bolts played dangerously in the roiling sky.

There was talk of tornadoes near the Austin area, which made him nervous for Beverly. Tornadoes struck swiftly and moved without logic.

A voice came over the PA system. "Flight 439 for Austin will be delayed for one more hour. Takeoff time will be at two-thirty."

Damn! Sonny thought. He'd better call Beverly. He rose, bored and frustrated, and found a phone.

He punched her number and waited. His heart was thudding hard in his chest, as if he'd been running. She answered on the third ring.

"Hello?" she said.

"Blondie, it's me. I'm stuck in Dallas. My flight's delayed till two-thirty. It's storming here. I'll get there as soon as I can."

He held his breath, wondering if she'd had a change of heart. "I hate waiting," she said. She sounded nervous. "It makes me feel so helpless."

"You still want me to come?"

"Of course," she said.

He exhaled and started breathing again.

She said, "Call me if you're delayed again, will you?"

"Absolutely." Again he had the frightening urge to say "I love you." The words choked in his throat, unspoken.

"Take care of yourself," he said instead, his voice gruff. "I hear Austin's under a tornado warning."

"Oh, so are we," she said, sounding unconcerned. "Three years ago it was the same thing. We were under warning so often it got boring. Don't worry. Nothing ever happens."

"Make sure it doesn't."

They said their goodbyes, and the distance between them seemed heavy with things unsaid.

CAROLYN MADE a brusque apology to Beverly, but Beverly was not appeased. For the first time in her life she sensed a split, perhaps unbridgeable, between herself and her mother.

Sonny called again at two-twenty. His flight had been delayed for another two hours. The storm in Dallas had not moved on; the rain had not lessened.

The tension made Beverly's nerves scream. "Do you have any idea of when you'll get here?" she asked. *God,* she thought, *even the weather wants to keep us apart.*

"It may be eight or nine tonight."

"Eight or nine?" She wanted to weep.

"At best. I'm sorry. But I'll get to you. I promise."

He hung up. Beverly was crushed. Eight or nine o'clock? It was unbearable. By then she would have spent more than twelve hours trapped in this house that tingled with discord.

She decided to ride Dandi until all the tension was galloped out of her system. As she pulled on her boots, it occurred to her that she hadn't tried to call Peggy Grimes's parents today.

She picked up the phone. She now knew the number by heart. Mechanically, like a well-programmed robot, she pushed the buttons. She waited for the answering machine's everlasting message.

But this time, on the third ring, the receiver was lifted and a woman's voice said, "The Burns residence. Bernice speaking."

Beverly was so taken aback that she couldn't speak.

"Hello?" said the woman. "Hello?"

"Mrs. Burns!" Beverly said, "How are you?"

"I'm fine," Bernice Burns said suspiciously. "Are you selling something? I don't want anything."

"No, no," Beverly protested. "I'm just calling about a Peggy Sue Burns."

The woman sounded more unfriendly than before. "Peggy? Did she put you up to this?"

Beverly was puzzled by the response. "I'm trying to get in touch with her. We went to school together in Galveston."

"Peggy doesn't live here anymore," Bernice Burns said coldly.

"She is your daughter?" Beverly asked.

"I don't want to talk about her."

"Have I got the right number? Peggy's your daughter?"

"Peggy *was* my daughter," Mrs. Burns said with bitterness. "If you're looking for the girl she was five years ago, forget it. That girl is gone."

Beverly pretended to misunderstand. "You mean Peggy's—passed on? I'm sorry. My sympathy. Whatever happened? Was it sudden?"

"She's not dead," Mrs. Burns retorted. "She's just not my daughter any longer. Not since she took up with that man. I don't acknowledge her."

Beverly thought, *God will strike me dead for this.* "Mrs. Burns, I'm shocked. Peggy's changed? How?"

The woman's voice was bitter. "He changed her. I warned her. Would she listen? Of course not. I'm only her mother."

"Something happened?" Beverly asked, all innocence. "How sad."

"I don't want to talk about it. Goodbye."

"Mrs. Burns, don't hang up," Beverly pleaded. "I hate to hear this. If I find Peggy, can I give her a message? Can I help in any way?"

"You won't find the Peggy you knew," Bernice Burns said with finality. "If you find her, ask her about Asa."

"Asia?" Beverly asked.

"Asa," the woman practically hissed. "Her son. The child she left for that man. That man. He probably still has his shed full of weights and drugs. She left her child. She left a wonderful husband. She did it for that man. Don't talk to me about her. I have her brother. I don't need her. She was always a user, always a liar."

"Mrs. Burns—"

But Bernice Burns did not answer. She did not even say goodbye. She hung up, and the line went dead.

Beverly stared at the receiver bewildered. Peggy, the pathetically childless and orphaned Peggy, not only had a family, but she had abandoned her own child?

She hesitated for a moment, then called the number again. But the phone rang six times, then there was a click, and the same old recorded message came on.

She's cut me off, Beverly thought, intrigued. A myriad of questions swarmed through her mind. What had happened in this family, and why had Peggy lied to the town so outrageously?

She glanced at her watch. It was just past two-thirty.

Bernice Burns had mentioned that Peggy had a brother. The Crystal Creek library would be open until five, and in its reference section was a shelf of phone books for different cities, including Dallas.

Sonny would not be in town for hours. She would go to the library. If she was lucky, she might track down some relative who was not as tight-mouthed as Bernice Burns.

She managed to avoid her mother, who was in the kitchen making hors d'oeuvres with Consuela, the woman she'd hired to help with the party. She backed the Cadillac out of the garage and rolled down the window. The car was hot, and the outside air sultry.

She saw Vern in the corral, putting Outlaw through his paces. The mettlesome black horse with its fine, tossing head and flowing mane brought back memories of her rides with Sonny. Sonny. Her heart jolted at the thought of him.

My God, she thought, bewildered by the strength of her emotion. *I do love him. But what good can come of it?*

The still air made no answer. It seemed only to crowd around her more oppressively.

AT THREE-TEN, one of the uniformed attendants at Sonny's gate took the microphone. *No,* he thought darkly. *Not another delay.* The rain had slowed to a drizzle, giving him a spark of false hope.

"The cloud cover's lifted somewhat, we've got a window of opportunity, and we're letting two flights go to Austin," the attendant announced.

Sonny's pulses speeded, and a sensation akin to light-headedness assailed him. He would get to her, at last.

There was not even time to phone her. It didn't matter. He would be with her in two hours.

TAP HOLLISTER had dressed as respectably as he could stand. But beneath his sport coat and white dress shirt, he'd worn a T-shirt that said TUNE IT OR DIE!

The concert band had been careless lately, and when their tune-up at the contest this morning proved listless, he'd angrily ripped open his dress shirt and flashed the band his lethal message.

"I mean it!" he cried. "No prisoners!"

The ploy worked. For a change the band tuned up perfectly.

Tap was a master of such dramatic gestures and unexpected actions. He had to be. Keeping control of thirty excitable, randy and ingenious teenagers was no job for a man of small imagination.

He demanded much from his students, and he got it. He did this partly by sheer cunning. He was always a step ahead of them and never predictable. Today the concert band had outdone itself. So before the final competition, he found himself making a rash promise.

"Get a perfect score, and I won't ride back on the bus with you," he said. He knew they'd do anything not to have him on the bus home. They would be chaperoned only by a few hapless volunteer band parents. What havoc could be wrought! He saw the glitter in the students' eyes. They were crazed with motivation.

The band got a perfect score. Too late Tap realized he'd backed himself into an awkward corner. He'd planned on riding home with the V-WAD. The V-WAD was the Volunteer Who Always Drove to competition separately, just in case the bus broke down and someone had to go for help.

In his fervor, he had forgotten that the V-WAD of the day was Belinda. How could he have forgotten such a thing?

While the students screamed and cheered and wept with happiness over their scores, Tap made his way to Belinda. "Look," he said, feeling like a rat, "I'm sorry. I didn't mean to put you in this spot. It was an accident. I forgot that you were the one—"

She squared her jaw and fixed him with her brown eyes. "Of course," she said with a cold shrug. "Why should you remember?"

"I didn't mean it that way," he said, miserable that he'd hurt her again. "If it bothers you, I'll go on the bus anyway. I'll give them a rain check."

She didn't so much as blink. She looked him up and down the way one might do an enemy. "No. You made a promise. You should keep it."

"I don't want you to feel—"

"I don't feel anything."

She waited, her face expressionless, for him to supervise the giddy band members packing up their instruments. Two boys had to be reprimanded for trying to stuff Gina Dalton into a tuba case.

"Arriba! Arriba!" one of the drummers screamed as the students finally boarded the bus. "Crystal Creek rules! We've going to state! We're gonna kick major butt!"

Tap heard somebody from another band say something about "Crystal Creek drug freaks." Somebody else laughed.

He followed Belinda to her compact car, his temper simmering. He swore, then said, "I wish this damn steroid thing was over and done with."

"It'll never be over and done with," Belinda said, her voice clipped. "Nobody can stop it."

"No?" Tap asked, his eyes still flashing. "They'll catch whoever supplies the junk one of these days."

"Get in the car, will you?" she said. "The bus is leaving."

He shut up, his heart beating hard. Anger and guilt warred in his chest. He got into the car.

Belinda said nothing. She rolled down the window to let fresh air in, but none stirred. The day was suffocatingly hot and close, like his own emotions.

SONNY'S PLANE landed in Austin at 4:08. The sky was weirdly clouded over, and the still air was heavy and humid. He made his way to a phone and tried to call Beverly. She didn't answer. He set his teeth and told himself to try again later.

He rented a car, a dark blue Chevy compact. He headed out of the lot and toward the highway that led to Crystal Creek. He wanted to see Beverly, he ached to see her.

AT 4:45, THE weary-looking librarian told Beverly she was sorry, but she had to close up for the weekend.

Beverly stood at the pay phone in the lobby. She had just placed her call, and the phone at the other end had just begun to ring. She gave Violet, the librarian, her most beseeching look.

"Violet," she said, "the sign says you're open until five o'clock. It's early."

"Beverly, you've been the only one in here for the last 45 minutes. And all you're doing is using the phone. You can do that at home."

"I don't want to do it at home," Beverly said.

"It's Saturday," Violet objected, looking put upon. "It's hot and muggy, and nobody else is coming in. Would the world end if I left a few minutes early?"

"Can't I finish this call?" Beverly asked.

"I want to close," Violet said with finality.

Beverly sighed and hung up. She had been trying to call everyone named Burns in the Dallas phone book, hoping to find a gossipy relative of Peggy Sue. She had failed.

She'd laboriously copied the list of Burnses from the Dallas phone book. There were at least fifteen more to call. But not now. It was too late.

She gave Violet her chilliest smile, then left the library and headed toward her Cadillac. She supposed she was extremely lucky to have connected with Peggy's mother. She couldn't wait to tell Sonny when he got here.

When he got here. Her heart plunged unhappily. He was delayed in Dallas and wouldn't arrive for hours. Those hours suddenly stretched before her like a trackless desert.

She had too much time, and she didn't want to go home. She would drive by the Grimes place and see if there actually was a shed such as Bernice Burns had mentioned. A shed full of "weights and drugs"? That might be just what authorities needed.

She headed east, toward Peggy's house. The Grimeses lived on the town's outskirts, on five prettily wooded acres.

Five wooded acres, Beverly thought, could conceal any number of secrets. She felt edgy but adventurous. At last she reached the mailbox that marked the Grimeses' lane.

Boldly she turned down the drive. If they saw her, she would say she'd pulled in to turn her car around. If they weren't at home, so much the better. She could explore.

She drew up before the neatly painted little clapboard house. The carport was empty. It appeared nobody was home. Beverly parked the car. Her heart racing, she got out.

It was 5:12. Not a breath of wind stirred.

CHAPTER FOURTEEN

THE GRIMESES' small house stood in a clearing of cedar, scrub oak and mesquite trees. Thickets of sumac and cow vine surrounded it.

Vegetation was thick because a section of the Crystal Creek made a perfect U-shaped loop through the property. An arm of the creek had been dammed to form a pond. Around the bank grew the ground-hugging plant known as flannel britches, and the purple flowers were already in bloom. Their pungent odor tickled Beverly's nostrils, and she caught the scent of rain, as well.

Rain, she thought and looked up. Wisps of cloud raced across the sky. She prayed that Sonny wouldn't be delayed by more bad weather.

At the far end of the pond, almost hidden by a screen of horsebean bushes, stood a large metal shed that perched on a foundation of concrete blocks.

A shed. That was what she'd come to find. When she approached it, she found the metal door was locked with two padlocks.

Double-locked? That was interesting. She walked around the building, hoping she could see into one of its windows. But they were all protected from the inside with something that resembled chain-link fencing.

Whatever was in the shed, the Grimeses wanted no one breaking in. A ditch ran behind the building. It was shrouded with vines, and gave off a dank, nasty smell.

Beverly shuddered delicately and moved to the building's rear. She peeked into a window, but could see only a large set of weights through the chain link.

A wind suddenly gusted. *Enough of this*, she thought. If she wasn't careful, she would be caught in a storm.

Just as she started toward her Cadillac, she heard a car coming down the lane. *Oh, no*, she thought in panic, *I'm going to get caught.* The wind gusted more menacingly.

A car entered the clearing. Beverly stood before the door of the shed, feeling like a trespassing child. The car was Peggy Grimes's silver Audi, and she wheeled up next to the shed like a woman with a vengeance. The front window rolled down automatically, and Peggy glared at her.

"What are you doing here?" she demanded.

Beverly did not feel frightened so much as guilty and stupid. But charm had always been her stock-in-trade, and she tried to ply it now.

"I was heading over to Amanda Munroe's," she said with a smile. "I forgot something. I used your drive to turn around."

Peggy's eyes were hard. "Why are you snooping around that shed?"

In the distance a siren sounded. Neither woman paid it any attention.

"Shed?" Beverly said innocently. "Oh—*this*. I hardly noticed it. I saw this big, lovely bird in your pond. This is the loveliest pond, by the way. I said to myself, 'My word, is that a sandhill crane?' I got out to look, but it flew away. I love birds, don't you?"

Peggy's face didn't soften. "Birds?"

"It's wonderful to see you," Beverly babbled. "But I should go. I declare, a storm's coming."

She glanced at the sky. Dark, ragged clouds streamed, and the wind, somehow, had suddenly gone cold.

"Yes," Peggy said tightly. "I think you ought—"

But such a strong, cold gust blasted the air that her words were swallowed up by it. The gale was so violent that Beverly staggered. Dust flew, and all around her she heard the crash of branches breaking.

A rumbling roar surrounded them. It seemed to shake and rack the very heavens. The earth trembled.

Peggy stared up, her face white. Instinctively Beverly dropped to the ground. *A tornado!* she thought in alarm. The sound was exactly as Grandpa Hank had once described it, a freight train from hell.

The air was dark with flying dust, leaves, twigs, pebbles. Beverly's instinct was to roll with the wind the way a fighter rolls with a punch. She did, even though the briars tore at her.

Somehow she hurtled into the ditch, a fall that knocked the air from her lungs. She clutched the vines, buried her face in the dank leaves and prayed, her eyes shut tightly.

She heard the cannonade of immense breakage. Metal shrieked and smashed. There was the explosive shattering of glass, the groan of things wrenching asunder.

Everything seemed to be happening in agonizingly slow motion, and Beverly was sure this was because she was dying, and she was crowding all the life she could into her last seconds. Objects thudded about her; dirt and gravel rained down on her, and she tasted blood in her mouth.

She wished she hadn't quarreled with her mother; she wished she'd been kinder and warmer to her stepfather; more honest with Jeff, more honest with everyone. She wished she could see Sonny one more time, even for an instant, before she died. *Oh, yes, Sonny most of all.*

Then, abruptly, the chaos was over. The roar of the world ending dulled.

Water poured over her, an icy drowning tide. For a moment she thought the pond was flooding the ditch, and she was going to drown.

But the water was falling from the sky, as if some heavenly floodgate had been loosed. *Rain,* she thought in dull wonder. *It can't rain during a tornado. . . . Is it over?*

Shaking, she rose on her elbows, wiping her damp hair back. A concrete block lay just a few inches from her head. Another block lay near her feet, as did an uprooted cedar tree.

She brushed debris from her body. She saw that her hands and arms were badly scratched, but she felt no pain. She supposed that she was in some sort of shock. She sat up, intending to put her head between her knees to get blood flowing again to her brain.

Something glittering caught her eye, and she paused. It lay right beside her, inches from her knee. A syringe. The force of the driving rain had rent its paper wrapper, exposing the clear plastic cylinder.

Next to it was another drenched white tube—another syringe, its wrapper dissolving in the rain. Beyond that was another and other; they were scattered like confetti along the ditch. In their midst was a small set of barbells, half-driven into the soft earth.

Lightning flashed, making her flinch. Its reflection bounced from glass she hadn't noticed before. Among the spill of syringes were two vials of yellowish liquid and a bottle of pills, half-buried in the sodden leaves.

Syringes. She tried to think straight. *Vials. Pill bottles.* She crawled down the ditch a few feet and picked up a pill bottle. The label was blurred from the rain, but not illegible.

She wiped the water from her eyes again and squinted at the bottle. Xanabolin, it said on the label. The name was one she had heard Sonny mention more than once. *Steroids,* she thought, shaking. She'd found a cache of steroids.

A strange, unreal elation swept through her. She crawled farther, picked up another bottle. Xanabolin again.

Farther down the ditch she could see another, larger set of barbells and the front door of the shed, lying ripped off and twisted.

Carefully, Beverly put the bottles in the back pocket of her jeans. Then, gingerly, she tried to stand. Her legs were weak, but they held her.

Take it easy, she told herself. She recalled she had something important in her pocket, something important to tell people, but she couldn't quite remember what.

The rain soaked and chilled her, but she hardly minded. She thought it might be pleasant to lie down again, even among brambles and rubble and mud. She wanted Sonny. That was foremost. She wanted Sonny very much.

Then a scream rang out. It shot through her system like an electric shock.

Peggy, she thought in alarm. *Peggy Grimes is screaming.*

BELINDA DUGAN HAD her cassette player on full blast, the better to ignore Tap.

"Look," he finally said to her. "I know I've done a lot of things that hurt you. I've been stupid and insensitive and imperceptive. I've been a lout, a jerk and a turd. But do you have to play the Bee Gees?"

"It's my car," Belinda said from between her teeth. "And I happen to like this album."

Tap sat back in grim silence. She turned up the volume a notch. "Disco Inferno" was about to play.

They were no longer within sight of the bus. Halfway back from Fredericksburg, the bus had pulled over for gas. The driver had signaled Belinda to go on, that there was no need for her to keep following.

Relieved, she'd taken to the highway again. Tap's presence scalded her nerve ends. She wanted only to get back to school, let him out and escape the disturbing force field he always created.

She glanced worriedly at the sky. Clouds had appeared, acting strangely. They grew steadily darker, swirling and twisting. She was glad she had music to distract her.

The voice on the tape admonished everyone to "get down," and Tap groaned. "Did you ever see this movie?" he demanded. "John Travolta prancing around in that white suit?"

"I *liked* John Travolta," she said stubbornly.

"Look," Tap said, "I'm not joking. Why don't you shut off that tape and get the weather. I don't like the look of that sky—"

Even as he spoke, the clouds boiled more furiously, a fresh influx of white ones mixing with the angry black ones. Black and white surged and wrestled, mingling into dirty gray. The churning and roiling grew more violent.

Suddenly, a huge portion of cloud streamed downward, like a funnel pouring the sky's violence onto the earth.

My God! Belinda thought in stunned disbelief. A tornado had formed before their eyes. It was vast, surreal and danced straight toward them, right down the highway.

"Jesus!" Tap said, his voice awed. She couldn't tell if he was praying or swearing.

She'd instinctively braked the car. Paralyzed, she sat, watching the cloud do its devil dance toward them. Automatically, she unbuckled her seat belt, possessed by the urge to run away.

"Don't stop," Tap practically screamed in her ear. "Keep moving! Drive at right angles to it!"

In numb obedience, she stepped on the gas again, but lunged forward.

"Right angles! Right angles!" Tap yelled. But how did one drive at right angles? There was no road down which to escape. They were surrounded by flat, uneven ground that gave way to hills in the distance.

"There aren't any roads," she cried.

"Don't wait for a road," he ordered, "just go—"

She jerked the wheel violently to the left and the car jolted off the road.

"Another left," Tap shouted, but the front tires hit an outcropping of stone, and she lost control of the car. It leapt into the air and thudded down, lurching out of control.

Tap snatched the steering wheel and jerked it left with all his might. "Keep your foot on the gas," he told her. He kept wrenching the car's course: left two hundred yards, then hard right for almost as far, then hard left again, hard right.

The jolting zigzag path threw her first this way, then that. But the little car wasn't made for such punishment, and after Tap had careered right to avoid a creekbed, something in the car's steering audibly snapped.

Tap's arm shot out to keep her from flying forward as they plunged into a shallow creekbed and balanced for a terrifying second on two tires.

The car shuddered upright again with a jarring crash. Belinda was flung against Tap so hard that it knocked the air from her lungs, and her ribs cracked painfully against the steering wheel.

Somehow Tap was out of his seat belt, out of the car, and pulling her free. They were halfway to their knees in water; a cold wind tore at them, and a distant roaring filled her ears.

She tried to break away from him, to hide behind one of the boulders that guarded the creek bank, but he jerked her away, running and dragging her with him.

"The rocks!" she screamed, struggling to pull him back. "We can hide!"

"No! Funnels *like* water—they follow it—"

Blindly she tried to keep up with him, but she lost first one shoe, then the other. They were racing through a cactus patch. Spikes slashed her legs, punctured her feet. She stumbled, fell.

He swept her up and carried her. Dust stung her eyes, choking her. The roaring swept down on them. He dived toward a shallow ravine.

Once again the air was walloped from her chest, and she thought she might pass out. Tap threw his body atop hers, and then the might of the storm seemed to swallow everything up—herself, Tap, consciousness itself.

SONNY HAD DRIVEN into Crystal Creek watching the clouds with a distrustful eye. He was concerned about Beverly's safety. The Circle T was out in the open, the sort of unprotected cluster of buildings that tornadoes liked to seize and gobble.

He decided to phone her from the Longhorn, and swung off the main highway. The sky had grown darker, a sign that he hoped meant only more rain. He heard a siren.

The wind gusted; the car shook. The grass flattened before the wind, and small trees bent.

He slowed for a stop sign and watched as a young woman sprinted from a house, snatched a toddler from his makeshift sandbox and ran back inside.

He was ready to step on the accelerator again, when something strange happened. The large metal toy truck that had been left in the child's sandbox jumped straight up in the air as if bewitched, then flew away.

What the hell? thought Sonny.

A plastic trash can sailed past him, and suddenly the Chevy, though stopped, was flung sideways. It smashed against something that cracked his windshield. The impact vibrated through his bones.

A primal rumbling shook the world. The car rocked and shivered like a buffeted ship.

For a split second, an unearthly quiet fell, then vanished in the gush of torrential rain. The car stopped shivering. The windshield had turned into an impossibly complex spiderweb of fractures.

Flying glass had cut him, but nothing serious. He got out of the ruined car. He stood in the chill, driving rain. What he saw appalled him.

Broken trees littered the street, the sidewalks and lawns. One tree had been hurled through a picture window and rested, half in and half out of the house.

His car, smashed, had been thrown against a pickup truck that lay on its side. One corner of the truck's twisted tailgate rested against his shattered windshield.

Cars and trucks were askew in the street. One lay upside down and wedged against a fallen oak.

The wind had sucked the window glass out of most of the houses, and the windows stared blindly at the street. Three houses had been scalped, their roofs ripped away.

Above the drumming of the rain he heard screaming. A man, dazed, climbed out of the overturned pickup truck. Blood ran from his face, one eye was swollen shut, and his arm hung at an unnatural angle.

He stumbled toward Sonny, grasped him by the shirtfront, then sank to his knees. "Help me," he begged. "Help me." He collapsed, groaning.

Sonny knelt beside him, checking his pulse. He ripped off his own shirt, tore off a strip and began cleaning the cuts on the man's face and scalp.

"Help me," the man sobbed.

"It's okay," Sonny said from between his teeth. "I got you. I'm a doctor."

The man was Horace Westerhaus, and he was hurt, perhaps mortally.

FROM THE KITCHEN WINDOW, Carolyn Townsend Trent had seen her husband lead Outlaw into the barn. She'd smiled to herself. Vern was like a kid with that horse.

She shook her head and began filling the crystal nut dishes with sugared pecans. In the living room, she heard Consuela rattling the silverware as she set it out.

The party, Carolyn thought sadly. It was a tradition that she throw J.T.'s birthday party, but Beverly might not attend. She had slipped off, probably to meet that man. What could Carolyn tell people?

Still, she wished to heaven she hadn't spoken to Beverly as she had. But what she'd told her was true—no interracial marriage could be easy.

Before Beverly had met this Dekker man, she'd been anxious to please. Approval and admiration were life's blood to her. Somehow this man had changed her. Carolyn prayed to God that—

A sound like the world ending shook the house. The window glass rattled, the light fixture swayed. Carolyn looked up in alarm.

The house gave a powerful shake that hurled her to the floor. Amid the roar, she heard the shattering of glass and the groan of tearing wood.

My God, it's a tornado! Beverly! she thought in terror. *Where's Beverly? And Vern? My God, where's Vern?*

She did not know how long the terrible noise lasted. It seemed interminable; it seemed like hell itself.

The next thing she was conscious of was the sound of rain rushing like a river. Rain blew in the window, splashed her hair and bare arms.

Fearfully she looked up. A fine dust of plaster hung in the air, and everything in the kitchen was powdered with it, taking on a ghostly aura. Mixed nuts and candy littered the floor, and shards of shattered crystal glittered.

J.T.'s birthday party's ruined, she thought dully.

"Mrs. Trent! Mrs. Trent!" Consuela's voice sounded close to hysteria.

"I'm all right," Carolyn said, sitting and wiping her eyes. "Are you?"

"Sí, sí," Consuela wept, "but the barn, he is down! I saw this tail come out of the sky and sting it to death—explode it!"

The barn, he is down, she thought numbly. *This tail come out of the sky and sting it to death...*

Suddenly an image pierced Carolyn's daze: Vern leading Outlaw into the barn. She became aware that she heard the screaming of horses.

Carolyn scrambled up from the floor. "Vern!" she cried and ran to the door. She jerked it open and stared out in horror.

Where the barn had stood was only rubble. Its roof lay tilted over the wreckage. The rest of the building was a caved-in ruin of timbers and broken boards.

She ran toward the barn. She saw Outlaw, terrified, kick his way through the boards of one corner of the building that still stood. He bucked free, then fled, galloping down the lane.

She made her way to the boards he had kicked loose. "Vern?" she cried. "Vern?"

"Carolyn?"

She went almost faint with relief. She started to inch through the opening in the boards, but his voice stopped her. "Don't!"

His tone was so tense with warning that she stopped. "Vern? Are you all right?"

"Don't!" he said more forcefully. "It sounds like the rest of it's going to cave in—don't come in."

She strained her ears. Between the screams of the horses, she heard an ominous creaking. She didn't care about the danger, she stepped inside. She had to find Vern. Vern, then Beverly.

"God let him be safe," she prayed. "And Beverly. Make Beverly be safe."

The air was dark and full of dust. Above her she heard the creaking, more ominous now. She saw that one half-fallen beam had kept a large section of roof from slamming into the ground, crushing everything beneath it.

"Carolyn?"

Vern's voice was agonized. "Go back, Caro—for God's sake."

She saw him now. *Oh, God,* she thought dizzily. He lay on his stomach, his face turned toward her. A beam pinned him to the floor.

The next thing she knew she was at his side, kneeling in the wreckage. The beam groaned above them, straining against the weight of the collapsing wall.

"Vern," she said, grasping his hand. "It's all right, sweetie. I'll get some men, and we'll get this off you."

"Caro," he said, "I can't feel anything from my waist down. I think my damn back's broke. *Please* get out—"

The beam groaned and shifted. Then there was the crash of timber caving in on them in a deadly, clattering fall.

CHAPTER FIFTEEN

BEVERLY CLAMBERED up the ditch's side, then stood, dumbstruck. The shed that had stood near the ditch was gone. Only a few of the concrete blocks that had supported it were still in place.

Her Cadillac, its hood sprung, had a fallen tree lying across it. Peggy's car had vanished.

Then she heard violent sounds of choking and splashing. She whirled toward the pond. Its surface churned, and an arm rose out of the water, grasping at the air. Peggy's contorted face appeared, then sank beneath the surface again.

Beverly plunged into the pond. When the water came to her chest, she grimaced and started swimming. She saw Peggy's arm strike out, clawing air, and her face break the surface. She choked, screamed, then sank again.

Beverly dived. She locked her arm around the other woman's neck in something resembling a lifeguard's hold. She dragged Peggy to the surface and held her face out of the water.

But when she tried to swim toward shore with her, she couldn't. "I'm stuck!" Peggy half screamed, half choked.

"How?" demanded Beverly.

"In the car," Peggy panted. "My foot. It's stuck in the car."

Beverly tightened her grip and cautiously stretched her toes. They touched metal. "Wait," she said. "Stop fighting. I think I can stand."

Gingerly, she settled her weight on the sunken car. She felt blindly with one foot. The door was open, but Peggy's ankle seemed wedged between the seat and the interior of the center post.

Trying to trace her foot along Peggy's, she lost her balance. She went under, taking Peggy with her. When they surfaced, Peggy coughed and swore.

Beverly struggled to keep her feet on the car. It was as hard as treading water. Already her legs ached.

"Get me out of here," Peggy said, starting to cry. "My foot hurts. I think it's broken."

"Hush," Beverly said. "Let me think."

Peggy wept harder. "My foot's broken, and it's raining. What if the water rises? What if it gets so high I can't keep my head up?"

"Why can't you keep it up now?" Beverly asked. "Could I let you go? And go for help?"

"No!" Peggy screamed. "I can't. It's the angle—I have to use all my strength. If you let me go I'll die."

Beverly's mind spun. If she couldn't go for help, help would have to come to them. But who knew how long that might take? "Where's Roger?"

"Austin."

"When's he supposed to be back?"

"After five. He may have gotten caught in this—this thing. Oh, God, what if I'm a w-w-widow?" Peggy blubbered.

Mercy, Beverly thought, *I've never been in such a fix.* The rain poured down. Peggy cried, great racking sobs.

"I'd bawl, too," Beverly muttered in anger. "If help comes, they'll see steroids up and down that ditch. Needles, too. Roger's little stash isn't secret anymore."

"Oh, God," Peggy wailed. "If he isn't dead, they'll take him away."

It occurred to Beverly that as uncomfortable as the situation was, she had Peggy at her mercy. She could demand anything of her. Beverly said, "The law knows a thing or two about you. So do I. What about that place in Austin—Nutricentaur? Is that where the kids get the stuff? Or from Roger, too?"

"No!" Peggy cried. "Roger didn't sell them anything. Honest to God!"

"But you called in the prescriptions, right?" Beverly accused. "And used real DEA numbers."

"No—no. I didn't do anything."

"I don't believe you."

"Honest." Peggy sniffled. "I swear on my mother's grave—"

Beverly was so angry she saw a red mist. "Your mother's as alive as I am. Her grave? Tell it to the fish." She pushed Peggy and held her down a good thirty seconds before dragging her up again.

"Don't you lie to me," Beverly ordered. "I want the facts. Tell, or I'll make you drink this whole pond."

Sputtering, terrified, Peggy Grimes began to tell the truth.

BELINDA LAY STUNNED in the dirt. The storm had passed, rain was falling, but she couldn't move.

Tap's body covered hers. His weight kept her from breathing deeply, but she didn't care. The simple human warmth of him was so comforting she didn't want to move.

The rain was cold, the dirt beneath them damp and sticky. She didn't care. They were alive.

The icy rain sluiced over them, and even Tap's body couldn't keep her dry. She was cold all over, except her neck. Something hot and sticky seeped against her neck.

"Tap?" she managed to say. "Is it really over?"

He didn't answer.

Her eyes fluttered open. A small, frigid rivulet ran down the ditch, lapping coldly against her cheek. The tiny stream was stained with red that turned to pink, then faded back to the muddy color of the water.

She watched it dully. *Blood,* she realized with a jolt. *Blood is running into the water.*

She touched her jaw, then examined her fingers with horror. They were scarlet with blood.

"Tap?" she said, frightened. "Who's hurt? You—or me?"

He didn't answer.

She squirmed from beneath his weight, struggled to a sitting position. His eyes were half open, focused on nothing. Blood flowed from his neck in a steady stream. His throat was cut.

"Tap!" she cried.

Using all her strength, she pulled him onto her lap. He was pale, his skin colder than hers. "My God, Tap," she said, "talk to me. Can you hear me?"

His eyes opened wider, looked blearily up at her. "Yo, Dugan. I mean—Belinda. You okay, little buddy?"

"I'm fine," she said, tears in her eyes. "But you're bleeding. What happened?"

He swallowed, shut his eyes. "Something hit me."

She unbuttoned her blouse, ripped it off and folded it into a compress. "Bleeding can almost always be stopped," she said, her voice shaking. "I learned that in Girl Scouts."

She pressed the cloth hard against his neck. She searched for the pulse of his carotid artery and put her other hand against it, applying pressure.

"So," he said, wincing with pain. "You were a Girl Scout. Didya sell a lot of cookies?"

Oh, Lord, she thought, only Tap would try to joke at a time like this. "Tons. I was the best cookie seller in Texas."

He stirred restlessly, as if fighting pain. "I bet you were," he said. "I bet—" He half rose and clutched her bare arm convulsively.

"Tap, be still," she begged.

"Jeez, little buddy," he said. "Something's wrong. More than my neck. Something's broken inside."

She forced him to lie back in her lap. "Shh. Hold still. You'll make it worse."

He'd kept hold of her arm. "You're warm. Jesus, this rain. If I don't die, I'll drown."

She bent above him, trying to shield him. "Do you know what happened? What hit you?"

"No. God!" He squeezed her arm so tightly that it hurt. "Talk to me," he said. "Okay? When I close my eyes I see this guy in black. Talk to me."

"A guy in black?" she said.

"Yeah," he panted. "Maybe it's Johnny Cash. What do you think?"

"Shh," she said. "Shh."

She struggled to keep the compress in place, her fingers against his. She looked about wildly.

The highway was deserted. Her car lay on its side, barely recognizable, smashed against boulders.

She stared down helplessly at Tap. If she went for help, he would bleed to death. She bit her lip and forced herself to stay calm.

"It felt—like somebody shot me," he said. "We were going down into the ditch. It just hit."

"Where?"

"My neck. My neck and my back, the left side."

"Let me see." She took her hand from his artery, ran it under his back. She found another sticky spot.

"Yes," she said. "You're bleeding there. It feels like a puncture wound. Maybe it was flying metal from the car or something."

He coughed. A pinkish froth bubbled at his lips. *Oh, God,* she thought. *He's bleeding internally. I can't do anything. Help has to come. Please, God, send help. Don't let him die.*

CAROLYN THREW her body across Vern's as the boards rained down. One struck her across the shoulders, so hard that she cried out.

"I love you," she said to Vern and waited to be crushed to death. But no more boards fell. She lay against his back, feeling both their hearts pound.

The beam creaked above them. A horse screamed, that terrible sound she couldn't get used to.

"Caro, are you all right?"

Her shoulders aching, she sat up, looked at the fresh rubble and thanked God that they were still alive.

She took his hand. "I'm fine."

He squeezed her hand hard. "Get out, Caro. Next time we may not be so lucky."

"I won't leave you."

"Think of Beverly."

"Beverly," she said, dazed. "I don't know where she is."

"Mrs. Trent!" The fearful voice was Consuela's.

"I'm here. Vern's trapped. Get help. Get an ambulance."

"Mrs. Trent, the roof on the house. She went up, she came down again. The roof is sitting crooked, and the curtains, they are hanging out of it."

"I don't care," Carolyn snapped. "Get help."

"¡Sí!"

The horse screamed again, and Carolyn shut her eyes, not wanting to imagine the creature's suffering.

"Caro, leave," Vernon begged.

"I'll never leave you," she swore. "Never." She lifted his hand and kissed it.

"I can't move my legs. I can't feel them."

She kissed his hand again. "We'll get you to a doctor. The best we can find."

"I don't want to be only a half a man for you."

"You're all man, and the only one I want. Don't talk that way."

"Get out. Do it for me. Please."

She smoothed his hair back from his forehead. "Shh. We'll both get out of this."

Above them the beam creaked.

EVERYWHERE SONNY LOOKED, there was destruction.

He'd carried Horace Westerhaus to the nearest porch to get him out of the rain. A steel splinter had pierced his skull, and Sonny suspected it might lie dangerously close to his brain. Yet he was conscious and in great pain.

A sixtyish woman came out of the house, a remarkably calm woman, for which Sonny thanked the gods.

She said she'd been a nurse. She had some pain pills left over from having a tooth pulled. Sonny mentally blessed her again and had her give two painkillers to Horace.

She had a first-aid kit, as well. They dressed Horace's wounds and splinted his arm as best they could.

By that time, somebody had recognized him as a doctor. A weeping woman carrying a child came running to him. The child had been hit by flying glass. Sonny removed it. "It's okay, Buddy," he said, "you're a brave guy. That's it, tiger."

The retired nurse, Hedda Wagner, made the mother sit and put her head between her knees. "Good heavens!" Hedda gasped. "She's got a piece of glass sticking out of her back like a dagger. She's so upset about the child, I don't think she even felt it."

"Let me have her," Sonny said. "Can you take the kid? She's more serious."

Hedda's next-door neighbor staggered over, leading his wife. They, too, had both been cut by flying glass, and the woman's wrist was sprained.

He worked frantically to tend them all.

A terrified-looking boy of eight or nine ran to Hedda's porch. He seized Sonny's arm. "My mama's having a baby," he said. "Come help."

Oh, God, Sonny thought and let the boy lead him to a small frame house. As they crossed the lawn, a middle-aged woman ran up to him. She grabbed his free arm. "You're a doctor? My father—he's had some kind of attack. I think it's his heart. You've got to come."

Next door a man staggered onto his porch. He clutched the railing and cried out. "My wife—help! I can't stop the bleeding! Somebody help, for God's sake!"

Sonny glanced across the street and thanked God that Hedda was back on her porch. He called to her, "We got a bleeder! Help her, will you?"

He patted the little boy's hand. "You tell your mother to hang on, okay? There's a sick guy I got to see. I'll be with your mom as soon as I can. Don't worry. Everything'll be fine."

Someone was screaming. "I can't find Leo! I can't find Leo!"

A woman sat on the curb sobbing, her face in her hands.

It's like a goddamn battlefield, Sonny thought. He could only pray that Beverly was all right.

PEGGY SUE SPILLED out much of the story. Roger had introduced certain members of the team to steroids when he came to Crystal Creek, three years ago. He had four pharmacists in Austin who would supply the drugs, including one at Nutricentaur. She admitted Roger used steroids, but refused to say for how long.

"The whole truth," Beverly snarled, tightening her hold on Peggy's neck. "I'm cold and wet, and I'm in a bad mood. How long has he used them?"

"Don't push me under again—please! Years. He's used them for years. They never hurt him. He didn't mean to hurt anybody else. He just wanted the team to win. He did it for the kids."

Beverly was sickened. "Why'd you lie about your family?"

"Roger didn't want anybody in touch with them," Peggy said, weeping again. "Why're you torturing me?"

"Why didn't he want them in touch?"

"They don't like him."

"Why?"

"They just don't."

Beverly moved as if to dunk her again. "Do you want to inhale some minnows?"

"No!" Peggy sobbed. "I left my first husband for Roger. I couldn't help it. He cast a spell on me. I'm innocent."

Beverly was filled with contempt for the woman. Somehow there was a child tangled up in all this. "You have a little boy, don't you? Your mother told me. You lied about that, too, didn't you? Why'd you leave your own child?"

"I told you," Peggy said, crying harder. "Roger made me. He didn't want a kid. I couldn't help it."

"If you were married, how'd you get involved with Roger?"

"I was working out. At a gym. He had the most beautiful body I ever saw. He cast a spell on me."

Beverly's lip curled in disdain. "Were you really in a car wreck?—the truth."

"No. Roger told me to say that."

"Why'd you lie about not being able to get pregnant?"

"Roger made me."

"You're going to be sucking pond scum in two seconds."

"Don't! I wanted people to feel sorry, to like me. That's all. I wanted people to like me."

You wanted to use people, Beverly thought. *And you had them all twisted around your little finger. Even Nate.*

"Did you really lose a baby?"

"Yes," Peggy wailed righteously. "It was Sonny Dekker's fault. Everybody knows it."

Beverly's heart was hardened. The woman was a pathological liar, a shameless manipulator, and she'd dragged Sonny into her web of deceit.

She didn't hesitate. She pushed Peggy underwater again and kept her there a good, long time. Then she hauled her back up. "That baby," she snapped. "The truth."

"All right!" Peggy sputtered. "I lied. Roger told me to say it. So people would feel sorry. Like they did for Ruth McKinney. He doesn't want kids. He doesn't want me to ruin my shape."

Suddenly, through the sound of the drumming rain, another sound came. A car was making its way down the lane.

Thank God, Beverly thought. Her legs ached, her arms were cramping, she was frozen and exhausted. All she wanted was to get home and make sure that Carolyn and Vern were all right. And Sonny. Desperately, more than anything, she wanted Sonny.

The sound of the car drew closer.

"Somebody's coming," Peggy said. "Roger. He'll save me. He'll make you sorry."

Fear shot through Beverly. If Roger Grimes was approaching, she was in trouble, very big trouble indeed.

SHIVERING, SHIRTLESS, Belinda sat in the rain, holding Tap. He was worse, she could tell. She'd had to rip up his dress shirt to use as an added compress. He lay, soaked, in his T-shirt that said TUNE IT OR DIE!

"You—you must be cold," Tap said, his teeth chattering.

"It's okay," she said. A spasm shook him, and she hugged him to keep him still.

When his shuddering subsided, he spoke, his voice strained. "Listen," he said, touching her arm. "I want to tell you something. If this had to happen, I'm glad it's you here. It's rotten for you, I know. But I'm glad it's you."

"Don't talk," she said. She knew he was only trying to make her feel good. *Oh, Tap, who wouldn't love you?*

He gripped her arm, his grasp surprisingly strong. "No. I am. Glad it's you. I was dumb."

"Shh," she said. "You don't have to say that."

"I want to. I've thought a lot about you. I—I dream of you. This whole last week. Sexy dreams. You're very pretty and sexy, you know?"

Another shudder ran through him. "Pretty and sexy," he said tightly. "I—I should have grabbed you when you gave me a chance. I was a damn fool."

"Tap, don't," she said, fighting back tears. "I threw myself at you. I should be the one apologizing, not you."

He shook his head, but the movement seemed to cause him pain. He grimaced. "No. I dreamed about you. Really. It was never better with anybody than you. You didn't act like it was just sex. You acted like it was l-love."

She swallowed hard. "I did it because I liked you so much. I don't regret it. Not really."

"Yeah," he said. "You did. I made you regret it. I was a first-class jackass. And then—just when I drove you off for good, I realized I wanted you."

Her heart jumped painfully. "You don't have to say these things."

"I'm not lying," he said. He gave her a crooked smile that was mixed with pain. "I don't think I got the leisure to lie. Will you forgive me? Can you?"

"I'd forgive you anything."

"Kiss and make up?" he asked, blinking against the rain.

"Kiss and make up," she said. She bent over him, placed her lips against his. His were cold.

"You're so warm," he said when she drew away. He winced in pain, his face twisting and his eyes shutting hard. When he opened them again, there was a wild look in their depths.

"I saw him again." The words seemed to stick in his throat. "The dude in black. Talk to me. Say anything."

"No dude in black is going to take you," she said, trying to keep her voice from shaking. "I won't let him."

A CAR PULLED into the clearing. It was not Roger Grimes's red Corvette. It was a gray compact, and the driver was Chuck Cooper. Barry Armbruster was with him. Chuck's mouth fell open when he saw the women in the pond. The two boys got out of the car and stood staring.

"Chuck!" cried Peggy. "Help! I'm trapped and she's trying to drown me—"

"Hush, you lying cat," Beverly snapped. "Barry, honey, we're in a fix. You come hold Peggy. I can't last much longer. Chuck, you drive me to town to get help, hear?"

"Jeez," Barry said, wading into the pond. "What the hell happened?"

"Her car got thrown in here," Beverly said. "Her foot's stuck. And my arms are like to fall off, holding her up."

"Jeez," he said again and swam to her side. He took Peggy from her grasp in a lifeguard's carry that was far more proficient than Beverly's. "Miz Grimes?" he said. "Are you okay?"

"No," she gasped. "That woman's making up stories about me. And you. All of you. She's vicious."

"The car's under us," Beverly said, ignoring her. "You can stand on it so you don't have to tread water all the time."

"Push her under—drown her!" Peggy screamed. "She's going to ruin us all. Stop her!"

Barry's mouth fell open again. He stared at Peggy.

"Stop her, you moron!" Peggy said. "She's going to ruin you. Drown her!"

"I can't do that," Barry said, clearly horrified.

Beverly swam away. She reached shore and staggered to the car. Peggy screamed, "Stop her! Don't let her leave! Kill the bitch! Stop her!"

Beverly leaned against Chuck's car and stared at the white-faced boy. "Well, Chuck," she said grimly. "Are you going to kill me?"

"No, ma'am," Chuck said, wide-eyed.

"Good," she said and shook the water from her hair. "Then let's get help."

A TOTAL OF NINE ranch hands, along with Carolyn and Consuela, labored to haul the weight of fallen boards from the single beam that protected Vern.

Mope Grizzard had said it would be easier to drag Vern out, but Carolyn refused to take the chance. If

Vern's back was broken, they might kill him moving him.

Carefully, nervously, they worked. Carolyn labored as hard as any of the men. She pulled away boards that ripped her hands with splinters and strained her muscles. She had but one thought: *Save Vern.*

She wept when they uncovered the horses. Three had been caught in the collapsing barn.

Two had died, and the third had two broken legs. It was Button, the first horse Beverly had ever ridden alone. Carolyn had to turn away when Mope shot it.

Beverly would cry when she learned Button was dead. *Beverly,* Carolyn thought, distraught. *Where's my Beverly?*

She bent and wrested up another piece of broken lumber, cast it out of the way.

"You be careful, Miz Townsend," Mope said. "You shouldn't do this. It ain't woman's work."

"I want my husband," Carolyn answered. And she went on dragging the heavy lumber, not caring that her hands bled.

"WHAT WAS SHE talking about, that you'd destroy us and stuff?" Chuck Cooper asked nervously.

Beverly was too tired to lie, and she refused to be frightened by a mere boy. "She means I know about the stupid steroids, Chuck," she said, leaning back against the headrest. "She told me almost everything. Except how many of you were involved. The truth's out. Finally. You want to tell me how many others were doing it beside you and Barry and Lester?"

Chuck was silent for a moment. "There were nine others. What'll happen to them?"

She sighed in exasperation. "We'll try to help them. If they'll let us."

"It was hard to quit," he said, his voice pained. "I hurt all over. I felt lousy. I felt terrible."

"You know what's sad?" she asked. "You all thought you were so great, so strong, so unbeatable. You weren't. You're victims. All you big, strong men, you're victims. I hope they throw the book at Roger Grimes."

Chuck sounded as if he was going to cry. "He told us to do it. He said we *should*. Especially me. He used to call me 'skinny' and 'wimp.' He kept calling Lester 'lard ass.' He told us to try stackin'. He gave us a Mexican address, so we could get more. Chuck and me and Lester all did. Coach said it wasn't cheatin'. Everybody does it, he said. He said, 'You want to be a wimp or a man?' I mean, what's a guy supposed to do?"

But then he had stopped talking and braked the car to a halt. The road was impassable. Utility poles were down, obstructing it, and a snaky tangle of wires twisted and sparked. The entrance to Crystal Creek was blocked and deadly.

SONNY PERFORMED CPR on the heart victim. He pounded his chest, he breathed in his mouth, he willed the man to cling to life. And cling to life he did.

"We'll get him to a hospital," he told the man's weeping daughter. "He's got a good chance. He's fighting. He's got spirit."

Then he went to check on the woman in labor. She lay on a couch, surrounded by broken glass from the living room's front windows. The baby was coming fast, too fast. He started to roll up his shirtsleeves, then realized he no longer wore a shirt, only a bloodstained T-shirt.

He knelt beside the couch, put his hand on the woman's sweaty brow. "It's all right," he said. "There was a tornado, but your house is standing. Your boy's fine. You're fine. I'm a doctor. I'll take care of you. How far along are you? Can you tell me?"

"I'm overdue," she panted. "Two weeks. Where's Nate Purdy? You're the Chinese one."

"Yeah," he said, trying to put her at ease. "If you have a pretty little girl, I'll give you a fortune cookie. Bear down. We're going to be fine here, just fine."

CHUCK SWORE and backed up the car. "We'll try another way," he said tensely.

Beverly's mind seemed under an eerie enchantment. She could think coldly and logically about some things, and others she did not allow to touch her consciousness. She was afraid to think about her mother and Vern.

She had to believe they were fine, untouched. Carolyn especially had always seemed immortal to her, too strong to be hurt by anything. As for the level of destruction she and Chuck saw, she did not let it register.

"You and Barry," she said to Chuck, "why were you at the Grimeses'?"

"Barry and me, we were just ridin' around," he said. "We saw the funnel come out of the sky. We saw a chicken house explode. Bam! It disappeared. Nothin' but feathers."

"You weren't scared?"

"Heck, yes," Chuck said. "I almost wet my pants. But what can you do? We were closer to the Grimeses' house than any place else. We stopped to see if they were all right."

"What about your family?"

He swallowed. "I don't know. Jeez, this way's blocked, too. Look at that phone pole. Those wires could be live. I'm not drivin' over that."

Two more utility poles were down, and wires lay crookedly across the road, hissing and crackling.

Impatiently Beverly raked her hand through her wet hair. "Try a different way," she ordered. "Your friend's back there up to his chin in cold water. Get me to the fire department. They'll know how to get her out."

"What if we can't get into town?" Chuck asked.

Beverly's head ached as if it were inhabited by a troll wielding a jackhammer. Decisions, decisions, why did she have to make them all?

"We'll do what we have to do," she said. She sounded braver than she felt. She wanted her home, her mother, Vern. Her only comfort was that Sonny was safe in Dallas, spared this madness.

SONNY LOST TRACK of the people he'd treated. What he remembered most vividly was the newborn baby, a lusty boy, at least eight pounds, healthy, and screaming his head off.

Then there was a young girl with a nosebleed that wouldn't stop. He stopped it.

There was a broken leg. He splinted it. There was a wounded scalp. He sewed it. There was a cut hand. He bandaged it.

There was a woman trapped in the second story of her house. Somebody produced a ladder, and he climbed up after her. Somehow, he got hit across the neck by a loose piece of drainpipe.

His throat was slashed open. He looked at the blood, realized it was from a vein, not an artery, so he wasn't in big trouble. He ripped off his T-shirt, knotted it around his bleeding neck and climbed into the window.

The woman was close to hysteria. Sonny caught her in his arms, held her tightly. "It's okay, it's okay," he told her.

"Doc!" a voice shouted from below. "We got a kid with a broken elbow. We need you. We need you *now*."

CHUCK AND BEVERLY couldn't find a way into town. Chuck finally took a circuitous route to a wreckage and salvage company.

"There's a woman trapped," Beverly told the salvage man, almost sobbing. "Her foot's caught in the car. She's in a pond, and a boy's trying to keep her safe. But somebody's got to help, to cut her free. Can you do it? Do you have a torch?" she pleaded. "One that would work underwater?"

"I've salvaged things out of the middle of the Pedernales River," the man said proudly. "But I ain't leavin' here. Thiefs could rob me blind."

"I'll guard the place," Beverly promised him. "My daddy taught me to shoot a rifle."

He stared at her, unimpressed. "I'm not leaving my place to be guarded by no woman."

"Then he'll guard it," Beverly said desperately, pointing at Chuck.

"Hey!" Chuck said in protest.

The man eyed him suspiciously. "Can you shoot, kid?"

"Well, yeah, but—"

"Okay. I'll get the shotgun. But if you ain't here when I get back, I'll hunt you down and turn you inside out. You hear me, boy?"

After the man had been given directions and left in his clattering truck, Chuck gave Beverly a resentful look. Once more he looked as if he might cry. He swallowed hard. "Why'd you do that? I want to go home. I want to see if my folks are all right."

She felt sorry for him, knowing exactly how scared and shaken he felt. Tears stung her eyes, and she was trembling with cold and fatigue.

"He wouldn't trust me to do it," she said. "I had to say you would. You can go. I'll take responsibility. But if you can get to my place, tell my folks I'm here, and I'm all right. Would you?"

Chuck cradled the shotgun uncomfortably in his arms. He looked her up and down. Then his eyes held hers for a long moment. Something strange and intimate seemed to vibrate between them.

He swallowed again. "No," he said tightly. "I'll stay. You been through enough. Take my car. But if you can get to my family's place, tell them I'm okay, will you?"

"No, Chuck," she said. "I got you into this, and I won't let you—"

"No," he said, drawing himself up to his full height. "You said I was a victim. Maybe I was. So let me be a man now, all right? Let me respect myself for something. You go. I'll stay. I should have volunteered in the first place."

He meant it, she could tell. She went to him, took his chin in her hand and stared into his eyes. "Thank you," she said softly.

She kissed him, because she somehow knew it was the right thing to do.

"You're a hero, you know that?" she said. "You keep your life on track from here on out, all right? Because things are always supposed to work out right for heroes."

She kissed him again, this time goodbye. Then she set out, trying to find a road to take her home.

CHAPTER SIXTEEN

SHERIFF WAYNE JACKSON found Sonny on Hedda Wagner's front porch, sewing an elderly man's shin wound. Sonny was bare-chested, with a bloody T-shirt wrapped around his neck.

"My God," Wayne said in wonder. "A real live doctor. In one piece. I thought you were gone. I need you like hell."

"Get me an ambulance," Sonny told Wayne. "I got two heart cases, a concussion and a new baby."

Wayne swore softly. "This street's bad. But downtown's worse. What's wrong with your neck?"

"It's nothing," said Sonny. "Attaboy," he said to his patient. "You're a man of iron."

"Sonny, come on," Wayne said. "I'm not screwing around. I need you bad."

"I told you—I need an ambulance. I got at least four patients that should be in the hospital."

Wayne's expression was strange, as if the big man himself was fighting shock. "There isn't any hospital," he said. "It got hit."

"*What?*" Sonny demanded.

Wayne said, "The hospital got hit. And the firehouse. We don't have an ambulance. It couldn't be worse."

"How bad is it? Anybody dead?"

"Four, at least," Wayne said. "All patients. We're still digging. And both doctors are out."

"What do you mean, out?"

"I mean *out*," said Wayne. "Womesh Godbole got durn near killed. A wall came down on him. He's laying on a table in the basement of the Baptist church with nurses trying to patch him up. He's hurt bad."

A sick frisson of alarm tingled through Sonny's system. "What about Nate?"

"He's in a bad way. I don't know if he'll make it."

Sonny swore, feeling sicker than before. "You've called for emergency help?"

"Austin can't get to us. Twister took the bridge out over the Claro River. Claroville's hit hard, too. I can't raise Blanco."

Sonny pushed his hand through his hair in exasperation. "Hedda!" he yelled. "Hedda?"

She came to the screen door. She'd turned her home into the neighborhood sick ward, God love her.

"Yes?" she said.

"The hospital's hit. I'm going there. Consider yourself block captain. I'll get back to you if I can."

"Right," she said. "Take care of your neck."

He nodded. He went with Wayne to the sheriff department car. Sonny shot a grim glance at the devastation up and down the street. "Is the rest of the town this bad?"

"No," Wayne said. "Except for downtown, this is the worst I've seen. Mainly, the hospital and the firehouse took the punishment. The fire truck's buried, and the ambulance is wrapped around the corner of the bank. God, what a mess."

"How many hurt?"

"I can't count 'em," Wayne said, "And I don't know when we'll get help, or where we'll get it from. Right now, you're the only doctor we got. And let me tell you, friend. It's hell."

AN OLD COWBOY in a pickup truck found Tap and Belinda. Tap had passed out, and Belinda was sure he was dying.

The rain had slacked off. Half-naked, she shivered and stared up at the stranger. He stood in the drizzle, gray-haired and unshaved, looking at her as if she were a creature from another planet.

"Please help," she begged. "I don't know what to do. Do we dare move him?"

"Girly," the man said, taking off his shirt, "I don't think we got much choice. Here, cover yourself up."

He put his shirt around her shoulders. "I'll drive the truck over here. We'll put him in back. You keep pressure on him. If we ain't got a road, we'll do without. We'll do hard travelin', little sister, but it's all we can do."

She nodded, flooded with gratitude at his kindness, his determination. She didn't know his name or where he had come from, but his simple humanity was like a gift from heaven itself.

SONNY FELT SICK to his stomach when he saw the hospital. The second story of the east side had caved in. The roof was partly torn off. A hospital bed, its frame tangled, hung out a second-story window.

Next door, the firehouse was in shambles, its roof lying upside down across the drive. Its flagpole was jerked halfway out of the ground and bent like a hairpin.

"Jesus," Sonny said.

"Yeah," Wayne muttered, "I've been talkin' to Him, too. This is bad."

"They're taking the injured to the church?"

"Yeah. The hospital's structurally unsafe. And there's people in there we haven't found yet. I don't know if they're dead or alive."

Sonny narrowed his eyes. A small group of volunteers and sheriff's deputies were searching through the rubble, trying to find survivors.

"I haven't got enough men," Wayne said helplessly. "We need to dig out the hospital, but we should be checking out the whole county. There may be places hit worse than this, God forbid."

"The east side of the building," Sonny said. "Did we lose the blood supply?"

"Yeah," Wayne said, pulling up in front of the church. "No ambulance. No hospital. No blood."

Sonny pulled the T-shirt tighter around his bleeding neck. "Okay," he said, looking at the ruined hospital. "That's what we don't have. What are our assets?"

"About twelve damn good nurses," Wayne said. "A couple of orderlies, two paramedics. Some medicine and surgical equipment. Some anesthesia. And you."

BEVERLY HAD to abandon the car. The road to the Circle T was badly torn up, and the broken pavement flattened two tires.

All right, I'll walk, she thought with determination. But she was starting to feel more and more like a woman moving through a nightmare. She was exhausted.

Chunks of the familiar landscape had been torn away. Trees were broken off, uprooted. Some of the houses she'd passed were untouched, but others were battered, their roofs askew, windows shattered.

No traffic was on the road, and she despaired of anyone finding her to give her a ride. She started cutting across fields to take a straighter route to her mother's ranch. The terrain was uneven, but she didn't care. All she wanted was to be home and for Sonny to come to her.

Sonny, Sonny, Sonny, she thought. She wanted his presence as much as food or drink or rest. Wanting him was so primal she wondered how she had ever doubted the strength of her need for him.

Trudging through a thin rain, she reached the old Heller place, deserted for years. Guy Heller had given it to Crystal Creek, and the town was considering turning the property into a rose garden once it raised money to tear the house down.

It no longer had to raise money. The house was reduced to rubble.

Beverly stared at it dully. She refused to think that this might have happened to her own home. She had to get to the ranch. To find her mother and to be found by Sonny. *Sonny, I need you. I can't keep on being brave.*

It was then that she saw what should not have been at the scene—a small, white car, nearly hidden by the wreckage of the house.

And it was then that she heard the cry for help, faint but eerie with desperation.

MOPE GRIZZARD had ingeniously engineered the removal of the rubble and collapsing roof that menaced Vern. He and the other men managed to lift the beam that pinned Vern and heave it aside.

Carolyn knelt at Vern's side. A truck pulled into the lane, and she recognized the man she'd sent for an ambulance. He stepped from the truck, his face grim.

"Where's the ambulance?" she demanded. "Is it coming?"

"There ain't none," he said.

"What do you mean?" Carolyn snapped. "We have to get him to the hospital."

"There ain't none," he repeated. "There ain't no ambulance, and there ain't no hospital no more. The town's hit bad. I was lucky to get back. Everybody wants help. I passed a car wreck, a bad one. I shoulda stopped. I didn't. I come back."

Carolyn stared at him in anger and bewilderment. "My husband needs a doctor."

"There's not enough. One got purt' near killed, and the other's not much better. That Chinese feller's the only one, and he can't leave. He's tryin' to get an ambulance set up. He's doin' his best. But, ma'am, it's hell there."

She stared at him, stunned. *That Chinese feller.* A few hours ago she had felt herself superior to Sonny Dekker, had wanted to hold herself and her family apart from him.

Now he was her only hope.

THE BASEMENT of the Baptist Church looked like an army hospital after a ghastly battle. The nurses had initiated a triage system. The most critically hurt patients were taken into the church, others sent to the elementary school, where a first-aid station had been set up.

The first thing Sonny did was bark orders for an ambulance—he said to outfit a hearse, a delivery truck, a van, anything. He didn't care. He couldn't spare a paramedic to go with it, but he had to. There was no choice.

The next thing he did was check Nate Purdy. Nate had thoracic injuries and was going to suffocate without an emergency tracheotomy. Sonny had no choice. He scrubbed up and did the best he could. He offered up a prayer of gratitude when he heard the sigh and suck of air rushing into Nate's lungs.

Next, he tended Dr. Womesh Godbole. The man was badly injured, but the nurses had patched him up remarkably well. Sonny removed a sliver of broken board that had pierced his lung and drew the air out of his chest cavity. He gave orders to find blood donors. Godbole would need a transfusion, and so would Nate.

Next was a paramedic, Farron Olsen, with a broken arm. He gave the man a shot of painkiller, set his arm and put him to work. "Jeez," Farron said, stumbling to his feet. "This is like the end of the world. Where do we start?"

"Just start," Sonny said.

BEVERLY DUG in the rubble, throwing boards aside. It was rough work, but she could not allow herself to slow. She was certain that she heard two voices crying. She lost track of time and didn't even realize that her face was wet with tears of fatigue.

Then, suddenly, she lifted a board, and there, as if by magic, lay a baby, perhaps a year old. It cried weakly. Its face was scratched, but otherwise it seemed whole and remarkably free from hurt. She snatched it up and held it tightly.

"Help me," a woman's voice whispered, seeming to rise out of the earth itself.

I can't go on, Beverly thought. *I haven't got any more strength.* But desperately she dug back into the wreckage, more awkwardly now, because she had the baby in one arm. The infant clenched its fists and wailed in protest.

At last Beverly uncovered a badly scraped arm that moved feebly. She kept tearing at the wreckage until she uncovered the woman's shoulder, chest and head.

But then she could dig no more. The timbers were too heavy, and the woman was trapped. Beverly was helpless to do more.

She seized the woman's hand and held it fast.

"My baby," the woman gasped, clinging to her. "How is he?"

"He seems fine, only scratched," Beverly said.

Oh, what, *what* in the name of heaven was she going to do now? She'd been through too much, she could take no more. She wanted Sonny. She wanted him more than she'd wanted anything in her life.

"Don't leave me," the woman begged. "I'm afraid to be alone. Don't leave me."

"I'm here," Beverly assured her. But her mind whirled. Who was this woman? How badly hurt was she? And how would anyone ever find them in this forsaken spot?

And how I can get home, now that I have this woman and this baby? she thought in despair.

The woman gripped Beverly's hand so hard that it hurt. "Don't leave me," she said again. "I'm scared."

"I'm here," Beverly said. The child cried more loudly and the cold rain drizzled down.

I'm in hell, she thought.

WAYNE JACKSON CAME into the hospital basement, carrying a small, weeping woman who clutched her side. "Busted ankle, she's in a lot of pain," he said, setting her down carefully. "We got a duplex caved in over on Cedar Street. Don't know who else is under there. And I'm out of men. Flat out."

"Get the football team," Sonny snapped, not even looking up from the patient he was treating.

"What?"

"Get the football team," Sonny repeated. "They're big, they're strong, they can take orders. Deputize 'em or something. The basketball team, too. The Scouts. Let's get this mess organized."

"Damn," Wayne said. "You're right. I'm not thinkin' straight. I keep worrying about my wife. Nobody seems to know where—"

"And I told you, get me a hearse, a van, anything. I've got to have an ambulance. At least four people on Persimmon Street need it. And God knows who else. There's a back case at one of the ranches. Ask Glenda, she's got the details, I don't. I need somebody there who knows how to move a back case."

"Right. Right."

"Get me anybody with first-aid experience. Anybody, young or old. And get on the radio and get me some blood."

There was a commotion as a big, dirty-looking man came in carrying Peggy Sue Grimes. Barry Armbruster followed, pale-faced and shivering. Peggy's left foot dangled uselessly. She was semiconscious.

"She was trapped in a car," the big man said. "Thought I was gonna have to take her foot off to get her out. She's hurt pretty bad."

Sonny swore under his breath. The foot looked cruelly injured, and he knew he was going to have to fight to save it. He signaled for an orderly to take her.

"Mister—" Barry Armbruster said.

"Hey, you're both big guys," Sonny said. "They need all the help they can get at the hospital. Get over there, will you? Just get."

He was so forceful that both the man and boy nodded and headed toward the door. "Hell," the big man said to Barry. "We're already heroes, huh, kid? Might as well go whole hog."

Then, like an apparition, Belinda Dugan appeared. She wore a man's shirt and looked so waiflike that Sonny didn't recognize her at first. She was pale and in tears.

"Sonny," she said, "Tap's outside. I think he's dying."

Fear twisted his stomach. Up to now, he'd made himself work like a machine, had cut off his feelings.

"What happened? Farron! Take a look at the Grimes woman's foot."

Then to Belinda he said, "Take me to him." He seized her hand and almost dragged her up the steps. In the truckbed, Tap lay motionless in a pool of his own blood. A grizzled old cowboy held a sodden compress in place.

"Sweet Christ," Sonny muttered and vaulted into the truck. He checked the vital signs. They were faint and irregular.

He turned him over. Tap had a puncture wound in his back between his bottom two ribs on the left side. It looked deep enough to kill.

"No, Tap! Please, buddy," he breathed.

No patient he'd seen on this hellish afternoon was as close to death as Tap Hollister.

CHAPTER SEVENTEEN

ALL SONNY HAD was a makeshift operating room in the kitchen of the church. But he still had an anesthesiologist, two good surgical nurses and a fair amount of drugs.

He took out a four-inch needle of ripped steel that had been driven into Tap's back. It had pierced his lung and nicked his spleen. Sonny patched him up as best he could.

Peggy Grimes's foot injury was less serious but more difficult. All he could do was ease the pain and splint her until they could get her to a team of specialists.

Barry Armbruster sent Sonny word that Beverly had saved Peggy from drowning, and the last time he'd seen her, she'd been with Chuck Cooper, going for help. Barry didn't know where she was, or Chuck either.

Glenda told him that it was Vern Trent, Beverly's stepfather, with the back injury, and it sounded as if the Circle T had been hit badly.

Sonny could only pray that Beverly was okay, and then he prayed again. He hadn't prayed in years. Now, during this long, bloody nightmare, he hardly stopped.

The patients seemed to come in waves. Familiar faces swam before him, and all had the same pleas in their eyes. "Help me," their desperate gazes said. Or, even more desperate, "Help my loved ones—for God's sake."

He worked without stopping.

Scott Harris, the owner of the Hole in the Wall, was brought in by his wife, Val. He had a fractured jaw, a broken collarbone, a collapsed lung.

A tearful Bubba Gibson brought in his wife, Mary, who was hemorrhaging from internal injuries.

One of the young Hiltz girls had a fractured pelvis. Brock Munroe, the big, gentle owner of the Double Bar Ranch, carried in his unconscious wife, Amanda. She had a serious head wound.

On and on the parade of patients came. Wendts, Hiltzes, Westerhauses, Dawkinses, Fletchers, Ditmarses. Betty Ann Bachmann, Liz Babcock's mother, came in with chest pains. June Pollock, a cocktail waitress at the Lonely Bull, had torn ligaments in her right arm. Shirley Jean Ditmars had two broken wrists. Cody Hendricks, the banker, had a fractured neck. And J. T. McKinney came in, sick with fear, bringing his cook, Lettie Mae Reese. Her skull had been fractured, her shoulder broken.

When two more patients were brought in from the rubble of the hospital, both in critical condition, Sonny didn't see how the strapped staff could handle any more. He wiped the sweat out of his eyes. He'd never had time to put on a shirt.

Farron, who'd been working one-handed and in a daze, suddenly pitched forward and fainted, hitting his head on a table corner.

"Get him," Sonny ordered. "Help him."

"Dr. Dekker!" called a nurse. "We've got a woman out here in hard labor."

Another baby, Sonny thought and took a deep breath. *God help me.*

BEVERLY SAT amid the rubble, holding the baby and trying to comfort the woman, keeping hold of her hand. Night had fallen, and there was no moon, no stars.

"Is the baby asleep?" the woman asked weakly.

"Yes," Beverly said. "He's fine." The child's downy head rested against her cheek.

"He'll be hungry when he wakes."

"We'll cross that bridge when we come to it."

"He must be cold. He'll be hungry. I think you should leave me. I'm not going to make it. Why make the baby suffer?"

Beverly took a deep breath. The woman's name was Sandra Thurman. She was a divorcée from Dallas who'd just moved to Austin. It had been a hot, muggy day, and she'd taken the baby for a ride. She'd found the deserted Heller house, thought the setting was pretty, and was picking wildflowers when the storm hit.

There was nobody in Austin to notice she was missing, and nobody in Claro County to know she was here. It was impossible for Beverly to tell how badly Sandra Thurman was hurt, but she feared the worst. Furthermore, Sandra was terrified, and Beverly was afraid to leave her. Sandra might simply give up and die.

"Sandra, you *will* make it," she said earnestly. "Somebody will come. Until then, hang on to me. I'm here. You're not alone. Hold on."

"Oh, dear Lord, I'm cold. I'm so cold—"

Shivering herself, Beverly felt Sandra's pulse. It was far too rapid and weak, and she was frightened that the woman was going into shock.

"Hang on," she begged Sandra. "Hang on, *please.*"

"I'm so cold," Sandra said and began to cry.

Beverly stretched out beside the woman and held her close, trying to warm her with her own body and to keep the baby warm between them.

"We're here," she said. "Your baby and I are here."

Please, God, Beverly prayed. *Send somebody to help. Please.*

SONNY DIDN'T KNOW precisely when the emergency blood supply arrived, airlifted from Austin. He'd lost track of time.

The helicopter that brought in the blood was equipped to take out the four worst-injured patients. Sonny settled on Amanda Munroe, Lettie Mae Reese, Horace Westerhaus and Tap Hollister.

Some time after the helicopter left, a fully equipped emergency vehicle arrived from Austin. Shortly after that, another ambulance came from Claroville, and with it one of Claroville's doctors, Margarita Gonzales. Sonny could have kissed her feet.

He wiped his brow and went back to operating. The Red Cross was moving in, thank God.

"This is the worst we've found," he overheard one paramedic with the Red Cross say. "When they start bringing people in from the outlying areas, it's gonna be even worse."

Worse, Sonny thought dismally. *How could it get worse?*

He didn't know what time it was when they brought Vernon Trent in. One of Sonny's makeshift ambulances had carried him.

Vern's condition was critical; he was numb from the waist down, and he was extremely weak.

Dread twisted Sonny's soul. He was exhausted himself; the little makeshift hospital was stretched to its limits, and Vern's injury was serious as hell.

Sonny took Carolyn upstairs into the foyer of the church. "All I can do is keep him comfortable until we can get him to Austin," he told her. "I'm sorry. I wish I could do more. But we haven't got the equipment."

Carolyn looked beaten and bone-weary. "Will he die?"

Sonny swallowed. "No. But he may never use his legs again. That'd be the worst."

"Never walk?" She started to cry.

He took her by the shoulders. "That's the *worst*. The best to hope for is that the paralysis is caused only by swelling. If it is, and he regains movement or sensation within a week, he may recover completely—or close to it."

"Can I hope for that?" she asked helplessly. "Can I? Tell me."

"You can pray. I'm not usually a praying man, but I've done a lot tonight. It hasn't seemed to hurt."

"I'm too frightened to pray," she said, crying harder. "I don't know where Beverly is. She might be sick, dead—anything."

"Don't think like that. She got through the tornado, we've got word of that," he said. "She's strong, she's smart, she's brave, she'll last. You've got to believe that."

"I love her," Carolyn said, weeping. "The two people I love most in the world, and he's hurt, and she's disappeared, and I—I—I—"

He put his arms around her, held her. *I love Beverly, too,* he thought, *where is she?* But he didn't want Carolyn to sense his fear.

Glenda came for him. "They just brought in another case," she said. "Bad head wound. This one's got your name on it. They need you."

"Yeah," he said tiredly. "Here, help Mrs. Trent. Is anybody from her family here?"

"Her brother-in-law and his wife," she said. "J.T. and Cynthia. Should they take her home?"

"No. Tell them to stand by."

"Mrs. Trent," Sonny said to Carolyn, drawing back and looking into her eyes, "I'll try to get your husband into Austin tonight. I'll do my best."

"Hurry, Sonny, the guy's in bad shape," Glenda said.

"Yeah, I'm on my way."

He made his way downstairs, and when he saw the patient, his nerve ends jumped. The man's face was badly swollen, but there was no mistaking his identity.

Roger Grimes lay in a coma. The new anesthesiologist from the Red Cross, Burk, shook his head pessimistically. "You can't save this one, Doc. He's too far gone."

"No," Sonny said, a muscle twitching in his jaw. "We've worked too hard. We're haven't lost anybody that they've brought in so far. We're not going to start now."

SONNY SAT ALONE in the last pew of the dark church, his head in his hands. He had worked eighteen straight hours, the last four of them on Roger Grimes. Grimes had an acute subdural hemorrhage that required a craniotomy, and fragments of metal had to be removed from his skull.

But he was going to make it. His Corvette had been crossing a bridge when the tornado sucked the bridge right out from under him.

There was, Sonny thought, nothing like mucking about in someone's brain to take it out of a man. As soon as the ambulance got back from its present run, he'd arranged for both Grimes and Vern to be taken into Austin.

Vern needed either CT scanning or MRI. He might need myelography or lumbar puncture, and Sonny wanted both men monitored closely. He himself wanted to sleep for a week.

That wasn't possible, of course, because he was supposed to be back in Denver tomorrow morning.

Being back in Denver wasn't possible, either; it wasn't morally right. He'd started this job, it was an emergency, and he needed to stick with it. Nate probably wouldn't be well enough to shoulder this mess for weeks. Godbole, too, could be of no help for a while.

He'd waited for Denver. Well, he thought tiredly, let Denver wait for him, now. He'd ask for six weeks' leave.

In the meantime, all he wanted besides sleep was to know that Beverly was all right. He'd heard the Mc-Kinney sons, Cal and Tyler, along with the Double C foreman, Ken Slattery, had organized a search for her.

Beverly, where are you? I want you safe in my arms, and if I get you, I won't let you go again.

He wanted her so much that he hurt from it, that he was ready to weep for it.

BEVERLY HELD both Sandra Thurman and her baby through the long night, trying to shelter them, give them warmth. Sandra kept passing in and out of consciousness. The baby would cry, then sleep, then cry again.

Beverly held them and tried to soothe them. She ached with cold, hunger and fatigue. Sometimes she dozed and had troubled dreams of searching for Sonny, but of being trapped, unable to reach him.

At one point she imagined Hank was there. She shuddered. "Hello, Hank," she thought she said. "Jeff just kissed me. How is he?" She shivered again.

Hank looked at her sternly. "That was his goodbye kiss. What you got now is plain old goose bumps. You hang on. Help's comin'. Calvin and Tyler are practically here."

Beverly couldn't stop shivering. "What do you mean, goodbye kiss? Where's Jeff?"

"He let go of you. It's time. He's got to move on. You let go of him, too. And me, too. And your daddy. All of us. It's time to set us free."

"But—" she said, not understanding. "Why?"

Hank shook his head. "You know why. You don't belong to us no more. You belong to *him*. That's the way it's supposed to be. Yes sir, you are absolutely, positively, godamighty certain supposed to belong to him. That's that. So there."

"I know," she said, somehow understanding the truth of his words, "but I don't want you to go."

Hank frowned. "Hell, I can't stay around here gabbin'. I gotta go with Jeff. We got business to tend."

"But—"

"Hush," Hank grumbled. "Behave. You got big things to do with that man. Go do 'em. You wondered if you was strong enough? Tough enough? Brave enough? Well, you are. You got my word on that. Love him right, and love him good. So long. Don't take no wooden nickels.''

He vanished. The next thing she knew she was in the arms of her cousin, Cal McKinney.

"It's all right, sugar," Cal was saying. "It's all right. She's gonna make it. She's gonna pull through. Baby's fine. You did great, sweetheart. You did great, champ."

"WAKE UP," said Burk, the Red Cross anesthesiologist. His voice was full of malevolent cheer. "You're famous."

"I don't want to be famous," Sonny said from the hellishly uncomfortable pew. "I want to sleep."

"There are reporters waiting. You're hot news."

"I hate reporters," he muttered.

"Too bad. They love you. They've been sniffing around like hound dogs. You smell like a hero."

"If I'm what a hero smells like, God help us all. Is there a shower in this joint? Has anybody got a spare toothbrush? I left my stuff on Persimmon Street. It's probably been stolen. Looted and pillaged."

"I'm not kidding. They like you. They really, really like you. Why not? You, almost single-handed, saved the whole town—"

"I wasn't single-handed," Sonny said, sitting up. He pulled off his white scrub jacket, which was blood spattered. He touched his neck where he'd bandaged his cut. "Everybody did what they could."

"Ah," said Burk, with the same malicious glee, "you're the one who was delivering babies, helping heart victims—"

"It wasn't my idea," he said, running his hand through his hair. "And remind me not to sleep on a church pew again. I've sprained my whole body. How long was I out?"

"Two hours."

Sonny yawned. "It'll have to do." He hoped he wouldn't have to work another eighteen hours straight, but he supposed it was inevitable.

"How is everybody?" he asked.

"They all made it through the night. Even Roger Grimes. We got word from Austin. Vern Trent's stabilized. So's Tap Hollister. You did it."

"Oh, quit that," Sonny muttered. "Where can I find a clean shirt?"

"I won't quit. You pulled off damn tricky stuff, Dekker. In a church basement, with only half the equipment you needed. The press wants to talk to you. They think you're maybe a movie of the week."

Sonny said something obscene about the movie of the week. A dark thought crossed his mind, jolting him to full wakefulness. He looked up sharply at Burk. "Beverly Townsend?" he asked. "Have they found her?"

Burk paused, as if for effect. It was morning now, and light streamed through the stained-glass windows that weren't broken. A bird sang, sounding ironically cheerful and at peace with the broken world.

"They're bringing her in," Burke said.

Sonny was on his feet. "Is she all right?"

"So we hear. A little the worse for wear. But that's why I woke you. She's conscious, she's asking about you."

"Conscious? What in hell happened to her?"

"She found a woman and kid out at some deserted farm. Had to see the woman through the night. Woman's going to be okay. The kid, too."

"My God," he said, wheeling toward the foyer. "I mean, thank you, God." He crossed himself, something he hadn't done since he was eleven.

He ran down the stairs to the church basement. It was still full of patients, but not as many. The Red Cross and the sheriff's department were working to ferry them to real hospital facilities. A staff of Red Cross people worked among the patients. A few gave him curious looks.

He went into the men's rest room, splashed water on his face and chest, then studied himself. His face was drawn, his eyes were red with lack of sleep, and he had a white hair he could have sworn wasn't there yesterday.

He rummaged through the haphazard linen supplies, but couldn't find another scrub shirt. He sighed and supposed he should hike over to Persimmon Street to see if his clothes were still in the rental car.

He started out the door, but a teenage girl stood there, as if waiting for him. She looked shyly at him. She nodded at the carry-on suitcase that rested at her feet. "This is yours," she said. "I brought it. We drew names. I won. We all wanted to thank you."

He stared at her, uncomprehending. She swallowed hard. "That was my grandfather who had the heart attack yesterday on Persimmon Street. You saved him. My boyfriend, you helped him, too. Mrs. Riggs? The woman who had the baby? She's our next-door neighbor. She says she's going to name him for you."

Sonny gave her a dubious look. "Dr. Dekker's a pretty weird name for a baby."

The girl blushed and shook her head. "No. Dekker Riggs. And we all want to say thank-you because we don't know what would have happened if you hadn't been there. You were wonderful."

"Uh," he said, embarrassed, "it's okay."

"And if you ever need anything," the girl said with feeling, "my dad says you call on us—the Mahoney family. The Riggs family says the same thing. Everybody does. Up and down the street. They're going to rename the street for you. Have a ceremony and everything."

"Jeez," he said. "No. Don't. No. Don't do that. Look, thanks a lot, but I've got to get dressed—"

"Sonny!" Burk's voice came from outside, clear and eager. "She's here. Her cousin says to tell you."

"Excuse me," Sonny said to the Mahoney girl. Still shirtless, he made his way outside. People crowded around the basement entrance, some of them reporters and cameramen. But others were citizens of the town, who acted as if they were waiting for someone.

With shock, he realized they seemed to be waiting for *him*. People were pressing around him, pumping his hand, trying to talk to him—

"Thank you for saving my husband—"

"Thank you for helping my son—"

"My daughter—"

"Our father—"

"My grandpa might have died—"

"Our aunt—"

"—he might have lost his arm—"

"—you pulled her through—"

Sonny saw them all hazily, as if they were obscured by a cloud of unreality. People kept pumping his hand, clapping him on the shoulder, trying to hug him. Somebody actually thrust flowers at him, and more than one microphone was shoved into his face.

But all he could focus on was the white truck across the street. It had the gold insignia of the Double C Ranch on its door panel. A tall, handsome cowboy whom Sonny recognized as Beverly's cousin Cal stood by it. He was helping someone out the passenger's side.

It was Beverly, and Cal hoisted her into his arms. He carried her toward Sonny. Her clothes were clean, but they looked borrowed because they didn't fit.

Her gold hair tumbled to her shoulders, and she wore no makeup. Her face was pale, but she broke into a brilliant smile when she saw him shouldering his way through the crowd.

A man with a microphone blocked his path. "Dr. Dekker. You'd left town. Why'd you return? How did you happen to appear at just the right time? Some people say it's a miracle."

"It's not a miracle," Sonny said, not taking his gaze from Beverly. "It's her."

"Who is she?" The reporter asked, turning to someone else. "Are you getting this on tape, Wendell?"

"Yeah," said the cameraman laconically.

"Who is she?" the reporter asked again.

"That," a woman said proudly, "is his girl. She used to be Miss Texas."

"Miss Texas," mumbled the reporter thoughtfully. "There's an angle. Hero doctor and beauty queen. Get 'em, Wendell. From the look in his eye he's gonna smooch her big-time."

Sonny broke away from the crowd and made his way to Beverly, a lump in his throat.

Cal McKinney held Beverly more securely against his chest and gave Sonny a devilish grin. "You lose something?"

"Yeah," Sonny answered, his heart hammering. "Almost."

"Well," Cal said cheerfully, "I found her. Watch out. She's a real handful, I guarantee, but she's awful cute."

He let her stand. She stepped toward Sonny, who pulled her into his arms. He wanted to ask her a hundred things, but none of them could make it past the knot in his throat.

She clung to him tightly. "I love you," she said. "Do you love me back?"

"Yeah," he said helplessly. "I do. Like crazy."

"Then kiss me," she whispered. "It's what I thought of, all night long. This moment. It kept me going."

He captured her lips and kissed her, blind to everything except her. She kissed him back just as passionately. They couldn't seem to stop.

"Boy-howdy," Cal said in admiration.

But neither of them heard him.

CHAPTER EIGHTEEN

WEAK AND EXHAUSTED as Beverly was, she forced herself to go to Austin. She had to see Carolyn and Vern. Cal took her because Sonny couldn't. Her reunion with her mother and stepfather was emotional, full of teary kisses and hugs.

But Carolyn, fearful that Beverly was close to collapse, told her not to stay. "Go back with Cal to the Double C and rest," she said.

"I'll go back," Beverly said, her face white and tense. "But not to the Double C. I'm going to Sonny."

Carolyn was silent a long moment. Then she nodded. "I understand."

"You thank him for me," Vern said weakly. "He's a good man, a good doctor. They say he called every shot right. That he couldn't have done better."

Again Carolyn said nothing. She nodded, but didn't meet Beverly's eyes.

In Crystal Creek, Sonny's landlady had gladly given him back his apartment for as long as he could use it. Beverly went back to the ravaged Circle T, gathered up a few belongings, then went to Sonny's. He came to her after another eighteen-hour day. The first thing he said was, "I love you."

They were both too spent to make love, but they held each other all night long, sometimes waking to touch and kiss. He had dreamed that this might happen. He had never supposed it would, and it was more wonderful than he could say.

The next morning, he woke when the first light of dawn spilled through the window. "I have to go back to the hospital soon," he whispered, holding her close.

"I love you," she whispered back, snuggling closer. She felt perfect in his arms, absolutely right, and he had to shut his eyes, because she made him so drunk with love and desire that the room spun.

"I love you, too," he said, raising her face to his. He kissed her soft mouth, and then slowly, with all the skill and patience he could will, he began to make love to her.

Each kiss, each touch seemed to bear them farther into some country of wild, loving bliss. It was crazy, it was enchanted, it was soul-shaking. It seemed that stars should sing and planets dance.

Afterward she lay in his arms, and he was so shaken by what had happened between them that he didn't speak. He could only hold her tighter. What if she vanished, and this was only a dream, after all? She lay with her back against his chest, her hands clasped on the arms he wound so possessively around her waist.

He buried his face in her silken hair and whispered against the back of her neck, "You're so quiet. Do you regret this?"

"I'm quiet because I'm happy," she said. "No. It felt so right."

He kissed her bare shoulder. The room was still dim, and he had pulled the sheets up to cover their bodies again.

She turned to him, put her hand to his face. He kissed the palm. She smiled at him and said, "You know, if we had a little boy, he'd probably look just like you."

"Yeah," he said huskily. "He probably would."

"Good," she breathed. "That's exactly how I'd want him to look. Him. And any brothers and sisters. All like you."

He kissed her, and they both knew they would make love again, even more fiercely, even more tenderly.

LATER IN THE MORNING, Beverly borrowed Sonny's rented car and drove to the Double C, where Carolyn was staying with J.T. and Cynthia. It would be weeks before the house at the Circle T was repaired.

"How is she?" Beverly asked anxiously when Cynthia answered the door.

"Fine, I think," Cynthia said. "But things are catching up with her. Vernon's doctors say he's better, but she needs rest. She's inside."

Beverly made her way to the living room. Carolyn sat alone in a wing chair, her head bowed, her hand to her eyes.

"Mama?" Beverly said, suddenly frightened. She'd never seen Carolyn look so helpless. "Is something wrong?"

"No," Carolyn said. "I think it's right, at last."

Beverly went to her and knelt by her chair. "I should have stayed with you in Austin."

"There was nothing you could do. And you were exhausted."

Beverly took her mother's hand. "Mama, I had to be with Sonny. It's where I belong. I love him. Can you understand about him and me? It's wonderful, it really is. The most wonderful thing that ever happened to me."

Carolyn raised her eyes and looked at her. She gave a shuddering sigh. "I asked myself a hundred times in the past forty-eight hours why I said those terrible things to you. When I saw him—Sonny—there in that church, and looked into his eyes, I knew that he would do everything in his power to save Vern, and that Vern was in the right hands."

"The best," Beverly said. "The very best."

Carolyn shook her head helplessly. "And I knew, just as surely, that if he asked you, you'd go away with him." She sighed tiredly again. "I should have seen it sooner. I should have been wiser. And kinder. And more generous."

Beverly took her mother by the shoulders. "Mama, I didn't know for a long time what he meant to me. I thought I'd just turned to him because of Jeff. When it was almost too late, I realized how much I needed him, wanted him—loved him."

Carolyn put her hand to Beverly's face. "I'll tell you something else I saw in his eyes. That he loves you very much. That he'll take care of you."

"He will. And I'll take care of him. Oh, you don't know how marvelous he is."

Carolyn almost managed to smile. "I suppose I'm going to have to learn, won't I?"

Beverly squeezed her mother's shoulders more tightly. "There's nobody like him. I never knew there could *be* anybody like him. He came into my life when I least expected. You see, that's the whole thing, Mama. He was so unexpected. I didn't expect him to be so wonderful. I never expected I'd love him or he'd love me. I thought we were too different. But we're not. We're like the same person.''

"Oh, Beverly," Carolyn said, drawing her near and holding her, "will you forgive?"

"Of course. I love you."

"Will he forgive me, do you think? Can he?"

"I know he will."

Carolyn held her closer. "I hope you're right."

Beverly was silent a moment. Then she smiled against her mother's shoulder. "And, Mama—Jeff? He set me free. And I did the same for him. It's like he gave me to Sonny. He knows it's right. And I do, too."

IT WAS TWO WEEKS later. Sonny and Beverly were giddy with triumph, silly with happiness.

For more than a week, Vernon had been wiggling his toes enthusiastically. He proudly stated that his bladder control was admired by nurses and interns all over the ward. Sensation was rapidly returning to his lower body.

Today he had taken his first unassisted steps. They were tottering, almost drunken, but they'd carried him directly to Carolyn's outstretched arms, and she'd hugged him.

Sonny had looked on with obvious satisfaction. He'd been called in, twelve days ago, to assist with Vernon's surgery, to remove a few splinters of bone and to decompress the spinal cord.

Now Beverly smiled up at him in fond admiration. Vern's steps were the second of Sonny's miracles this week.

The first was that four days ago, Tap Hollister had been released. An elated Belinda Dugan had driven him home.

The borrowed car had been full of flowers, plants, balloons, teddy bears, boxes and jars of candy, posters and cards the band students had showered on him.

Roger Grimes was recovering, although he experienced giddiness, headaches and attention-span difficulties. He could remember nothing of the accident, and he would be in therapy for at least six months. But he was alive, and doctors in Austin were confident he would recover. He hadn't been told yet of the charges pending against him.

His wife, Peggy Sue, was already out of the hospital. She had been taken into custody, questioned and finally arrested for falsifying prescriptions. The townspeople of Crystal Creek were appalled by her lies and duplicity, and felt betrayed by both her and Roger.

Wayne Jackson had ruefully told Sonny and Beverly that Texas drug agents and DEA men had been watching Nutricentaur for some time. They'd been moving slowly, secretly and carefully, waiting for the right break in the case. Peggy Sue's confession had been that break. Eager to save her own skin, she had sacrificed Roger's, pouring out details of his guilt and Nutricentaur's involvement.

But today, the important news to Sonny and Beverly was Vern's walking, and they didn't dwell on the Grimeses. The steroid business was in the open now, and many of the boys involved had come forward with the truth.

A number of them had been instrumental in digging out survivors from the hospital debris. They were real heroes now, not just gridiron idols. Chuck Cooper and Barry Armbruster had helped save Peggy Grimes. And Lester Fletcher, who knew first aid, had saved one of his neighbors from bleeding to death. Mayor Martin Avery was giving citations of honor to each boy involved.

Physically, Crystal Creek had been battered. But spiritually and emotionally the crisis had been healing, and a new sense of unity coursed through the town. People helped each other recover. They worked together, and their resolve was strong.

Now Beverly and Sonny strolled down the corridor of the Austin hospital, hand in hand. They had left Vern and Carolyn to themselves. It had seemed the right thing to do.

The corridor, a side one, was oddly deserted. Ahead of them, two nurses walked purposefully, and then disappeared around the corner.

Beverly and Sonny passed a supply closet, its door slightly ajar. "Hey," Sonny said, "I've got an inspiration."

Deftly he spirited Beverly inside, pulled her into his arms and kissed her. He kissed her quite thoroughly, until she was pleasantly dizzy from it.

"What is this?" she asked with a laugh when he let her come up for air. She twined her arms around his neck and gazed up into his eyes.

"A sentimental journey," he said with a crooked smile. "The first time I ever held you was in a supply closet. It's like revisiting the place where we really met."

She stared up at him, drinking him in. *God,* she thought, *I love him. I love everything about him.*

She raised her hand so her forefinger could trace the line of one straight eyebrow, the sculpted curve of his cheekbone, the curve of his upper lip.

Beneath her other hand, his shoulder was warm and hard with muscle. He smiled and drew her closer again.

"You feel good," she whispered.

She raised herself and kissed him again. The touch of his mouth was more exciting than any she had ever known. She let her tongue flirt lightly along his parted lips and was delighted when he gasped in pleasure.

"You taste good," she breathed against his mouth.

"Be careful." He growled deep in his throat. "Or I'll have my way with you among the paper towels and mop buckets."

She nuzzled against his chest, inhaling his scent, which was soap and sandalwood. "You smell good," she mused, and breathed in again dreamily.

"I love you," he whispered, kissing her ear. "How's that sound?"

"It sounds wonderful," she said, winding her arms around him more tightly, burying her nose in the curve of his throat. "You sound good, you look good, you smell good, you taste good, you feel good. I love you."

"You're no slouch yourself," he said. "Good grief, don't be so sexy. I'll disintegrate if I can't have you."

"Then take me home," she said, her lips against the pulse in his throat. "You've got the whole day off."

"Beverly," he said with a groan, "you've got on that damned gardenia perfume again. Why'd you do this to me? We've got that stupid ceremony to go to. And all I want is to make love to you."

"It's not a stupid ceremony," she said, kissing the hollow of his neck. "It's for you, and you deserve it. And afterward we'll go to the house on Lake Travis."

"Yeah," he said, kissing her hair. "The house on Lake Travis. All weekend."

"I know," she said softly. "It'll be heaven."

The Hopkins-Sloane Clinic had given him emergency leave until May to help Crystal Creek through its medical crisis. Beverly was aflutter with happiness. In May, she would be done with her classes. She would transfer to Denver and finish her course work there. And in May, before she left with him, she would become Mrs. Sunarjo J. Dekker.

She already had the engagement ring, a square-cut diamond, two carats. She'd been astonished when he gave it to her, and told him it was far too big.

"Hey," he'd said, kissing her. "I've been saving for years. It's time to spend a little. When I finally get out of this damn town, I'm going to make a lot of money. And I'm going to spoil you, Blondie. I'll buy you rubies in Bangkok and pearls in Tahiti. Count on it."

"Umm," said Beverly, "the perfect husband."

To Beverly's joy, Carolyn seemed actually to be growing fond of Sonny. "I don't know how I'd have gotten through this without him," she said. "He was always there, to explain, to support."

Vernon and the McKinneys, too, went out of their way to make Sonny feel welcome to the family. J. T. McKinney had told Sonny he could have the McKinneys' vacation home on Lake Travis "any damned weekend" he wanted. This was the first chance Sonny had had to take him up on it, the first weekend he and Beverly could steal.

He kissed her again. "I want to go to the lake *now*. I don't want to go to any ceremony." He winced at the thought. "Then we've got to go to this cocktail party at your uncle's. When do I get you alone?"

"Tonight," she promised, locking her hands behind his neck. "As soon as we can. I promise."

"All this stuff makes me feel stupid," he said with distaste. "I'm no hero. I did my job, that's all. One night doesn't change things. I'm the same guy I was."

She kissed a corner of his mouth. "No," she said. "You're not. You changed me. But this town changed you. You're not the same cynical, 'I worship science only' guy you used to be. You admit you care for people now."

"No," he objected, "only you."

"That's not true," she said. "You cared for every single person that was brought to you. You cared passionately. That's always been your deep, dark secret, hasn't it? That you care so much."

He stared down at her a moment. He smiled his cynical smile. "Keep it quiet, will you?"

"It's too late, sugar," she said, raising her lips to his. "The secret's out."

SONNY SAT, looking supremely uncomfortable, on the stage in the high school auditorium. Beverly had pressured him into buying a dark blue suit and insisted he looked "handsome enough to die for" in it.

He'd replied rather sourly that being a doctor, it was against his best interests to be "to die for."

"You thing," she'd said, and swatted him on the arm.

Now she sat by his side, looking beautiful, of course. She wore some little silk suit thing, and she kept smiling at him as if he were the only man in the place. This embarrassed him even more.

The auditorium was full, which touched Sonny in spite of himself. But the damned reporters were all over the place, snapping flash bulbs and trailing wires and making him feel like a freak.

The only thing that kept him from fidgeting completely off the stage was that behind him, in folding seats, were ranged all the nurses and orderlies and volunteers who had served that night. Sonny had stated flatly that he wouldn't sit on that stage if they didn't, too.

Reverend Howard Blake took the speaker's podium first. He began with a solemn prayer of thanks that Sonny found too long, but then he felt guilty. He'd asked God for enough favors that long night; he guessed the least he could do was let Howard give The Big Guy his due.

Then Mayor Martin Avery took the speakers' podium. He commended the nurses, the orderlies, the paramedics, Hedda Wagner and all the volunteers, and he asked for an ovation for them. The audience rose to its feet applauding. So did Sonny and Beverly. When the audience settled again, Martin went on, his face serious.

"A town is like a family," he said. "It can have its disagreements, its misunderstandings, its pettiness, even its scandals."

He paused and looked out at the audience. "The people who make up a town are only human, and like all humans, frail. On Saturday afternoon, March sixth, we were given a demonstration of just how frail our little lives are.''

He stood straighter, his voice growing stronger. ''But when a crisis strikes, a town, like a family, can forget its differences and pull together. We look into each other's human faces and no longer say, 'ally' or 'foe,' but 'brother' and 'sister.'''

He took a deep breath. ''At times during the past year, I've seen this town divided against itself. But on the afternoon of March sixth, and during that long night, I saw it come together. I saw the best, the bravest, the highest, the most dedicated and generous that human nature can give. And you are still giving to one another. I'm proud of you.

''So many of you showed courage and compassion during those terrible hours, it's impossible to single everyone out. But it's equally impossible *not* to single out one man.

''He came to us last summer as a stranger, he did his job, and sometimes he was given little gratitude for doing it. He left. Some of you were glad. But somehow, and Reverend Blake says he thinks it was a miracle, he returned to us, precisely at the time of our greatest need.

''I have a letter here from Dr. Nate Purdy. He's still resting, gathering strength for all the challenges ahead for the hospital. Rose says the hardest job she's ever had is to *keep* him resting.

''This is what his letter says in part. 'I hate that I could not help my town in its hour of crisis. But if I could have wished for one man to be there in my place, I would have asked for Sunarjo Dekker. I know he did better than I could have done. Perhaps he did better than anyone could.'

"Ladies and gentlemen, I'm sure I have already embarrassed Dr. Dekker. I'm afraid to say much more. It was hard enough to get him here in the first place. I don't want to drive him off.

"So let me say simply, that the following people are still alive primarily because of this man."

Solemnly Martin read a list of names, including Horace Westerhaus, Jackson Mahoney, Tap Hollister, Roger Grimes, David Ditmars, Mary Gibson, Amanda Brock and Lettie Mae Reese.

"And," Martin added with a smile, "two people were brought into the world on March sixth by this same man. They are a boy and a girl, Dekker John Riggs and Maria Teresa Dekker Rameriz.

"These names don't begin to approach the number of lives he touched that night. With gratitude, Crystal Creek salutes its honorary son, Dr. Sunarjo Dekker."

Sonny suffered through more agonies of embarrassment when the audience, joined by the people on stage, rose to give him a standing ovation.

What do I do? Sit here like a toad and look smug? he thought. *Or do I rise, like I'm saluting me, too? No, that's gotta be wrong—*

Beverly nearly hauled him to his feet. "Bow," she said. "And give your speech."

"I don't do bows," he said tightly, but he managed to execute one that he hoped did not resemble a curtsy.

He made his way to the speaker's podium. His heart pounded. He fumbled in the breast pocket of the unfamiliar suit and discovered he couldn't find his speech.

He shrugged and looked more uncomfortable. "I can't find my speech," he said. "For which you should probably be profoundly grateful."

A laugh rippled through the audience. "All I can tell you is that everything Martin said is gross exaggeration. I showed up and had the good sense to stay out of the nurses' and orderlies' and paramedics' way.

"They're the ones who deserve your thanks. I was honored to work with them."

He set his jaw in determination. "I've only got one more thing to say. I come from another country, one of diverse peoples and cultures. On our crest are the Sanskrit words, 'Bhineka Tunggal Ika.' They mean, 'We are many, but we are one.'

"On the sixth of March, you proved this town is like my nation. 'We were many, but we were one.' I was honored to be a part of that, too. Thank you."

"That's all you're going to say?" Beverly whispered in his ear when he sat down. "What happened to your speech?"

"My suit ate it," he said miserably.

SOMEHOW HE SUFFERED through the whole thing. There was a commendation sent by the governor of Texas and one from the Red Cross. There seemed to be an interminable number of speeches, but at last they were over.

Then there was the cocktail party to get through. He sagged against the wall in the McKinneys' living room, trying to be inconspicuous. Beverly had gone to say good-night to someone. He waited, stuggling to be patient.

Tap Hollister limped over and stood by his side. He had his arm around Belinda, who beamed up at him. Tap cuffed Sonny's arm. "Bet you think you're something, huh?"

"No, I don't," Sonny returned. "I meant it. This is all blown out of proportion."

"That's not what I meant," Tap said with an irreverent smirk. "I mean you think you're smart getting the prettiest blonde in town. You're not the only sly fox. *I* got the prettiest brunette."

Shyly Belinda showed Sonny her left hand. A diamond gleamed from her finger. "We're engaged," she said, her eyes shining.

Sonny smiled at her happiness. "Congratulations. When's it happen?"

"This summer," Tap said. "As soon as school's out. God, can you imagine all those band kids throwing rice? We'll be *killed*."

Sonny cocked an eyebrow. "So elope."

"No way," Tap said, pulling her closer. "I want the world to see me go into harness with this little filly. I'm proud she'll have me."

"You should be," Sonny said. "I always thought she was too good for you."

"Absolutely," Tap admitted. "But where's anybody who is good enough? She settled for me."

Beverly joined them. "What's this? Did I see a diamond on that hand?" she said to Belinda. "When did this happen?"

"Last night," Belinda said.

"As soon as I was well enough to stagger to the jewelry store and fall deeply into debt," Tap said. "And if our firstborn's a boy, we're going to name him Dekker, for you, old buddy. It's the vogue these days."

"Spare me that," Sonny said.

"No way," Tap said, shaking his head. "It's like the fable. Like I'm a lion, and you're the Roman who took

the thorn out of my paw, so I've got to show my gratitude. Except it was a metal sliver, and it wasn't my paw,
and I'm not a lion, and you're not a Roman."

"I'm frightened," Sonny said. "Because that almost makes sense."

AT THE LAKE HOUSE, as Beverly lay in Sonny's arms,
she let her forefinger trail dreamily down his chest. "I'm
so lucky to have found you. I almost didn't. How did I
ever let you go? What if you hadn't come back?"

He took her face between his hands and kissed her
lips. "I would have come back. I had to. We've had this
date from the start of time."

"You think so?" she asked, snuggling closer.

"Oh, yeah," he said, his breath fanning her cheek.
"Ever since I was a little kid in Jakarta, I think I was
meant to find you. That's why I had to cross all those
lands and seas. To find you. So you could make me
whole."

"Do you really believe that?" she said. "Because
that's how I feel. Ever since I was a little girl, my heart's
been looking for something I couldn't name. Until you
came along. You're what I wanted, needed, waited for.
What if we'd missed each other?"

"Shh," he said, laying his finger against her lips.
"We didn't. It's okay. We're here, and we're finally together. And you know what happens next?"

"What?" she said, enjoying the feel of his strong
body so intimately close, so infinitely desirable.

"We live happily ever after," he said, lowering his
lips to hers.